GRAVELY CONCERNED

A DCI WARLOW CRIME THRILLER

RHYS DYLAN

WYRMWOOD
BOOKS

COPYRIGHT

ISBN 978-1-915185-09-9
eBook ISBN 978-1-915185-08-2

Published by Wyrmwood Books.
An imprint of Wyrmwood Media.

EXCLUSIVE OFFER

Please look out for the link near the end of the book for your chance to sign up to the no-spam guaranteed VIP Reader's Club and receive a FREE DCI Warlow novella as well as news of upcoming releases.

Or you can go direct to my website: https://rhysdylan.com and sign up now.

Remember, you can unsubscribe at any time and I promise won't send you any spam. Ever.

BOOKS by RHYS DYLAN

The Engine House

Caution Death At Work

Ice Cold Malice

Suffer The Dead

CHAPTER ONE

'MAM! Mam! The chickens are on fire.'

Nerys Howells heard her daughter Fflur shouting from the backyard and squeezed her eyes shut. Day one of the Whitsun school holidays was in full swing, but at least the weather had relented and the sun, though hardly blazing, shone down. That meant the kids could be outside. Thank God.

Nerys had just come back from a big shop in Aldi with both kids in tow. They'd be wanting lunch in ten minutes. Plus, she had a wash to hang out. The last thing she needed now was for Fflur to start playing silly buggers.

She sighed, opened the fridge door, and tried to make room for the dozen yoghurts she balanced in her other hand.

Both front and back doors were open. Osian, her six-year-old son, wore a cycle helmet and a cape as he fought aliens with a stick in the front garden. He'd built a space-ship out of cardboard boxes and a wooden crate in the access way running up the side of the house joining front and back yards. She'd warned him it had better be gone by the time his dad got home or there'd be trouble.

There wouldn't be, but Osian left a mess wherever he went, and he needed to be reminded to clear things away. His sister, on the other hand, had a thing for animals. Nerys forgave her that because it was one of her weaknesses, too. They had almost two-thirds of an acre on the edge of the village of Cwrt Y Waun. Plenty of room for the rabbit hutches and the chickens at the bottom where a hedge separated them from the farm fields they backed onto.

'Mam!' Fflur's urgent yell reached her again. And this time Nerys listened because something in her daughter's voice lent a sudden, urgent credence to her cries.

But how could the chickens be on fire?

Nerys hurried out of the back door and stared down across the area of lawn sectioned off by laurels from the vegetable patch to the lower garden that fell away towards fields. The smell reached her even before she saw the smoke. An acrid whiff of burning straw and then a column of grey smoke spiralling upwards.

'Fflur?' she shouted, panic flaring. 'Where are you?'

Her daughter, ten and leggy in her jeans and a 'This Girl Is Double Digits' T-shirt, sprinted around the laurels, tears streaming down her terrified face.

'We've got to get them out. We've got to get them, Mam.'

'Shit,' Nerys muttered, and ran.

The wind wafted the smoke north, away from the house, but the odd gust sent some of it towards her as she neared the wired-off chicken run. No flames, only thick billowing smoke.

The chickens clucked in full voice, fear stoking them into a terror-filled cacophony.

'Get the hose,' Nerys yelled to Fflur.

Having the vegetable garden nearby meant they had water to hand. Nerys took off her sweatshirt and tied the sleeves around her mouth, then opened the latch to the run and shooed the chickens out into the garden. Squatting low under the wafting smoke, she looked in to locate the source of the fire.

Not in the coop.

She backed out, coughing, tears streaming down her face, and moved around the coop towards where their garden led on to a field. The hedge needed cutting, but this was fledgling time, and the hedge would continue growing for a few more months before the farmer trimmed it. The blackthorn and hazel were already in full leaf, but she could see enough through the gaps to make out the remnants of a pile of straw smoking furiously. And she could smell something.

Was that petrol?

Fflur appeared next to her, hose in hand, adjustable spray nozzle attached.

'Look after the chickens, make sure none of them get out onto the lane.'

Maes Awelon, the Howells' property, sat next to an access lane leading to a path that went all the way to a water treatment works for the village. The property on the other side of the lane had a big paddock and a manège at the rear, so there would always be straw lying about. But this... this didn't make any sense.

Nerys couldn't see over the overgrown hedge. But by squatting and turning her face away from the smoke, she found a gap wide enough to get a good jet of water through and onto the straw. To begin with, all it did was make the smoke worse, but after a couple of minutes of steady dousing, the smoking eased, and the few flames died away.

She stood up. Behind her, Fflur waved her arms about, herding the chickens. They'd all forgotten about the fire and were busy finding new bugs to eat in her potato patch.

The fence bordering the lane, tanalised shiplap mostly, gave way to beech hedge towards the bottom of the garden where Nerys now stood.

No sign of anyone in the Madge's place opposite. They had teenage kids, but they were sensible. Studious and horsey. The last thing they would want to do was set a fire near animals.

But lighting up half a bale might be some of the more reckless kids from the village's idea of fun over half term. She couldn't think of anyone, but some properties were council owned. Social housing on a small site.

She shook her head. What was she like? Nerys Howells, Thomas as was, born and bred in a council house in the Gwendraeth Valley. Still, some houses on the site sheltered people who were not local. People brought in from outside for reasons best known to themselves and the council officers who put them there. Interlopers, as one of the fussier old biddies she sometimes met at the post office called them.

She turned back to her daughter. 'Right, come on, let's get these chickens back inside.'

'Is the coop alright, Mam?'

'It's fine. Get your brother and tell him I want him to help.'

Fflur ran back to the house, opening the door to the little side entrance and exposing her brother's rocket ship, or 'Moony Module' as he'd christened it, shouting his name as she went.

'Osh? Osh? Mam wants you.'

Nerys waved her hands, scooting the chickens back to the bottom of the garden. Behind her, she could hear Fflur calling, frustration growing in her tone.

'Osian? Come on. Stop messing about.'

'Look in the spaceship,' Nerys called over her shoulder.

'I have,' Fflur yelled back.

A minute went by, or was it only thirty seconds? Long enough for the first tiny spark of concern to press Nerys's anxiety button. Osian could be a little sod, always playing games, hiding from his sister, or, when asked to do something he didn't want to, from Nerys. Bloody good at it, too, he was. But she knew his hiding places.

When Fflur appeared in the open doorway in front of the Moony Module, shaking her head, the little spark of worry in Nerys turned into a hot, gnawing anxiety.

She left the chickens and ran back towards the house, calling her son's name as she went.

'Osian! Come here, now. Osian?'

She joined Fflur and pushed past the haphazard arrangement of boxes to where she'd last seen Osian waving his lightsabre – a yellow-painted stick. A 'weapon' that hadn't been out of his hands for the whole of the weekend.

'Osian!' No longer a plea, her bellow turned into an angry demand.

She hurried into the house, checking through the usual places she knew he liked to hide. Behind the sofa, upstairs under his bed, his sister's toy chest. Fflur followed her, looking in the other rooms, calling her brother's name.

'Where is he, Mam?'

Nerys shook her head, not trusting herself to say anything. Not yet. He'd be outside. Of course he would. Hiding in the garden somewhere. The only place they hadn't looked.

Nerys ran out through the back door, down through the vegetable patch and the clucking chickens that squawked in alarm as she scattered them and squawked again as she retraced her steps back to the spaceship and the front garden.

Her knees bumped against the stupid cardboard boxes and dislodged something from underneath. A yellow stick and a bike helmet skittered across the ground. Osian's weapons and protection... abandoned.

The gnawing heat inside Nerys died instantly, only to be replaced by a cold, twisting fear. She picked up the stick, stared at it, ran out to the gate, and stood, staring up at the quiet, empty road and the nearest houses to the south a hundred yards away.

She waved the stick. A ridiculous movement, trying to conjure up something, anything that would change what she suddenly felt, the fear of what she intuitively knew.

'Mam, where's Osian?' Fflur's voice held all the terror that Nerys felt. But she didn't answer because the world hummed around her, the colours in it painfully bright as she pieced together the little charade. The smoke had been a distraction. Someone had set it. Someone who'd wanted her away from the house for five minutes.

The five minutes that it took to steal a child.

The denial from Nerys, when it came, shattered the afternoon quiet and set a dog barking somewhere.

'No, no, no...' She ran through the gate, ran down the lane towards the field with the burning straw.

Empty.

Ran into the Madge's.

Empty.

Ran up the road, calling Osian's name every ten yards. Fflur followed, crying openly, but invisible to her mother, whose eyes had taken on a strange absence as if she was no longer there.

People heard the shouts, heard the desperation in Nerys's voice.

They came out of their houses and stared. Asked what was wrong.

Those same people flinched when they heard. Turned to one another and murmured. Many of them joined Nerys and shouted Osian's name.

But no one had seen him.

Fflur was still crying and Nerys still running fifteen minutes later when they got back to Maes Awelon after searching the handful of lanes that made up Cwrt Y Waun village and finding nothing.

'Mam.' Fflur wailed. 'Where is—'

'Check the chickens,' blurted Nerys by way of distraction and with such feigned exuberance that it stopped Fflur in her emotional tracks. 'Make sure they're okay,' Nerys nodded, smiling. Or at least showing her teeth in a way that made Fflur frown. But the little girl didn't argue. She turned and ran out.

Nerys didn't give a flying fowl about the hens. But she wanted Fflur out of her mind for a moment because she had no room for her there. Not now.

The world started to slide around her and all she could think of was doing what needed to be done before the gigantic black hole expanding in her mind swallowed her whole.

Fflur ran through the garden, still calling her brother's name. Nerys picked up the phone, dropped it, picked it up again and, with trembling fingers, dialled 999.

CHAPTER TWO

DCI Evan Warlow didn't like funerals much. He realised that if he met anyone who did, he'd recommend a psychiatric formulation. Except for undertakers of course. He glanced back. A couple of them stood at the rear, hands clasped in front of them, dark-suited and professionally sombre. End of life – or rather end of existence as flesh and bone given, they were in a crematorium – was their bread and butter.

Still, unless you were an undertaker or a relative, you mostly went to funerals out of a sense of duty. And this funeral, the cremation of his ex-wife, 'Jeez' Denise Foley, plucked at the old duty strings with a discordant vengeance. It wasn't the surroundings that troubled him. In fact, Llanelli Crematorium did this sort of thing pretty well. A modern red-brick building designed with a nod to divinity, thanks to a high vaulted wooden ceiling and huge gable windows letting in masses of light, while the dearly departed – suitably encased in flammable wood – turned to ash. It also had a memorial garden where those same ashes could be scattered, or urns buried. All aimed at the need to have something physical as a link to remembrance.

He understood all that. Just as he accepted the need for a ceremony. The craving for a formal farewell went back millennia. All very human.

What was harder to swallow was the belief, by some, that after a lifetime of blasphemy and booze, Denise needed a member of the church to send her off. He doubted it would have been what she'd wanted. But then neither he nor she had any say in it. The arrangements were the remit of her current partner, Martin Foyles. And good old Martin found a vicar from somewhere, crossed his palm with silver – hopefully not thirty pieces – and got him to stand up there to wax lyrical about Denise and ask them all to pray for her.

They'd even sung a hymn.

Denise would have laughed her socks off.

In fact, Warlow kept one eye on the coffin to make sure it didn't start revolving at speed to the accompaniment of maniacal laughter.

But in the main, he, like everyone else, was here to remember the woman Denise used to be. And, more than that, because his sons, Alun and Tom, were sitting in the front row, one pew ahead of him. They were saying goodbye to their mother, and he kept that thought firmly at the front of his mind while the ancient vicar began rabbiting on about how Denise struggled with her illness.

Struggled with opening a bottle of vodka more like. The 'illness', in the form of a devastatingly acute pancre-atitis, blew in like a desert storm and wiped her away in a matter of days. Hardly any struggle had taken place at all in the end. One day Warlow was WhatsApping her at the hospital, the next thing she'd been in a coma, never to return from massive multi-organ failure.

The boys sat to the right, Tom with his partner Jodie, Alun on his own because his partner was too pregnant to travel and stayed in sunny Western Australia. Martin's daughter from a previous marriage sat next to him and held his hand.

Warlow could have squeezed in there between the daughter and his own boys but opted for tier two when it came to seating. Close, but with the requisite amount of distance for decorum in his own mind.

At last, the coffin sank out of sight on its way to the furnace and the music changed to Earth, Wind and Fire's *September*, the first two bars of which were guaranteed to get Denise out on the dance floor no matter where or when. Martin had got that one right at least.

Warlow glanced back again. The place was two-thirds full of people he knew. Some better than others. Relatives and friends paying their respects. Right at the back, he glimpsed his colleagues: the towering figure of Superintendent Sion Buchanan, difficult to miss at six-foot-four when standing, a big man even sitting down. Next to him sat a man with a barrel chest and Michelin Man girth. Sergeant Gil Jones's baritone voice echoed through the building when they'd launched into the hymn, and that had made Warlow smile. Why it had taken a funeral for him to learn that the bloke could sing, he'd never know. Next to Gil sat a woman with dark hair and olive skin, smart in a dark-navy suit and a white blouse. But then, DI Jess Allanby would look smart in a hessian sack. The Italian genes mixed in with a little Celtic blood somewhere along the immigrant line blended into an eye-catching combination.

All three worked with him in Dyfed Powys Police. Sion, 'The Buccaneer' Buchannan, his immediate boss in the BOSU he was attached to, Gil and Jess, part of the team that had somehow morphed into a mini–Major Crimes Unit. All there out of politeness. Only Sion had ever met Denise, back in the day when Warlow and she were still together. And so, The Buccaneer had seen her at her worst; the functioning alcoholic that sometimes accompanied Warlow to the odd 'do'. Gatherings they'd always exit early from before too much damage could be done by Denise's brash, piss-artist exuberance.

A new movement caught Warlow's eye. The undertaker walked slowly up the aisle in his tails and motioned to Martin that he could now walk out into the little cloister where close family met with the other mourners. Warlow wasn't looking forward to this. He felt a little like a spare wheel here. He didn't want to be there as Denise's ex. But he needed to be there as the boys' father.

Of course, they weren't boys anymore. They were men. Alun, the engineer, married with a child already and another on the way. Tom, the doctor, burrowing head-first into a surgical career with a partner in London.

They'd done both him and their mother proud. If you're up there, Denise, be glad of that at least, thought Warlow.

He followed his sons out and stood with them, a little apart from Martin and his daughter, while people in dark clothes filed past, shook his hand, mouthed sympathies, and mumbled uncomfortable small talk that always felt somehow too light or too maudlin. Rare was the mourner who hit just the right note. Walking the mourner's tightrope was a skill, but who in their right minds would ever want to be good at this sort of situation?

Warlow kept an eye out for Buchanan and Gil and Jess, but they'd avoided the procession. So, he listened, acted suitably morose, shook hands, and nodded at faces grown old by the years.

Not that all of it was an act. The boys were sad, and he felt for them. But his and Denise's relationship had died and been buried long before this official ceremony. No sense pretending otherwise.

At last, the final few stragglers drifted away and Warlow tapped Alun, his eldest son, on the shoulder.

'You coming with me? Or riding with Tom and Jodie.'

'No, I'll come with you,' Alun said.

Martin arranged for a post-cremation bite to eat in a pub on the outskirts of Pontarddulais. Tom and Jodie were heading back to London with Alun immediately after. This would be Warlow's last chance to chat with his son before he went back to Australia. And though more chit-chat with long lost in-laws in the King's Arms was the last thing Warlow wanted to do, it would be a worthwhile sacrifice for a few more minutes with the boys.

———

'WHAT DID you think of the hymn?' Warlow asked, as they drove back up the A4138.

'I told Martin not to bother. But he insisted. Said it wouldn't be a proper funeral without a hymn.' Alun shook his head.

Warlow glanced across at his son and chuckled. Taller than Warlow and tanned from the Australian sun, Alun bore his mother's mouth and fine features. Her short fuse, too.

'Spoken to Reba today?'

'Yeah. She's fine. Leo's playing up a bit. Keeps pointing at the bump and asking when his sister can come out to play.' Alun sighed but kept a wistful smile on his lips.

'He's a handful.' Warlow wasn't talking from personal experience, but it was obvious from the videos and photographs he'd received since Leo's birth. Alun picked up on it.

'So, come on, Dad, when are you going to come out to find out just how much of a handful he is?'

'Good question.'

'You can't use the cottage as an excuse. That's all done. And there's no need to worry about upsetting Mum, now.'

Visiting Alun had been a bone of some contention between Warlow and Denise. Alun had been up-front about not wanting her to come out. And more than once she'd ring Warlow up at some ungodly hour to make sure he didn't go without her.

'Don't you dare, Evan Warlow. Don't you dare visit your grand-child without me.'

But since Alun had put a moratorium on her going anywhere near his child, Warlow, too, had effectively been banned. So, he'd crouched down in that dark emotional crevice between a rock and a hard place and waited. But the rock had moved, and daylight was flooding in. For someone used to the murk of indecision, all this light was proving uncomfortable.

Not that Alun had accepted Warlow's desire not to upset Denise as a very good excuse. He'd been unable to see his father's need to play nice, and Warlow's unwilling-ness to visit became an equally contentious bone. Warlow himself had been happy to keep his head well-buried in the sand, using Denise as the convenient excuse to start with, Covid after that, not wanting to tell Alun the real reason for his reluctance to visit. Worried that if he did, he might face an equivalent ban; Alun had a strong will and equally strong opinions. And Warlow had told neither of his sons about why he'd retired early from the police. It was a conversation he'd rehearsed in his mind a thousand times and yet still could not bring himself to have.

Oh, and by the way, Tom and Alun, I'm HIV positive. Did I mention that?

Tom, the doctor, would understand. Alun, non-medical father of one, soon to be two, might not. Might want to keep Warlow at arm's length from his children for a lot longer.

And so Warlow kept everything tightly stoppered, waiting for the right moment. It had not appeared yet.

'I'd need to give work enough notice,' Warlow said.

'Oh yeah, work. The thing you've retired from once already.' Alun didn't exactly sneer, but a trace of it sneaked into his tone.

'I'd probably want a month at least, wouldn't I?'

'At least.'

'Okay. How about October or November? Early summer for you lot, isn't it?'

Alun nodded. 'Lovely that time of year. Before it gets ridiculously hot.'

Now would be a good time, Warlow thought. Get it over with. Just say it. But he wanted to have both his sons in front of him when he did. Maybe this afternoon, when all the guests had left the King's Arms.

'Right. I'll start looking at flights now that things have opened up again.' Warlow drove under the M4 towards Hendy, one eye on the cars behind full of mourners on their way to a free meal and a pint.

'So, you've settled on Amber as Leo's sister's name?'

'Yes. Amber Melanie Warlow. Melanie after Reba's gran.'

'So long as it's not Nectar,' Warlow said.

Alun snorted. 'I suggested that, but it wasn't appreciated.'

'No. The Warlow sense of humour seldom is.'

CHAPTER THREE

THE BUFFET HAD BEEN LAID out in the King's Arms' function room, complete with staffed bar and trestle tables for the food. A couple of young wait-staff dressed in black offered people wine or orange juice on their way into the room.

Warlow stuck with the fruit juice and mingled. Which meant walking around with a plate of sandwiches as a prop, nodding to people occasionally, and trying desperately to remember if the faces in front of him had names. They undoubtedly did, but since Warlow had last seen most of them the day he got married to Denise, the chance of him remembering was miniscule.

Of course, they knew who he was. Not only because of Denise, but because of his profession as a Detective Chief Inspector whose photo, much to his chagrin, appeared now and again in the newspapers. And though that put some people at an advantage over him in the name stakes, it also meant that several of Denise's shadier relatives quickly walked the other way when they saw him coming.

Some of them regretted ever having met him, and certainly had no intention of jogging his memory.

Eventually, he found the Buccaneer, Jess and Gil, sitting at a table near the back of the room. Only Gil had anything resembling a proper drink in a pint glass. When Warlow's gaze lingered a little too long, the detective sergeant said, 'Non-alcoholic lager in case you were wondering.'

All three sat with their backs to the wall in a classic copper's pose, watching the room.

'See anyone you want to arrest?' Warlow asked.

'There is a woman over there wearing a dress that deserves a caution,' Jess said.

Warlow followed her gaze. A heavy-set young woman in a blue patterned dress sat head down over a brimming plate of food, concentrating hard on cramming as much into her mouth as she could and hoping, in vain, that no one would notice. The dress looked like someone had taken three different sets of clothes and sewn them randomly together.

'That's Denise's niece, the designer,' Warlow said. 'She's apparently incredibly talented.'

The Buccaneer spoke for everyone when he said, 'Eye of the beholder, I suppose.'

Gil turned the conversation towards more important matters. 'Lovely salmon sandwiches. Vinegar and brown bread, mmm. Always liked this pub.'

'We've already spoken to your sons,' the Buccaneer declared.

'Nice looking boys,' Jess added.

'Must take after their mother,' Gil muttered before biting a mini sausage roll in half.

Warlow smiled. 'You were in good voice this morning, Gil.'

'I tried to tell him to shut up, but it's water off a duck's back.' Jess shook her head.

'A hymn is there for the singing,' Gil protested through

a mouthful of pastry. 'Too many times I've been to funerals where only the tone-deaf vicar has sung. It's not natural.'

'Watching you eat that sausage roll isn't natural either,' Jess murmured.

'Homemade,' Gil protested. 'I asked the barmaid. This'll get them four stars on Trip Advisor.'

'Thanks for making the effort. I appreciate it. I'm here on sufferance, too.' Warlow glanced around. 'Denise's relatives have not forgiven me for leaving her, not to mention marrying her in the first place.' He nodded at a table of three women who'd been glowering in their direction. 'Her sisters. I can feel the heat from here.'

'Bloody Nora, they must be on the eye out for newt and toe of frog sandwiches,' Gil commented.

Jess snorted. 'I'll keep a look out for a bubbling cauldron.'

From somewhere under the table, the opening bars of The Jungle Book's 'I wanna be like you' warbled up. The Buccaneer reached for his pocket as he stood, took out his phone and answered the call, hastening to a quiet corner to take it.

Gil used the tip of his finger to pick up the last remaining crumbs off his plate and looked across at the buffet before throwing Jess a questioning glance. 'Profiteroles or Victoria sponge?'

Jess waved a hand. 'I'm fine.'

'Evan?'

'Go ahead, I'm full of ham and mustard.'

Gil nodded. 'Not quite on a par with the salmon, but very delectable.'

'Anything you haven't tried?' Warlow asked.

'Profiteroles and Victoria sponge.' Gil wandered off, plate in hand.

Warlow took the vacated seat and sat next to Jess. 'I'm

getting some grief from Alun about Australia. He wants me to go out and visit.'

'Why don't you?' Jess's eyebrows arched.

'Denise wouldn't let me go without her. Besides, Alun… he didn't want her pissed around his wife and child.'

Jess nodded. 'No excuse now though.'

There wasn't.

Jess narrowed her eyes. 'You still haven't told them, have you?'

Only two people in the world apart from his doctors knew Warlow was HIV positive. One of them was talking to him now, the other was the man with The Jungle Book ringtone, with his back to the room on the phone.

'No,' Warlow admitted, finally acknowledging Jess's penetrating gaze.

'You will have to, you know that?'

'Will I though?'

Jess's trill of laughter sounded accusatory. 'Of course you will. Because it's eating you from the inside out.'

She was right. But it wasn't his concern over his own well-being that held him back. He simply didn't know how they'd react. Of how his illness – though it hadn't made him ill at all yet thanks to the antivirals – would alter how they saw him. Admittedly, it hadn't altered the way Buchannan and Jess treated him, but family was different. And Warlow had never come top of the class when it came to dealing with personal issues openly. He only had to think of Denise to realise that. For years, he'd shielded the boys from the worst of her excesses. Played that role until they were both old enough to fly the nest. He'd followed soon after. Abandoning the sinking ship before he, too, drowned.

'It's on my list,' Warlow said.

Jess gave him a wan smile in return. But he was saved any further discomfort by Buchannan striding back towards them. Judging by his expression, it didn't look like the call had been from the National Lottery announcing his winnings.

'That was Catrin Richards. A bad one. A child's gone missing.'

'Oh, God,' Jess whispered.

But she got no further as Gil appeared with two young men.

'Ah, so this is where you're hiding.' Alun nodded towards his father. 'In the thin-blue-line corner.'

Warlow stood up. 'You know everyone?'

'We do,' Tom answered. 'But we wanted to track down the voice.' He threw Gil a grin.

The sergeant slid his plate – profiterole and Victoria sponge laden – back onto the table. 'Brought enough for everyone to sample.'

But before he could tuck in, Buchannan stood back up and took Gil to one side with an apology to Tom and Alun. 'Excuse us for one minute.'

'Oh dear,' Alun said, as they moved out of earshot. 'Criminal activity?'

'It never stops,' Warlow said.

'Not even for your wife's funeral?' Alun's grin was a little forced and his eyes flashed with challenge.

Warlow wanted to correct him with the word 'ex' but held back. The glass in Alun's hand swirled with something dark amber that had ice floating in it. Tom's held nothing but clear water.

'I'm driving.' Tom grinned. 'Al isn't.'

Out of the corner of his eye, Warlow saw Gil's face change as the Buccaneer filled him in on what he'd been about to tell him and Jess before the boys arrived. But a moment later, they were back at the table. Neither man sat down. The Buccaneer held out his hand towards the boys.

'Alun, Tom, I'm sorry for your loss. And I'm even more

sorry to have to take your dad away. Something serious has come up and we're needed.'

Tom took the superintendent's hand, looking shocked, but Alun's hand stayed down and all he could do was scowl and snort out his derision. 'Really? What can't wait another hour?'

Warlow froze. Alun was not a child, yet in his petulant response, he saw Denise's legacy. One drink and her belligerence came to the fore. Warlow did not want to fall out with his son, today, of all days.

But he was spared from responding by Gil who turned to Alun, the customary genial smile tempered by something else. Something dangerous.

'You have a child, don't you, Alun?'

'Yes. What's that got to do with—'

'How old?'

'Eighteen months.'

'Leo, isn't it?'

Alun nodded.

'So, imagine you go out to the garden to fetch something and when you come back, Leo is gone. The front gate is shut, so you look everywhere. But there is no sign of him. I expect you'd panic. I expect you'd run around wildly, calling his name. And when there's no response, you'd call the police because it's us that deals with such things. People like me and your father. How would you feel if, when you rang, the person on the other side of the phone told you they'd be there to help once they'd finished their alcohol-free lager and sandwiches?'

Alun's face paled. 'I—'

Gil kept going. 'Your dad leads a team that answers calls like that, Alun. I'm sorry about your mother, too. It's tough. But as of this minute – and yes, every minute counts – the living need Evan more than the dead.'

Alun put his drink down. It clattered onto the table, the

ice clanking in the glass. Shock had replaced the argumentative sneer. Gil spoke a few whispered words into Warlow's ear.

The Buccaneer offered a few more condolences to Alun and Tom, and when Warlow turned back, he said, 'We could go, and you follow, Evan.'

Warlow shook his head. They all knew that the hours following an abduction were the most important. 'I'll say my goodbyes and follow you in.'

This time Alun shook everyone's hands as the police officers left, leaving Warlow alone with his sons.

'Not what I'd planned for today,' he said.

Tom shrugged. 'Sounds like they need you.' He opened his arms and Warlow stepped in.

Alun looked a little sick. 'How old?'

'What?' Warlow asked.

Alun swallowed loudly. 'The kid.'

'Six. A boy.'

'Christ.' Alun held out his hand. Warlow pushed it away and pulled him into a hug.

'I am coming to Oz.' Warlow announced this as he stepped back. 'That's a promise.'

Tom's eyes lit up. 'Jodie and I are thinking of going, too. Maybe we could go together?'

'I'd like that.' Warlow nodded. 'The Warlows on the beach together.' He smiled at his boys. 'Can you give everyone my apologies?' He glanced up at the mourners. Not his world. Not anymore.

The boys nodded in unison.

'Go do your thing, Dad,' Alun said with feeling.

Warlow nodded. Then he turned and left the pub.

CHAPTER FOUR

WARLOW GOT BACK on to the M4 at junction 48 and joined a string of cars heading west. Tourists flocking to the Pembrokeshire and Cardiganshire coasts no doubt, some to the ferries for Ireland. Traffic moved quickly, but not quickly enough for Warlow as he waited for a gap to push into the middle lane. At the same time, he found Catrin Richards's number in his contacts and called her up via the Jeep's Bluetooth link to his phone.

He steered over to the middle lane, passing caravans and motorhomes which seemed to make up every other vehicle. Catrin answered after five rings.

'Afternoon, sir.'

'Superintendent Buchannan and Gil gave me nothing but the bare details. What have you got?'

'This one's close to home, sir. Osian Howells is the boy's name. The family live at Cwrt Y Waun, a dozen miles up the valley.'

'I know it.' A small village off the A40, closer to the market town of Llandeilo than Carmarthen, where Dyfed Powys had their HQ.

'The mother and both children had come back from a shopping trip. Someone had set fire to a load of straw in a field at the rear of the property. Next to a chicken coop.'

'A distraction?'

'Looks like it, sir. By the time the mother had dealt with that and got the chickens out, the boy was gone.'

Warlow's grip on the steering wheel tightened. He pulled out to overtake an orange VW Camper van. Behind him, a red Jaguar flashed its lights in warning. Warlow ignored it and powered on past the van. 'How long ago?'

'Three hours and counting, sir.'

'House to house?'

'Ongoing, sir. But few houses to call on. It's a small place.'

'I'm on my way in.'

'I'll get the kettle on.'

Warlow ended the call. The day had stayed dry. An even greater draw for the holidaymakers keen to get a bit of early sun on their backs. That got him wondering how much the weather played a part in everything. Clichéd though it might be as to how obsessed the British were with the weather, it was always something you factored in. Showers were forecast, but he'd seen nothing of them yet. In this part of the world, the fronts came and went vigorously. The weather could change in an instant. What if it had rained when whoever had taken Osian had set the fire? The boy would still be in his house watching Paw Patrol. Warlow would still be at Jeez Denise's funeral. The day would not yet have soured.

But it had not rained yet. And Osian was not in front of the TV. He was somewhere else. With someone else. Someone he didn't want to be with.

Warlow felt his chest tighten. Not his first ride on this roundabout. He'd been involved with investigating missing children before. Once, memorably, he'd caught a dog thief and found a shoe belonging to a kidnapped girl in the dark hole the thief used to keep the dogs in. That shoe led to them finding the little girl alive in the thief's cellar.

That had been a good day.

But he knew how rare such positive results were. Most of the time, the endings in cases like this were everything but positive. Families destroyed; questions left unanswered. Lives ruined and often, lost.

But the sooner you got into the hunt the better. You maximised your chances that way.

He floored the accelerator.

———

Three and half hours missing…

HQ SPRAWLED in a greenfield site outside the town of Carmarthen. Its official address was Llangunnor, but access off the A48 was at Nantycaws, the literal translation of which was cheese stream. No problems parking all the way out here. Yet, the downside of situating it this far south meant much of the area that HQ administered stretched a bloody long way west and north. Three hundred and fifty miles of coastline and almost three and a half thousand square miles of land in total. Ideally, if you took a pin and dropped it in the middle of the patch, HQ should have been inland and southeast of Aberystwyth, somewhere around Llanwrtyd Wells. The trouble was that most of the people that needed policing lived around the edges. The very middle of the area was almost empty. It made no sense to have a lot of resources there.

And so, everything stemmed from the south. And Catrin had been right when she'd said, with a little relief, that this one was close to home. Close to HQ anyway. Far from home for Warlow, of course. Because 'home' was now a renovated cottage in Nevern on an estuary in Pembrokeshire. A space he shared with his dog, Cadi. Far enough to sometimes not make it back to the cottage at night. Luckily, he had a great support network for the dog. Molly Allanby, Jess's daughter, helped, as did his neighbours, the Dawes', who were more than willing to take the black lab whenever Warlow got caught up on the job.

Jobs like finding Osian Howells, which, Warlow already knew, would mean not sleeping in his own bed tonight.

When he pushed open the door to the Incident Room, for once, most of the desks were occupied. More often than not, major crimes started off slowly and built as the investigation gathered pace. But not this one. Warlow walked into a room buzzing with activity, busy with co-opted CID officers and some Uniforms staffing phones and bent over monitors.

DC Rhys Harries, clean cut and as tall as the Buccaneer but a lot younger and fitter, handed him a cup of tea as soon as Warlow threw his coat on a chair. He took the cup, still steaming, and smiled in appreciation.

'Saw me arrive in the car park, right?'

Rhys grinned. 'I did, sir. I can spot that Jeep a mile off.'

The other members of the investigating team that Superintendent Buchanan had put together stood in expectation. They knew full well what needed to be done at this stage. No need for introductions.

Warlow glanced up at the two boards at the end of the room. One beige, the other white. The Gallery for photographs, the Job Centre for actions.

'Right,' he said. 'Let's get to it.'

Catrin took the lead. Normally Gil ran the office, but since she had been the one who'd taken the shout, and since she took pride in how she set out the information on the boards, logic dictated Catrin did the needful.

No one argued because everyone agreed she was good at it.

She walked over to the Gallery and the posted-up photograph held in place by a little silver Maglite she'd found to be more powerful than the cheap stuff HQ provided. Next to it, she'd printed a name and a date of birth.

Osian Howells. 08/01/2016.

Hair cropped, a naughty, toothless smile. Osian looked like a bundle of trouble. The good kind.

Posted underneath were the other members of the family. But Warlow's eyes drifted further down to the map Catrin had posted up. She'd circled the village, and the A40 sat well within that circle. A fast road joining Carmarthen with the other towns of east Carmarthenshire; Llandeilo, Ammanford, Llandovery and then on to Brecon and the Beacons, linking these to the south and west where the coast sucked in tourists by the thousands. South lay Swansea and Llanelli, and to the north, the more rural roads ran up towards farmlands and forest.

Warlow ground his teeth. Easy to be overwhelmed in this sort of situation. Best to control what they could.

'Who's the Liaison Officer?'

'PC Mellings, sir,' Catrin said.

Warlow threw Rhys a glance. He and Mellings were a couple. Rhys held up his hands. 'Nothing to do with me, sir.'

'The Buccaneer asked for her,' Gil said.

'Good choice. At least we'll have someone competent with the family.' Warlow nodded.

Rhys's face beamed.

'Anything from forensics?'

'They're looking at the fire.' Jess walked to the board and pointed to a diagram of the property. 'So far, all they have said is that there is no doubt an accelerant was used.

The straw was dragged across from the property on the other side of an access lane. They keep horses so there's lots of straw about the place.'

'Anything come in as evidence?'

Gil shook his head but pointed at two more photographs. One of a bicycle helmet. The other a yellow-painted stick. 'Stormtrooper helmet and lightsabre,' Gil said, and his voice sounded tight. 'Didn't do him much good. They're with the techs.'

'Shame the Force wasn't with him,' Rhys muttered.

'True. But it is now,' Warlow said. He felt the knot that had formed in his stomach as he'd driven in tightening a little more. He looked at Gil. Something in the way he breathed hinted at an anger building within him. The same anger that was building in Warlow. The kind of anger that didn't do you any favours as a police officer. Being professional required a certain detachment. An ability to dissociate yourself from the crime and the person perpetrating it. The trouble was that when it came to kids or animals, that damned nuisance of a thing called 'being human' kept getting in the way. Because being human meant that if you ever caught someone beating on their dog, or hitting a child, you couldn't help but want to step in and intervene. Ask them what they thought they were doing, and if they didn't oblige, punch the miserable bastards in the face.

Or punch the miserable bastards in the face and then ask them what they thought they were doing.

And in a case like this, you could multiply that anger by a factor of a hundred. Someone had taken a six-year-old child for a purpose that could only be wicked. The Americans favoured the term nefarious. The trick was to rein that anger in and do your job. At least until you found the sod. Then, if you were lucky, you could rein it all out again while no one was looking.

So Warlow knew he needed to keep all that in check if he was to be useful. And so did Gil, who had come across many more than his fair share of such people.

Though the word "people" was stretching things a bit, Warlow often thought.

'Okay, it sounds planned.' Warlow motioned back at the boards, waving his finger at the images. 'How much do the press know?'

Catrin's mouth turned down. 'Mrs Howells turned to social media early on. Facebook and Insta. She contacted friends and neighbours. Unfortunately, the press is all over it.'

Warlow turned back to Rhys. 'Tell Gina to make sure the family does not talk to the press until we've spoken to them.'

Rhys nodded and picked up his mobile.

'Is he a wanderer?' Warlow looked at Osian's photo.

'His mother says no. Osian's a home bird. Star Wars obsessed,' Catrin replied.

'Anything of interest with the mother or father?'

Jess shook her head. 'No exes. Nothing on the PNC. They seem like a completely normal family.'

A normal family whose world had just turned upside down.

Warlow went through his checklist. 'What about health issues?'

Catrin shook her head.

'And Social Care has nothing to add?'

'Nothing,' Jess said.

'Then we treat this as elevated risk until proven otherwise.'

Nods all round.

Warlow sucked in a deep breath and let it out in the same tempo. 'Right. Best I get out there as soon as possible and take a look. Then I'll talk to the parents. Gil, you keep a lid on things here for now?'

The sergeant nodded. 'For now.'

Warlow looked down at his tea, still too hot to drink. 'And someone get me a paper cup for this. I'll drink it on the way.'

CHAPTER FIVE

Four hours missing…

WARLOW WALKED down the lane between the Howells' property and the Madge's. The tarmac ended after fifty yards at a second entrance into the Madge place and gave on to a stoned path running next to a stream. Warlow pushed away some overhanging branches and followed the sound of running water. Wild garlic grew in clumps everywhere, shaded from the sun and the wind by hedges and trees. The path descended to the stable block of the Madge's property, stood high on one side. On the other, the field where the fire had been lit stretched away. Warlow kept walking. The path opened out under a green sign with an image of a white walking man on it. Here, a locked gate barred entry into a treatment works under a Welsh Water sign and a new access lane led back to a tarmac road and the A40.

A secret passage of sorts, then.

One not frequented by many, he guessed.

Warlow turned around and retraced his steps. Uniforms had already searched all of this, but he'd needed to see for himself. He re-joined the stone lane and walked up towards the road fronting the Howells' property. On the other side, an empty field of rushes and rough pasture gave on to a copse. Lots of places to get away quickly, out of sight.

An initial search hadn't thrown up anything of any use and the PolSA was looking to extend the search area.

The crime scene bods had long gone, too. There'd been no trace of violence, and petrol had been confirmed as the accelerant for the straw fire. In the road outside the Howells' house, a few Uniforms stood around, making sure no one poked their nose in where it wasn't wanted. The press had set up at the edge of the fifty yards cordon at either side of the entrance. But even now, a reporter was doing a piece to camera.

Jess was talking to some Uniforms who'd done the house to house in the village. Catrin had her phone to her ear, busy listening. Eventually, Jess came back to where Warlow stood.

'Anything?' he asked, as she approached.

'Something and nothing. The local primary school had a nature day just before they broke up for the holidays. A kid went missing for half an hour, but then turned up unharmed. Said she'd been playing with a new friend. They were on the point of ringing us when it all fizzled out.'

Warlow shrugged. 'I'll leave that with you to follow up.'

Catrin put her phone away and joined them. 'PolSA says that they sent the dogs in, and they followed a scent up towards the trees here.' She pointed to the field opposite. 'The dogs went through the copse and out the other end to a road. They lost track at a passing place.'

Warlow nodded. 'Nothing spinning off from that. No forensics?'

'It's grassed all the way through. No muddy prints. They're having a look at the passing place for tyre tracks.'

'What about the fire?'

Jess shook her head. 'Whoever set it could have got in from two or three points.'

Warlow let his gaze drift up the road and swivelled to a one-eighty to look back to where the houses started. 'CCTV anywhere?'

'Nothing on the Howells' property,' Catrin said. 'The Madge's next door have some out back but that's to protect the horses. We're checking the houses up the street. If the abductor came in from this side, there's no chance.'

Rhys appeared, vaulting over a gate into the field opposite, twenty yards down the road.

Catrin shook her head. 'Looks like the steeplechase is on then.'

Warlow called across to him. 'Stay there. I want you to show me the route.' He turned to Jess. 'You okay to talk to the Madge's?'

'Of course.'

Jess turned away. 'I'm talking to neighbours, still. Catrin's liaising with Gil who is chasing up the sex offenders' register. See what rodents there are in the vicinity.' Another unpleasant box that needed ticking.

Warlow joined Rhys. 'If you think I'm jumping over that gate like a bloody racehorse, you've got another think coming.'

'You probably could, sir.' Rhys grinned.

'And I could fall on my head. No need to give the Uniforms something to laugh at.'

The DCI climbed over and stood in the field, studying the latch. He knew the type. A spring fastener comprising a vertical rod you pulled to release from the catch. The gate itself was not locked, but as was so often the way, the owner had tied some nylon rope around the gate and post as a deterrent and to let walkers know they should not enter.

'Who owns the field?'

'A farmer called Gwilym, sir. This is the southern edge of his land. The sheep in the field next door are his.'

Warlow looked up across the rough ground to a greener pasture a hundred yards away, where sheep were quietly grazing along with at least twenty lambs. 'How much did Osian weigh?'

Rhys consulted his notebook. 'Around three stone, sir.'

Warlow nodded. 'Get a photo of this tie. Ask the farmer if it looks like the knot is his.'

'But anyone could untie this, sir.'

'That's why we need to ask. He'd know. If no one messed with the tie, it means Osian was carried over. And if that's the case, it would need to be someone strong. If the tie were loosened, anyone could have opened the gate and taken Osian through.'

Rhys nodded, scribbling in his notebook. 'Good point, sir.'

'Lead on.'

Warlow followed Rhys with the hedge on their left, following yellow markers in the ground where the dogs had signalled. They reached the copse and a ditch that separated it from the field itself. Agricultural fencing topped with a single strand of barbed wire marked the boundary.

'Any sign of where they crossed?'

Rhys pointed to a white marker. 'They think there, sir. Where the fence post is angled.'

The fence looked too tall to step over. Warlow reached the marked point. A thick carpet of dried leaves covered the ground. There'd be no footprints here. Above, the branches of an oak reached down. Close enough to act as a handhold for someone wanting to climb over. 'If he crossed here, then he had Osian tied up so that he wouldn't run. So, he placed him over the fence before he climbed over himself.' An aluminium fence ladder placed by the PolSA straddled the fence a few yards further on and Warlow climbed it. He stood on top, above the barbed wire, and took in the view.

Through the trees, the distant foothills of the Beacons were visible. Grey-blue mounds against the paler sky. Further west, across the valley, Paxton's Tower stood tall, like a chess piece on the horizon. A folly straight out of a *Game of Thrones* set.

The copse had a mixture of old deciduous and a few evergreen trees scattered over a shallow area of only twenty yards in depth, sloping down to the narrow road and the passing place pull in. No other properties within sight. No traffic. No sign of anyone. If someone had parked here, they'd taken a gamble. Anyone passing would have noticed the vehicle. But then who would be passing up here in this remote spot?

'Knew what he was doing alright,' Warlow muttered. 'Whoever did this had done their homework.'

'Is that how you see it, sir?'

'You tell me, Rhys?' The young detective was shaping up well and despite the situation and the hum of urgency buzzing away at the back of Warlow's brain, one day Rhys might oversee an investigation like this.

Rhys paused, considering the question. 'It means someone must have reconnoitred, sir. If this is a stranger abduction, then Osian was chosen for where he lived rather than who he was.'

'Exactly,' Warlow said. 'But most abductions aren't stranger abductions, are they?'

They were about to turn back and retrace their steps when a bright yellow Astra with a black stripe running lengthwise along the bonnet and roof turned into the lane and sped towards them before screeching to a halt in the pull in.

One man got out. Young, dressed in clothes that in Warlow's day would have been classed as gym wear, but these days passed for everyday wear. He had his hair shaved at the sides, leaving a curly mop on top. His T-shirt and trousers had matching stripes down the sides.

The driver stayed in the car; baseball hat clamped on.

Warlow turned to Rhys. 'Why haven't they shut off this road?'

'Don't know, sir.'

'Get on to them now. This is still a crime scene.'

Curly Top was out of the car, already making strides up the bank and into the copse, his face alight with excitement.

Warlow shouted across. 'You asked permission to be in that copse?'

The youth turned, annoyed. 'There's no fence. Why would I need permission?'

Warlow stood below him and saw the driver put up his phone. Video recorder on, no doubt.

'It is someone's land though, so you are trespassing.'

'What the fuck has it got to do with you?' Curly Top yelled back.

Warlow smiled. 'As it happens, quite a lot.' He took out his warrant card and held it out for the man to see and then stepped over to the car so that the driver could take a closeup. 'Detective Chief Inspector Warlow. And who might you be?'

'We don't have to give you our names,' the driver said.

'You're right. But Rhys here has your car registration. And I also have the right to arrest you for trespass. Be up to the owner to press charges, of course.'

The first brief flare of doubt bunched up Curly Top's

brows. 'Fuck's sake, I only want to get to the top and take some photos. Be worth a shitload to the papers.'

'Oh? And why is that?'

'Cos of the kid, innit? It's all over fucking Facebook.'

'Right. So, you know this area?' Warlow was reasonableness personified.

'Yeah.' Curly Top ticked up the end of the word in defiance.

'That's interesting. Because we think whoever is involved in the abduction knew the area. And you know what these criminals are like. They're always coming back to the scene of the crime to gloat or to find out how useless the police are.'

The arrogant defiance on Curly Top's face froze.

'Whoa,' he said, his confidence sliding from under him. 'Hang on a minute.'

'I didn't know you could get to the house from here. But you seem to.' Warlow turned again to smile at the driver. 'You too?'

The phone dropped away. The driver, his head shaved, stuttered, 'I— I'm not from around here.'

'Yet here you are. Parked in a spot no more than a few hundred yards from where a child went missing.' Warlow turned back to Curly Top. 'So that leaves you knowing more about this case than the police. Care to explain that to us down at HQ?'

Curly Top's mouth dropped open. He hurried back down the slope. 'I've only been up there once. We were just messing about. Looking for mushrooms we were. Last year sometime. I recognised it from the description.'

Rhys joined Warlow. 'We're running the plates now, sir.' He nodded towards the Astra.

Curly Top had his hands up now. 'I don't know anything about the kid. I thought we could get some quick snaps is all. Get 'em up on Insta.'

Rhys's phone rang. He answered and stepped away, relaying the information he received out loud as it came to him. 'Josh Stebbings, aged 24. 17 Corris Street, Cross Hands.'

The driver paled. 'Shit, Ben. Come on, man. Forget it.'

Curly Top's swagger was now a hands-up apology as he sidled past Warlow towards the passenger door. 'Sorry, man. I hope you catch the bastard. I swear I don't know shit about this.'

Warlow stepped closer to the driver's side. 'I know who you are now, Josh.' He looked up towards Curly Top, grinning as he added, 'And Ben. If I see that video anywhere, I'll be sure to call and discuss its artistic merits with you.'

The car fired up and Josh drove off with due care and attention. Once it cleared the corner, Warlow heard it roar away.

'Nice guys,' Rhys said, not meaning a word of it.

'Idiots,' Warlow replied. 'Come on. We need to speak to Osian's parents.'

CHAPTER SIX

Four hours and twenty-five minutes missing…

WARLOW RETRACED his steps through the copse and across the field, Rhys in tow. He climbed over the gate with one more look at the knotted nylon rope securing it and crossed to Maes Awelon. They'd painted it white as a nod to the whitewashed farmhouses dotted over the landscape, though it was a more modern build. The house name sat on the picket gate that led to a concrete path through the front garden. A second path branched right to the side of the property, where an open wooden door marked the entrance to the side passage. A jumble of cardboard boxes sat in the gap between the wall of the house and the hedge bordering the property.

Osian Howells' imaginary spaceship.

The front garden looked used. Nothing twee, no lovingly tended borders here. Just flattened grass stamped down by little feet. Warlow noted a rugby ball and a football and a plastic hoop. The Uniform guarding the gate opened it for Warlow and the two detectives walked up the path to the front door, which opened without them having to knock. The woman who stood there wore the black uniform of Dyfed Powys Police and, despite the circumstances, smiled a greeting. PC Gina Mellings' eyes slid past Warlow to Rhys. Her eyebrows shot up, but, to her credit, she gave nothing away.

Though he'd been already told, Warlow felt a rush of relief on seeing Mellings as the FLO. He'd worked with her before. Knew how capable she was. 'Gina, how are they holding up?'

'Not too bad until Mrs Howells' brother arrived, sir.' Gina's mouth turned down.

'Is he here now?'

Gina nodded. 'Tea, sir?'

'Silly question. Milk and one.'

Gina's blue eyes strayed to Rhys. 'Tea or coffee?'

'Coffee, if it's going.'

'One sugar or two?'

'You know it's only one—'

Gina stifled a grin and turned away.

Warlow sent Rhys an over-the-shoulder glance. 'Word to the wise. Coffee is always a risk. Bound to be instant. So could be anything. Better to stick with tea. And how come your girlfriend doesn't know how many sugars you take?'

'She does, sir. She just—'

Warlow's turn to flicker a smile.

Once the FLO had made the introductions, they all congregated in the living room. Warlow and Rhys sat on a brown leather sofa, the cushions sagging in the corners, and the backrest angling back in such a way that anyone sitting in it would be comatose in fifteen minutes. But this was no time for sleep.

Gina came back with the tea and put it on a coaster on a low table. Warlow sat forward, his coat still on. He didn't intend to spend too much time here if he could help it.

Talking to the relatives was important, but Osian wasn't here.

It was now after 4pm. The boy had been missing for almost five hours. From the look on Nerys Howells' face, it could well have been five years. It had probably felt that long to her. She wasn't a small woman. Chunky, as one of Warlow's old sergeants might have said. But worry had ravaged an attractive face, fed by what her imagination was no doubt throwing into the mix every few seconds. She had mascara-smudged eyes and lids puffy from tears. She held on to the hand of a big man sitting next to her. Nerys's husband, Lloyd, was broad in the chest and sat with his thick arms folded in his lap. His expression had the lost look of someone stuck in a waking nightmare, struggling to find a foothold in reality.

'Would you like a biscuit?' Nerys asked.

'Not for me, thanks, Nerys,' Warlow answered.

'I'm fine, too,' Rhys said.

Nerys ignored them. 'There's a box in the cupboard over the sink. We keep it up there so that Osian can't...' She caught herself, pulled in air with a ragged intake of breath and kept talking. 'I could put a plate out, if—'

Gina cut her off. 'No need, Nerys. Everyone is fine.'

'Yes, forget the bloody biscuits, Ner.' This irritable warning came from the third member of the family standing silhouetted against the window. James Ryan was everything his sister wasn't. Wiry, with an angular face and tattoos on his neck and wrist and many more under his plaid shirt.

Warlow sent him a neutral glance, which Ryan returned with belligerent interest.

The DCI reengaged Nerys and Lloyd. 'I realise you've had nothing but people asking you questions all day, but I'm the Senior Investigating Officer and I would like to ask you some more. It is frustrating for you, but it's all a part of the process. If that's alright?'

Nerys nodded, eager to cooperate. And Lloyd nodded dully and muttered, 'Whatever we need to do.'

But James Ryan, standing behind his sister, glared at the DCI and shook his head, his pent-up anger keen to find a target. 'How many times are you lot going to badger my sister? Jesus. Osian isn't here. He's out there somewhere.'

Warlow nodded. 'I know. But it's the little things that usually add up to something big in an investigation like this—'

'Little things?' Ryan spat. 'What bloody little things?'

This time Warlow blanked Ryan. 'You have two children, Nerys?'

Nerys nodded. 'Osian and Fflur.'

'It's half term so they're off school. Does Osian play outside much? In the front garden, I mean?'

Lloyd shook his head. 'No. Not much. We've got a lot more room at the back. He practises taking penalties or converting tries out back.'

'But he's been watching Star Wars,' Nerys added. 'He decided that the front garden was in space.' She snorted. 'It sounds pathetic.'

Warlow gave her half a smile. 'It's not. It sounds like he has a great imagination.'

Nerys smiled in return. A brave effort that faltered as soon as it formed. 'He built a spaceship, and he began fighting aliens. He shut the door into the backyard because he wanted to be on a different planet.'

'So, it's new, this playing in the front garden?' Warlow asked.

'Yes,' Nerys explained. 'New this weekend.'

She looked at her husband. He squeezed his eyes shut. Playing the if only game, Warlow guessed. If only they hadn't let him watch Star Wars. If only it had been raining today. If only…if only.

'Can you run through what happened today? Right from the beginning. Right from when you got up. Mr Howells—'

'Lloyd.'

'Okay, Lloyd. You got up first?'

'Seven. I'm off to work by half seven. I'd normally wake the kids up, but it's the holidays.'

Warlow gave him an encouraging nod. 'Right. And when you left for work, you saw no one? You didn't pass any cars?'

'No. The road was empty,' Lloyd confirmed.

Warlow flicked his eyes to Nerys. 'And you took the children shopping?'

'Aldi. We were there by nine.'

'Again, you saw no one parked on the road?'

'No.'

Rhys had his notebook out, scribbling down details.

'We were back by half past ten.'

'And you've seen nothing odd, no one driving past or hanging about?'

Lloyd shook his head. 'There are some Airbnbs in the area. Not unusual to see the odd tourist driving around.'

'But nothing that aroused your suspicion?' Warlow enquired.

'Christ's sake,' Ryan muttered. 'What is this? Spot the bloody kidnapper?'

Nerys's head jerked around at him. But he remained defiant. 'Well, Jesus, come on?'

'Why are you being such a pain, James?' Nerys said, the words pitiful and pleading.

Warlow watched the dynamics, deciding already that Ryan had relinquished his membership of the Dyfed

Powys Police Fan Club somewhere along the way. But his negativity finally proved too much for his brother-in-law.

'They're bloody clueless, Ner. I told you—'

For a big man, Lloyd moved quickly. The sapping lethargy of a moment ago gone in an instant and replaced with a seething anger as he sprang to his feet 'Why don't you go home, James.'

It struck Warlow that Lloyd didn't need to shout much. The rumble of fury in his voice required no volume to convey its meaning.

'I'm only saying—'

'Yeah, and I've heard it too many bloody times,' Lloyd said.

'I can get some of the boys. Someone knows something. We can drive around—'

'Jesus, James.' Lloyd shook his head. Fear and sadness drained all his anger in an instant. 'You think you can do better than the police? Is that it?'

'They're not doing much, are they?'

Lloyd's head snapped up again, the anger back, his cheeks flaring bright red. 'Go home. You being here isn't helping.'

'What? Ner?'

But Nerys didn't turn around. She'd given in to misery and fat dollops of tears ran down her face, her lower lip trembling violently. She didn't look at her brother. All she could do was shake her head. No room in there for family squabbles. Not now.

Ryan hissed out air like the brakes on a double decker and left the room.

Warlow waited for the mood to stabilise.

'Sorry,' Nerys whispered after a while.

'No need to apologise. There is no right way to react in a situation like this.' And it was true. He'd seen people collapse in hysterics, withdraw and become virtually catatonic. Others ranted and raved at anyone within earshot. That 'anyone' usually being a member of the constabulary tasked with getting near to a situation that most sane people would run a mile from. 'Is James close to Osian?'

'He takes him fishing,' Lloyd explained. 'They get on.'

'Back to today,' Warlow pushed things back on track.

Nerys sniffed. 'No, I didn't see anyone odd or different. Not when I left for the supermarket. Not when I got home. But whoever did it lit the fire, didn't they?'

Warlow held her gaze. 'Someone lit the fire. No doubt about that.'

More tears came then. Silent ones. Nerys didn't even bother wiping them away. 'That's so evil. So—'

'Planned, yes.' Warlow couldn't pull the punches here. He wouldn't lie to these people. 'And you haven't fallen out with anyone in the area. Not even in the most trivial way?'

Lloyd shook his head. 'No. I don't owe anyone money if that's what you're asking.'

'Why?' Nerys's expression crumpled in disbelief. 'You think someone could do this for money?'

'It's possible,' Warlow told them. 'There's a reason Osian has been taken.'

Lloyd's head dipped onto his chest. 'Not likely though, is it? A ransom?'

'It's still a possibility.'

'What about the other reasons?' Lloyd asked.

'There are other reasons. None of them good.' Again, Warlow couldn't lie. 'And we face that fact.' He fell short of giving them the stats. That if this turned out to be a stranger abduction and a predator, there was a significant chance that Osian might be already dead. Taken, and used, for nefarious purposes. He'd shoulder that burden himself for now. These people, these victims in front of him, needed hope. 'We're going to talk to all your neighbours, ask them the same questions. The dogs have traced

Osian over the field to the copse so we know he went there. We have men searching in case he's wandered off and got lost.'

Nerys squeezed a couple more tears from her eyes. There was more Warlow needed to ask, but not now. 'Gina is going to stay with you. She'll answer all your questions and answer the phone to the press if you want her to. She'll be able to tell you anything you need to know.'

Nerys looked up into Gina's face. The PC smiled and put a hand on her shoulder.

Warlow turned to Rhys. 'Anything you want to ask, Constable Harries?'

Six months ago, such a question would have made Rhys flush a bright red and stammer out a standard. 'No.' But that was then.

Rhys looked up and addressed Lloyd. 'Does James live locally?'

'No. Why?'

'We'll want to talk to him when he's calmer. See if he has any ideas.'

'He has a lot of ideas,' Nerys said.

Rhys nodded. 'And one of them might help. We leave nothing to chance, Nerys.'

'Right now, the only idea James has is what knot he'll use to string up the bastard who did this,' Lloyd muttered. 'He's a hothead.'

Warlow nodded. 'He's allowed to be. I have no idea how I'd react in a situation like this. None of us do.'

Nerys stepped in to defend her brother. 'He's angry. He loves the kids, and he wants to find who did this.'

'We all do, Nerys,' Warlow told her. 'And I promise the both of you we'll do whatever it takes to bring Osian back to you. I give you my word on that.'

Nerys nodded, and her mouth formed a trembling smile of gratitude. 'Gina says you won't give up. Ever.'

'She's right.' Warlow looked Nerys in the eye when he answered.

Rhys hadn't given up on his question. 'What's James's address?'

Lloyd answered, 'He lives in Whitland with his partner.' He made to get up, but Rhys put a hand up. 'Don't trouble yourself now. Give it to Gina.'

'No, I'll do it now.' Lloyd got up and walked to the kitchen table, glad, it looked like to Warlow, of something to do. Rhys had managed that well. All three of the officers in this room knew the stats. Fifty per cent of all kidnapping cases involved a relative of the victim. Of the remaining abductions, half were acquaintance abductions by someone who was known to the victim. The rest, the most feared, were stranger abductions. Warlow was keeping an open mind. People were innocent until proven guilty, but in Warlow's head, everyone was capable of doing anything. That included James Ryan. It also included Lloyd and Nerys Howells. Though if they were involved in this, they'd missed their vocation as actors. One look at them told him they'd been stripped raw by events.

Still, Warlow had crossed no one off his list yet.

They would certainly need to talk to hothead James Ryan. And they'd be double-checking Lloyd Howells' movements. They wouldn't be doing their jobs if they didn't.

Lloyd came back with a post-it note with James Ryan's address written on it.

Warlow finished his tea and put down the mug. 'One more thing. The press.'

'I'm not talking to them,' Lloyd muttered, his brows gathering.

'Good idea. For now, at least. Gina can screen all the calls that come in if you'd like her to. We may decide to use the press if and when. But it'll be on our terms.'

'An appeal, you mean?' Nerys asked, her mouth curling in distaste.

'I don't like the idea either. But there'll be forensic psychologists who'll be advising us on all of that. For now, we'll have Uniforms stationed to keep the piranhas at bay. And Gina is a great Rottweiler when it comes to dealing with them.'

Gina nodded with a grim smile.

'Thanks.' Lloyd sat down next to his wife. She reached out for his hand, and he took it. But Nerys had one more question to ask. The big one. The one that rasped at her throat when she voiced it.

'Do you think he's dead?'

Warlow held her gaze. 'The truth? We cannot know. But as far as I am concerned, Osian is alive. I've already promised you we'll do everything we can to get him back and I'm sticking to that.'

The fingers of Nerys's hand were white where she was squeezing Lloyd's. But she nodded on hearing Warlow's words. Hardly a cast iron reassurance but the God's honest truth.

'We're going to find him,' the DCI said again. 'We are.'

CHAPTER SEVEN

Five Hours missing…

RHYS'S PHONE buzzed the minute he and Warlow left Maes Awelon. Warlow waited while the DC looked at the message, his eyes flicking between the garden and the Uniform guarding the gate. The fence bordering garden and road could not have been more than three feet tall. Easy enough for a strong adult to lean over and pick up a child.

'That was Catrin, sir,' Rhys said. 'She says they'll be another few minutes.'

'Text her back and ask them to meet us in the Reading Room.'

Rhys's finger moved over the touchscreen as Warlow left the garden and stood once again looking up and down the quiet road before walking to the Jeep. It was only half a mile or so. Easily walkable, but that would have meant running the gauntlet of the waiting press, hovering on the edge of the cordon like a line of racing snakes.

Bugger that. Warlow didn't trust himself to ignore the inanities.

Who do you think has Osian, Detective Chief Inspector?
What's your plan of action?
Where do you think Osian is?
Is it likely Osian is already dead?
Fair questions, all of them.

It was simply that the scum asking them and the way they would be asked pressed all Warlow's sod-off buttons.

They parked up a hundred yards past the driveway to the Reading Room, near a gate that led through a field to a church perched on a hill.

Rhys got out of the car and stood looking around. Opposite them stood the tall and incredibly old wall of a private house. 'Posh here, isn't it, sir?'

Warlow nodded. 'Lots of big estates out this way. Land carved up for the gentry back in the day.'

They walked back along the road, staying close to the line of parked cars to avoid the traffic flowing steadily through. Warlow wondered how much of this unusual level of traffic contained rubberneckers out to see what all the fuss was about.

'Why is it called a Reading Room, sir?' Rhys asked.

Warlow didn't stop walking but allowed himself a little smile. 'I thought you were the history buff in our team.'

'I'm more World Wars, sir.'

'You old romantic you. But you need to go back a little further for this. Reading Rooms were set up by the Great and the Good to educate the masses. Books and newspapers were made available to be read only in these rooms. Difficult to believe in the Google age. But if you wanted news or information as a worker, you came here under strict regulations. In other words, they were temperance rooms. No drunks or drinking. The idea was to provide an alternative to the pub.'

'I can't see a pub, sir.'

'Not now. Though there is one at the crossroads a mile

away towards Llanfynydd. But we're a few miles from Llandeilo. A market town with twenty-three pubs in the mid-nineteenth century. And yes, you may well ask how I know this? Thank Sergeant Jones for these bits of useless information which, over a cup of tea and a biscuit or three, he keeps telling me all about. But the point is, the pub was the focal point of the working man's entertainment before TV and films came along. And with that came a whole slew of bad health choices thrown into the bargain.'

'Sergeant Jones has moved back there hasn't he, sir?'

'He has. There aren't twenty-three pubs in Llandeilo now. But that is not the point. They explain the Reading Room.'

'Weird to think you had to go to a certain place to find out things?'

'There speaks the man with an iPhone glued to his hand,' Warlow said.

Someone had put cones out to stop people from parking. A complete joke since the road for a hundred and fifty yards either way and the little lane up to the small Reading Room car park was stuffed with response vehicles, Canine units, CSI vans and the search hunt Sprinter vans that had delivered the Uniforms who were now combing the area, picking over anything that might hint at what had happened to Osian Howells.

Inside, the room – more a small hall – had been taken over by the PolSA and his teams. Warlow nodded to the Crime Scene Manager, who shook his head in response.

'Nothing yet, sir.'

Tables had been pushed to the walls and chairs lay in a rough half-circle three rows deep in front of a flip chart. The place had a musty smell that old floorboards sometimes had. It took Warlow back to his primary school days. But nothing remotely childish could be mistaken for the desperate search the PolSA was coordinating from here. Warlow saw no reason for not making use of the building, too. Behind the flipchart stood a small stage with steps leading up to it on both sides with a table and chairs in the middle.

'We'll use that,' he said to Rhys. 'Take a couple more chairs up there.'

While the DC did that, Warlow studied the map the PolSA had laid out on one of the tables next to the chart. A big circle had been drawn around Cwrt Y Waun for two miles. Marked to indicate where outbuildings needed searching. And they were only the abandoned ones. Others might need warrants. Then there were the driveways, rivers and streams, lanes, and hedgerows. As always, it seemed a massive undertaking. And they were doing it in the figurative dark. With nothing to lead or guide them.

At some stage, there'd be a press conference. Mellings would have a chat with Nerys and Lloyd Howells and choose a photograph to release to the media through HQ's support unit. That photograph would then appear in all the newspapers and on TV. The official acknowledgement of a family's nightmare. But it hadn't happened yet. They still had time to see if someone, somewhere, had seen something. The one advantage of being out here in the countryside came in the form of habitual behaviour. People tended to get up at the same time, walk their dogs at the same time, get to work, open the shop, wave at the postman. Boring, some might say, but it wasn't the chaotic buzz of the city where everything happened fast and with exponential possibilities. Warlow clung to the hope that something would turn up.

Though there were tea-making facilities out back, no one had done anything about them. When Jess and Catrin arrived a few minutes later, the four members of the investigating team sat on the little stage, tea-less, and spoke in low voices while down below the Crime Scene Manager and an evidence officer got on with the business of organising men and facilities.

Warlow filled them in on their interview with the Howells. He mentioned James Ryan as someone they'd need to keep an interest in, but his gut feeling was that neither Nerys nor Lloyd Howells was directly involved. 'What about the Madges?' he asked.

Jess shrugged. 'Two teenage kids. Both away. One staying with a friend, the other on a chemistry refresher course. We spoke to the parents. He is some kind of financial consultant who works from home, she is the horsey person. They were both at home this morning when Osian went missing. Both can vouch for each other and neither of them saw or heard anything different until Nerys Howells raised the alarm.'

'What about the straw for the fire?' Rhys asked.

Catrin nodded. 'They keep bales dotted around. We went out into the paddock. There is a path that runs past the property, slightly lower down.'

'I know it,' Warlow said. 'Leads to a water treatment works.'

Catrin elaborated. 'It wouldn't take more than a minute to scramble up the bank from the path and reach over a fence to grab some straw. The field where the fire was set is only a few yards away. A couple of forensic techs are examining the fence for signs of scuff marks or a boot print.'

'And they're happy for us to search the property?'

Catrin nodded.

'Do we think that the abductor knew about the straw and the path?' Rhys asked.

Jess undid her coat. 'He's scoped out the area. It's a

public footpath. He could have done all that yesterday or a week or a month ago. The one thing that came up again was this incident a couple of weeks ago when a child went missing for half an hour.'

'From the school, was it?' Rhys asked.

'Not quite.' Jess explained, while Catrin flicked through her notebook. 'Mrs Madge is a primary school governor, so she knew all about it.'

Catrin looked up, her face serious. 'Small school. Forty-nine kids, three teachers. The week before end of term, the whole lot of them went out on a nature trail walk. Near to the school and the Howells' property, in fact.' She reached into a messenger bag and pulled out a sheet of A4 paper on which a crude map had been drawn with a few crosses dotted along the snaking lines for roads labelled School, Maes Awelon and Nature Woods. Warlow peered at it, frowning. The woods between the school and Maes Awelon formed a rough triangle, with each side measuring two-thirds of a mile.

'What could she tell you about what happened?' Warlow asked.

Jess sighed. 'Not much. The child was six, the same age as Osian. Three adults and almost fifty kids in a woodland and suddenly, they couldn't find one. They made the kids sit down in one area and one teacher stayed with them while the other two searched. It took them half an hour, but it appeared she'd strayed close to a stream near where the woods began and they found her there, unharmed, saying she'd been playing with a Green Man.'

'A Green Man?'

'That's what the kid said.'

Warlow's senses sat up. 'Did they report this? The teachers, I mean.'

Jess shook her head. 'No. I mean, the child was

unharmed. They were embarrassed, and the kid has a vivid imagination. They spoke to the parents, apologised, but nothing has come of it. No reason it should have appeared on our radar.'

'No reason until now,' Rhys muttered.

Jess winced and, for once, grabbed the fingers of one hand in the palm of the other. 'But then the parents posted something on social media and other parents joined in. Beware the Green Man, that sort of stuff. Warnings to look out for strangers. You know the kind of thing.'

Warlow nodded. All entirely understandable. Yet his mind was churning, trying to make sense of this. Trying to fit these two pieces of the jigsaw together. But his thoughts were interrupted by his phone. Gil wanted to FaceTime. Catrin put her messenger bag on the table and Warlow used it to prop up his phone. He shifted his chair around next to Jess's, and Catrin and Rhys stood behind it as if they were in a bizarre family photo. Gil's face appeared distorted from the phone camera angle and with half his chin missing.

'Stand back from the phone a bit, Gil,' Jess told him. 'You look like something Picasso painted.'

'My arm isn't long enough.'

'Prop the phone on the desk,' Catrin said, her tolerance of Gil's tech cack-handedness thin at the best of times.

Gil adjusted the phone, and the image danced giddily, stabilised, then danced again as the device slid to the desk. Finally, he reappeared, upright but angled with the wall of the Incident Room forming a background behind him.

'Glad to see you trimmed your nose hairs, Sarge,' Rhys said.

'You're a fine one to talk. It's like the Addams family look-alike contest. I'm not going to say which one of you looks most like Cousin Itt. Where are you?'

Warlow explained about the Reading Room.

'Right, so you've set up an outpost,' Gil commented.

'We have.' Jess replied.

'Tidy. I've found one SO registered within five miles of the abduction.' Gil's eyes flicked up to the troubled expression on Rhys's face and shot out an explanation to the young officer. 'SO. Sex Offender. Thought I'd go out there and pay him a visit.'

'Good idea,' Warlow said. Of all the people in the team, Gil would be the best placed to do this. His experience in Operation Alice gave him a better-than-average insight into this side of things. Not that such knowledge was anything to brag about. Far from it. Gil kept his powder dry when it came to all things Alice related. 'I'll send Rhys back to HQ and he can go with you.'

'What?' Rhys said behind him, sounding like a kid who'd just been told he had to go to school.

Warlow rode over his protests. 'It'll be valuable experience, Rhys.'

'They give me the creeps, sir. Sex Offenders.'

'Then you need to face your demons,' Jess said. 'There's no picking and choosing in this job.'

'Right.' Gil nodded. 'But don't bother coming back. It's further up the valley. Stay there, Rhys, I'll pick you up on the way through.'

'Sounds like a plan,' Warlow said, pleased that they all had actions to follow. 'Jess and Catrin are going to talk to a teacher about a nature trail, and I'm going to talk to a little girl about a Green Man.'

'Simples,' Gil said. 'I'll get the Transplant box out. Bring a little curated sample along.'

Rhys, whose face had fallen at the prospect of visiting someone on the sexual offender's register, brightened at the prospect of Gil's HUMAN TISSUE FOR TRANS-

PLANT box since it hid a selection of handpicked biscuits. 'There's a post office seventy yards off the main road. I'll walk there. Will you be bringing a flask for the biscuits, Sarge?'

'Is the Pope a catalyst?'

CHAPTER EIGHT

CATRIN AND JESS headed back to the A40 crossroads, with the sergeant driving the Focus and the DI in the passenger seat. The straight road on the other side looked Roman. It took them underneath the ruins of a castle perched on a rocky hill with commanding views of the river valley.

'What's the story there?' Jess asked, glancing up as the road curved beneath.

'That's Dryslwyn Castle, ma'am. I'm ashamed to say I don't know the story. Never been up there. You ought to ask Rhys if you've got a spare twenty minutes.'

'Of course. I'll do that.'

They crossed the River Towy before climbing out of the valley on the other side. 'Molly would love all this,' Jess commented. 'It's almost alpine here. Very *Lord of the Rings*.'

She was looking at the broad sweep of the valley floor and another, bigger, ruined castle at Dinefwr. This one stood north of the river, on the edge of the town of Llandeilo with its multicoloured houses marching up the hill.

But then the road swept around and climbed still higher towards Maesybont.

Catrin kept up a commentary. 'All change here. Still

farmland, but it becomes more industrial. A few more miles and we're in the coalfields.'

'Where are we heading?'

'Ammanford, ma'am. Nice coffee shop there if you'd like?'

'The one opposite the station?'

Catrin nodded.

'I do like. And I need a caffeine hit. Why not.'

––––––

ARMED WITH AN AMERICANO and a flat white from Coaltown Coffee Roasters, the two officers took the Llandybie road back out of Ammanford towards a development at Tir Y Dail and pulled up in front of a red house on a street called Ffordd Yr Afon. Most of the houses they'd passed had been thirties semis, but this little block was newly built. Number eight was all red from the bricks to the colour of the roofing tiles. Faux wood uPVC windows and doors in a porch lent it a Lego-built vibe.

Dewi Boyce opened the door before Catrin had a chance to ring. Mid-fifties, average height, with a receding hairline and a sincere expression, he delivered the invitation in a half whisper. 'Come in, please.'

A woman hovered in the background, clad in a skirt and blouse, her smile a mix of invitation and concern. The kind that undertakers specialised in.

Boyce led the way into a conservatory at the back of the house, looking out onto a neat garden with a snooker-table lawn and raised beds.

'Thank you for seeing us,' Jess said.

'Of course.' Boyce replied, earnestly.

'I'll put the kettle on,' the woman said.

'*Diolch, cariad,*' Boyce said, before his face fell at realising that he had not introduced her. 'Oh, this is my wife, Meinir.'

Nods were exchanged and Catrin responded with, 'Sergeant Catrin Richards and Detective Inspector Jess Allanby.'

As they walked through the house to the rear Catrin glanced at some photographs of a family unit, two adults and a child, that same child in cap and gown and then a wedding as the bride. They ended up sitting in wicker chairs, watching the leaves from a silver birch dance in the breeze at the bottom of the well-tended garden.

'You'll know why we're here, Mr Boyce,' Catrin said.

'Dewi, please. And of course, anything I can do. You have no news of Osian *bach*?'

'Not yet.'

Dewi Boyce slumped. The movement more like a slow flinch as he recoiled from the news. 'He's such a bright boy. Full of life.'

'We wanted to ask you about the incident that took place a couple of weeks ago when you took the school on a nature trail.'

'Yes. The day we almost lost Nia Owen.' He shook his head before frowning as he put two and two together. 'You don't think there's any link—'

'Could you tell us what happened that day, Dewi?' Catrin pressed him before he could get side-tracked.

'It takes a bit of planning with fifty children across all age groups from five to eleven.' Dewi did a lot of his talking with his hands, conducting the orchestra of words animatedly. 'But we try to do it a couple of times a year. Different seasons, you see. And the woods are owned by one of the school governors. They've even made a little play area there with tables and chairs carved out of fallen trees.'

Catrin waited impassively.

Boyce caught the look in her eye and concentrated. 'We went over at nine-thirty. A dry day after two previous dry days. A rare event. Three teachers and forty-three pupils. Three of our pupils were off sick that day.' His fingers walked through the air. 'We crossed the road as a crocodile, two abreast, and then we were on the lane that leads to the treatment works. Across a stile, and a field and we were in the woods.'

'And when did you realise Nia was missing?'

Dewi made a shape in the air with his hand. 'It's a circular walk. It's not far. We stop and look at the trees and the flowers. Some of the older children have sketchbooks. We divide them up into three groups of fifteen or so. Myself, Lowri Williams and Janice Fyles.'

'The other two teachers?' Jess asked.

Boyce nodded. 'I take the older children, Janice the little ones under seven and Lowri those in between. We set tasks for them and follow it up in class.'

Catrin wrote in her notebook before looking up. 'What happened to Nia?'

'It's a small wood,' Dewi explained. 'The groups are never separated by more than a hundred yards. And there are head counts every time we move on. Janice's head-count was one short. She shouted for me, so I took my group and left them with Lowri. Janice's group was nearest to the entrance. She'd counted them in and, as she was about to move on, counted again. Nia wasn't there.'

'She's what, six?' Jess asked.

'Six. And a character.' He shook his head. 'We re-counted. I wanted no one to panic, though I will tell you that the old heart was racing. We took the other children over to Lowri to keep them all together, while Janice and I searched. It's not a big area. I thought Nia had fallen or passed out. All kinds of things go through your mind. The other children and Lowri were in the dead centre of the wood now. I sent Janice one way, I went the other, looking into bushes, behind logs. Six-year-olds are small.'

Mrs Boyce came back in with a teapot and left it on the conservatory table.

Dewi smiled up at his wife.

Meinir put her hand on his arm and left, closing the door behind her.

'Was it you who found her?' Jess asked.

Dewi nodded. 'Fifteen minutes went by and there was still no sign of her. I knew we couldn't wait any longer. I needed to do something and dreading it. I needed to phone you and then phone Nia's parents. I didn't want to do it from the woods – the signal can be patchy there – and the only place we hadn't looked was the road back to the school. As I crossed the stile that led to a field, there's a stream. She was there, squatting down with a stick in her hand, playing in the water. Busy making a cake mixture was what she said to me.' He huffed out air and mimed stirring a bowl.

Jess smiled.

'I was so relieved, I wouldn't have cared if she'd been making a bomb,' Dewi continued. 'I brought her back to the other children, and we carried on with the trail. It was only afterwards, when we were back at school, that Janice told me about the Green Man.'

'That's what we're here about,' Catrin said. 'This Green Man.'

Dewi nodded. 'From what I've already told you, you realise that Nia clearly has an imagination. She called it *Y Dyn Gwyrdd*. That's the Welsh equivalent. What she said was that she'd been on the edge of the wood and looked back to see a Green Man standing by the stile. When she saw him, he waved and crossed the stile to the stream.'

'So, she wandered off to find him?'

Dewi sighed and looked up at the ceiling. 'I can't tell you

how many times we emphasise making sure never to wander off and never ever to talk to strangers. We teach even the younger ones, *Clever Never Goes*. It makes my stomach turn to think that one of ours…' Dewi squeezed his eyes shut.

'But you saw no one?'

'No. Nothing and no one in the field, on the lane, or on the road back to the school. Of course, we did not go back to the school right away. Since we were all back together, I saw no reason for the others to suffer. Nia was unharmed and not at all perturbed.'

'And afterwards, you spoke to the parents?'

Dewi leaned forwards to pour the tea. 'I felt obliged. Nia is a chatterbox. She would have told her parents about the Green Man. It was my duty to nip all that in the bud and apologise. They were very understanding. Knew that Nia had a very independent spirit. And as for the Green Man, well, Nia's mother did post something. A mild warning about her daughter having seen a stranger hanging around the school outing, though of course, none of the adults or the other children saw anything.'

Jess accepted the cup Dewi offered and poured in a splash of milk. 'Are you saying that Nia didn't see anything?'

'Who knows? We always assume the children are telling the truth. Always err on the side of caution. We have to. But Nia has an imagination, as I've explained.' He offered a plate of Welsh cakes with an encouraging smile. 'Meinir's own. She adds a little something to the mix. Delicious.'

Jess declined with a shake of her head. Catrin took one and a serviette to catch the crumbs.

'But you weren't concerned enough to report it to us?' Jess asked.

'No. I decided not to simply because there was nothing to report other than what Nia had told us. I know how busy you are. And yes, before you ask, of course I regret not doing that now. After what's happened to Osian...it's all I can think about.'

Jess nodded. Hindsight was indeed a wonderful thing, though from what she'd learned here, there would not have been much to investigate.

'And the stream is how far from Osian Howells' house?' Jess asked.

'Half a mile I'd say.' He stopped, pondering his reply, and realising its significance. 'That is close, isn't it?'

'Close enough to merit our interest,' Catrin said.

'I feel such a fool in not reporting this.' Dewi's cup clattered onto the table. He glanced at the two officers with a pleading look.

Jess gave him a half smile. 'If it's any consolation, the way you and Nia have described things is at odds with the careful way Osian was abducted. It seems the Green Man, if there is one, made little effort to hide himself. Not the pattern whoever abducted Osian adopted.'

Dewi grabbed on to this little straw of consolation and nodded gratefully.

Catrin reached into the messenger bag and pulled out a printed section of OS map. 'If you could show me where the woods are and where Nia was found, we'd appreciate it.'

'Of course. Let me get some highlighters.' He stood up and paused, smiling at the women. 'The one thing about being a primary school head is that I do have an excellent selection of colours.'

He left the room and the two officers exchanged glances. 'What do you think?' Jess asked.

'I think Warlow is right to want to speak to the little girl.'

'Dewi?'

Catrin wrinkled her nose. 'For now, we keep him on the list.'

'Agreed.' She'd known of cases where there'd been an accomplice. Though Dewi Boyce looked and sounded like the good, kind man he projected, when it came to kids, all bets were off. Obviously, he had not been the Green Man. But the question remained: did he know him?

'You should eat one of these, ma'am. They're delicious.' Catrin took a second slice.

Dewi appeared in the door, clutching an assortment of pens. 'Green for the woods, I think. And red for the lane.'

Catrin slid the map across and waited for Dewi Boyce to start colouring it in.

CHAPTER NINE

Five hours thirty minutes missing…

THIRTY MINUTES after his video call to Warlow and the team, Sergeant Gil Jones picked Rhys up from outside the local post office half a mile from the Reading Room. The registered Sex Offender's address was in Llansawel, between Llandeilo and Llandovery. 'L of a place,' Gil had quipped.

The post office doubled as a shop, now unfortunately shut, and, while he waited, Rhys gazed longingly in through the window at the shelves, his stomach rumbling. He sat on a low wall and watched people driving in and out of the little retail area next to the post office which had a hairdresser and a solicitor's office as its main attractions. Music drifted out of one parked vehicle, a mud-spattered pick-up. Rhys looked across and saw a baseball-hatted James Ryan smoking with the window open, glaring back at him.

When Rhys returned his gaze, Ryan put out his cigarette and wound the window up.

Gil's car, a Chrysler people carrier that had seen better days, smelled of bubble gum and prawn cocktail crisps.

'Folly Farm visit last weekend. Me, the missus, and a murder of grandchildren. So, thank your lucky stars it is only bubble gum and crisps you can smell. Given their eating habits and age, that no one threw up was a bonus.'

'It's a murder of crows, Sarge,' Rhys said. 'Not grand-children.'

'You haven't met my lot. *Diawled bach*, the lot of them.' Gil's brawny arms and thick fingers clutching the wheel made it look tiny as they sped east along the A40, shad-owing the river.

Rhys spied a wrapper on the floor, picked it up, and smoothed it out on his lap.

'I used to love Curly Wurlys.'

'I used to weigh eleven stone,' Gil replied. 'But the past, as they say—'

'Is a foreign country?' Rhys offered.

'No, has buggered off on a Saturn rocket never to return.'

'Is that a quote?'

Gil sent the younger man a look. 'Yes. One of mine.'

'Didn't know you were a poet, Sarge.'

'Whereas I have many and varied qualities and strengths, DC Harries, verse, unfortunately, is not one of them. My poetry extends only to a few choice limericks that can turn the air a darker shade of navy, but that's about all.'

Rhys nodded. 'They'd posted some poems from the kids at the *meithrin* in the Reading Room.'

Gil raised an eyebrow and smiled. Wales's education system used to induct children at three years old. That had changed to five and the gap had been filled by *meithrins* where Welsh was the primary language.

'Any budding laureates?' Gil asked.

'I think they must have been on a farm visit because "*moch*" and "*coch*" featured in most of them.'

Gil snorted. *Moch* was pig and *coch* was red. 'Artistic licence they call that.'

They drove on in contemplative silence, bypassing Llandeilo and winding their way east. But finally, Rhys opened up and asked the question.

'This man we're going to see, he's on the sex offenders' register?'

'Not anymore. But he's still on the PNC and still under an SHPO. You know what that is, right?'

Rhys's face told a different story.

'Sexual Harm Prevention Order,' Gil explained. 'Prohibitions such as using a computer capable of accessing the internet, being anywhere near a child for longer than a certain time. That sort of thing.'

'And he's a suspect in the abduction?'

'We need to tick a box, Rhys. If we didn't and it turns out he was in the area, we'd never forgive ourselves now, would we?'

Rhys nodded.

'It's not glamorous. Sometimes it's downright unpleasant. But got to be done. Now, find that address and put it into your phone.'

———

Leighton Pitcher lived in a pebble-dashed bungalow at the end of a cul-de-sac in the village. The narrow front garden needed attention and straggly bushes would block the path once summer growth kicked in. A green plastic bunded oil tank took up much of the remaining space. Gil parked on the street outside and walked up to a blue front door, looked for a bell, didn't find one and so knocked and waited.

The woman who opened the door had greasy hair tied up in a bun. The yellowed fingers of the hand holding the door open matched the ravaged skin of a lifelong smoker. The shapeless sweatshirt and jeans she wore hung off her, and Rhys wondered if the cigarettes were now demanding payment for the years of neurochemical enjoyment they had given.

'Help you?' the woman rasped.

Gil held out his warrant card. The woman looked at it and turned away to call out, 'Leighton, it's them.' She walked away, leaving the door open. From the dim interior, a man appeared. No more than a boy in stature, Gil would later use the adjective scrawny to describe Pitcher. Rhys put him at early twenties dressed in a clean T-shirt and jeans, hair clipped short and clean shaven. Not the image the DC had conjured for someone on the Sex Offenders Register. He'd imagined someone older, bearded, and unwashed. Pitcher looked at the warrant card and nodded, a dull acceptance hardening his features. He reached for a padded coat and stepped outside.

'Come around the back to the shed. Stuff's there.'

Gil exchanged a quick glance with Rhys and flicked his eyebrows up. Pitcher wasn't tall and looked even more like a boy behind Gil's ample girth and Rhys's six-feet-plus height. They followed the contour of the building's gable end and Rhys glimpsed a modern kitchen through the window before they got to the back garden and a path leading down towards a large, shiplapped building with double-glazed windows and a black chimney pipe sticking up from the roof. More a garden office than a shed.

Inside, the space was divided into two areas: in one sat a desk with a computer, a franking machine and packaging equipment, and in the other, a couple of chairs and a table.

'It's been a while,' Pitcher said. 'But I haven't changed anything since the last time you were out.'

Gil nodded. 'We're not from the VISOR team, Leighton.'

Pitcher frowned. 'No?'

Rhys looked around the room and the EBAY logos on the envelopes. 'You run a business from here?'

Pitcher nodded. 'Vintage toy cars mainly. Some records, other bits, and bobs.'

When Rhys frowned, Pitcher walked past him and outside to a smaller padlocked shed. He fished out a key and opened the door. Inside, arranged on racks of shelves, were dozens of small vehicles, some boxed, others not. On a different rack sat stacks of vinyl records in their sleeves.

'It's okay, I don't sell any toys to kids,' Pitcher added quickly. 'The cars sell to collectors, mostly.'

Gil stepped back from the doorway and let Pitcher lead them back into his 'office'. Only then did curiosity get the better of the man they'd come to visit. 'If you two are not from VISOR checking on my computer, why are you here?'

'Sit down, Leighton,' Gil suggested.

Pitcher complied.

'Today between nine and midday, where were you?'

'Today?' Leighton frowned. 'We went to Sainsbury's in Lampeter. Me and my mam. Weekly shop.'

'If we track the CCTV from the store, you'd be on it?'

'I suppose.' Pitcher kept frowning. 'If you're not here to check my browser, why are you...' Realisation spread like a mudslide over Pitcher's face. 'It's not the missing kid, is it? For Christ's sake...'

'What do you know, Leighton?'

'Only what's on the news. A kid's gone missing.' He shook his head as the reality bit home. 'I should have bloody known. All the usual suspects, is it?' His aggrieved gaze slid from Gil to Rhys and back again on a tennis match loop.

'What time did you leave and what time did you get back?' Gil asked.

'Really?' Pitcher's eyebrows shot skywards.

Gil waited.

'Like I said, we left at nine, back at around eleven thirty.'

'And it was Sainsbury's in Lampeter. Not Aldi?'

'There is no Aldi yet,' Pitcher said grudgingly. 'They say there's one on the way.'

'That your mum who opened the door, was it?' Gil asked.

'Yeah.' The word came out as a whisper heavy with defeat.

'Right, we'll have a quick word with her and then we'll be on our way.'

'Every time.'

'What?' Rhys asked.

'Every time some shit happens you lot come calling.'

'We're only doing our jobs, Mr Pitcher,' Rhys said.

'Yeah. Just like you were when I was arrested.' Pitcher's lips were a thin white line. 'Makes no difference that she was the one who sent me the photos. She said she was seventeen. I didn't ask for a selfie of her tits. She sent it. I only showed my mate to see if he thought they were genuine. Turns out she was fifteen. And ever since I've had to put up with this crap.' Pitcher looked on the verge of tears. 'Distributing pornographic images of a minor, for Christ's sake. A caution and two years on the Sex Offenders Register because some girl lied to me. Haven't you fucked up my life enough already? I'm not a bloody paedophile. When are you lot going to stop treating me like one?'

Rhys looked at Gil, but the sergeant's face showed no emotion.

'We'll have a quick word with your mother. If there's anything else, we'll be in touch.'

'Thanks a lot.' Pitcher's bitterness soured his expression.

As they prepared to drive away, having had Mrs Pitcher confirm everything that her son had said, Gil wrote a few lines in his notebook, but Rhys looked unhappy.

'Penny for them, detective constable,' Gil said.

'Is it true? Was he cautioned because of sending a photo of an underage girl?'

'I didn't read the details of the case. He was nineteen when it happened.'

'That's why he's on the register?'

Gil dotted an I, flicked off the ballpoint and closed his notebook. 'He is, but the SHPO ensures he doesn't delete his internet history and that his computer is for work. We can confiscate his hard drive at any point, too. And, of course, he can't be in contact with any child for over twelve hours.'

Rhys nodded, and Gil sent him a sideways glance. 'You think it's harsh?'

'I don't know, Sarge. I don't know the guy.'

Gil nodded. 'The law's the law, Rhys. And, if he keeps his nose clean, he may get the prohibitions revoked. He's young. I'd be delighted if he had nothing to do with Osian Howells. In the meantime, we'll get the nerds to chat with Sainsbury's in Lampeter and get some CCTV footage from this morning to make sure Mr Pitcher is telling us the truth. Sympathy is one thing. Catching a lying bastard is another. And believe me, some of these buggers are good at it. Now, let's break out the flask and biscuits.' He pronounced the last word the French way. 'I'm starving.'

Rhys nodded. Gil had been around the block and dealt

with this sort of thing many more times than Rhys had ever done. Something to consider. So much so that as Rhys gazed out of the window at the passing countryside and tried to put his inexperienced thoughts in order and remember that VISOR stood for Violent *and* Sex Offender Register, he didn't notice the mud-spattered pick-up parked in a bus bay next to a chapel fifty yards up the street.

An omission he would live to regret.

CHAPTER TEN

Six hours missing…

NIA OWEN SAT at the kitchen table of her family home on a couple of cushions to add height so that she could comfortably reach the surface. Dressed in pink jeans and a light-blue sweater with her hair in two pigtails, she sat next to two women. One, her mother Lois, a taller version of Nia, with enormous eyes and sculpted eyebrows, the other, a woman named Kerry Shingler that Warlow knew from the Child Abuse and Sexual Offences team. A trained and experienced officer who would interview Nia on Warlow's behalf.

Now Shingler sat encouraging Nia to draw pictures while her mother looked on. They spoke in Welsh, Nia's first language. Warlow was fluent, and he'd briefed Shingler on what he wanted to know. Even so, with a six-year-old, you couldn't rush things.

'So,' Shingler said, 'that's the big tree with the tunnel through it on the way into the woods?'

Nia nodded.

'And that's where you saw the Green Man?'

Nia nodded again.

'And you were waiting your turn to walk through the tunnel?'

Another nod.

'Were you the last one to go through?'

'Yes, I was picking flowers.'

Shingler beamed. Lois, on the other side of Nia, shook her head exasperatedly.

'And you were picking flowers when you saw the Green Man?'

'He waved at me from by the fence.'

'Did you wave back?'

Nia nodded.

'Were you scared?'

Nia shook her head slowly.

Lois squeezed her eyes shut. Warlow, standing at the sink, observing, caught her expression. Innocence was a wonderful thing. Something to be cherished in a chatty little girl like Nia. But he sensed the despair in Lois's expression. The what ifs and the dreaded imaginings all over again.

'Right, Nia,' Shingler said. 'Let's play a game. I want you to close your eyes and pretend you're picking flowers all over again. Then I want you to open your eyes and see the Green Man. Straight away, I want you to draw him for us. Can you do that?'

Nia nodded; her expression solemn in that way that trusting kids had. Warlow smiled. She was a sweetie.

'Now then,' the Child Abuse and Sexual Offences officer said, 'shut your eyes and hear the other children in the woods. You're picking those flowers and then you open your eyes and…there, you see the Green Man?'

Nia opened her eyes. She didn't need telling twice. She reached for the crayons and started drawing. Warlow didn't move. Nia's colouring in technique was slow and deliberate. He waited as she reached for distinct colours, carefully, methodically.

He caught Shingler's eye. They ought to wait until Nia had finished, but time was slipping by. They'd need to chance making Nia work a little harder.

'Wow,' Shingler said. 'You can see him. That's very good. And did he wave again?'

Nia didn't stop drawing. But she tilted her head and said, wistfully, 'No. He did this.' She held up both hands, palms towards her chest, pulling them towards her in a single come hither movement.

'Oh, did he now?'

Nia nodded. 'Then he was part of the tree again.'

Warlow frowned. The report he'd read had been nowhere near as detailed as this.

Nia kept colouring in.

'Then you walked across to find the Green Man?' Shingler continued probing.

Nia nodded. 'But when I got to the fence, he was gone. He left a face in the mud by the water.'

'A face?'

'In leaves. With eyes and a mouth.'

More detail. Nia finally sat back, contemplating the drawing. The CASO officer looked on, frowning. 'Shall we show this to Mr Warlow? I know he wants to see what you've drawn.'

Nia nodded.

The CASO sergeant turned and handed over the A4 sheet. Warlow grinned and held it up.

'Thank you, Nia. This is great. Let me take it over to the window to look at it properly.' He walked over and put it down on the drainer under the light from a window. The Green Man's figure had a dense block of green for legs and arms. But Nia had put a round head on a big torso, and, instead of block colouring, she'd used more than one shade of green for the body and face. Warlow took out his phone and took a quick snap.

He turned back, smiling broadly, feeling something vague and unsettling signal its significance in the back of his head. 'This is really good, Nia. Was the Green Man wearing a coat?'

Nia nodded, unperturbed.

Warlow turned away, pretending to study the drawing again, but really scrolling to Safari on his phone and punching letters into the search engine. A series of images came up. He picked one and used his fingers to enlarge it before walking over to Nia.

'Is this like what the Green Man was wearing?' He put the phone on the table in front of her. She took one look and nodded.

Warlow flicked to the next image. 'And is this what his face was like?'

Nia, beaming, looked at all three of the adults in turn, delighted that her drawing had explained everything so clearly.

'Well done, Nia,' Shingler said. 'Well done, you.'

'Right, I think this clever girl deserves a hot chocolate.' Lois stood up and made for the kettle. Warlow glimpsed her expression as she stood. What he read there was terror for what might have been.

'Thank you, Nia.' Warlow gave her back the drawing. 'Why don't you finish this one off for us.'

Nia nodded, pleased.

Warlow took his phone and walked out of the house, still with the image he'd found, and which Nia had confirmed as showing what the Green Man looked like on the screen. He punched in a number and made a call.

He had no idea how significant this was, but something at least had come from speaking to the little girl. Something they could work with.

The Green Man was now only a man after all. One dressed in a camouflage jacket and makeup.

———

Six hours, thirty-five minutes missing...

THEY CONVENED in the Reading Room. In the hour since Warlow had been there, the place had filled up with more people, including the PolSA coordinating the search, a stocky uniformed sergeant with a shaved head and thick glasses called Ken Morris whom Warlow had worked with only a couple of times before, but whose reputation as a thorough workhorse went before him.

The DCI joined Morris as he peered at the map just as Jess and Catrin walked in.

'How's it going?' Warlow asked the PolSA.

'Nothing yet.'

'Right, well, I may have something worth hearing.' He explained what had happened with Nia Owen. When he'd finished, he looked around, bemused by the numbers. 'Who the hell are all these other people?'

The PolSA looked up. 'We have three teams out, so I've called back the leaders as per your call. Then there's Child Protection, some volunteers from the Reading Room sorting out teas and coffees, and Social Services.' The PolSA nodded towards a man who, on a cursory glance, couldn't really have been anything else. Tall, anorak, thicker glasses even than the PolSA, long hair and beard with an ID hanging from his neck on a lanyard.

'What the hell are they doing here?'

'Something about sheltered housing. I didn't really understand it.'

The man had a clipboard and hovered near a trestle

table where a big silver urn of hot water sat next to paper cups and tea bags.

Warlow walked across and introduced himself.

The man looked up; his eyes magnified by the lenses of his glasses. 'And you are?' Warlow asked.

The man stuck out a hand. 'Pete Grimshaw. Social Housing Liaison.'

Warlow noted the English accent and the ID which, for once, had an image that looked a lot like the man standing in front of him. Warlow wondered if the hair and the beard had been forged in a university somewhere and had remained un-styled by human hand ever since.

'Don't take this the wrong way, but why are you here?'

Grimshaw smiled. 'I was asked to come up here by the powers-that-be in case I might be needed.'

'For what? Do you have a cape and underpants in that briefcase?'

Grimshaw shook his head, grinning. 'Good one. No, we have a couple of families housed on the Caeglas estate from outside the catchment. We sometimes help out other areas in the country who need to re-house vulnerable families.'

'Vulnerable how?' Warlow narrowed his eyes.

'Domestic abuse. Families escaping violence or an abusive relationship. They come here to get away. One step short of witness protection. They haven't changed their names, but no one knows they're here.'

'What's that got to do with Osian Howells?'

'Nothing. But if you felt the need to interview these families, knock on their doors, we think it's best that one of us speaks to them first to explain.'

'Right,' Warlow said, understanding flooding his brain, but not reaching the intonation in his speech.

Grimshaw detected the scepticism. 'Obviously, I know

the priority has to be the missing child, but these families have been through a lot themselves.'

Warlow wanted to object, but Grimshaw was right. There would be fallout from an operation like this and damage limitation was never a bad thing. Just as well to have someone as a buffer. Grimshaw took a card out from his wallet. The phone number on the back had been crossed out and replaced with handwritten digits.

'Changed my service provider,' Grimshaw explained with a grimace.

Warlow looked up, caught Catrin's eye. She came over. 'How did it go with the headmaster?'

'Nothing of note.'

Warlow sensed the brief hesitation in her voice. But then he turned to the man next to him. 'This is Pete Grimshaw, Social Services. He's here to make sure we don't scare the living daylights out of some vulnerables on the estate. I think it's best he liaises with you.' He handed her the card.

Catrin took it, nodded, and reached for her own business card to give to Grimshaw.

'Let's hope we don't have to disturb your charges,' Warlow said, and walked away.

He walked over to the flipchart and clapped his hands. The buzz of noise died away.

Warlow turned to the volunteers refilling the milk jugs. 'I'm going to have to ask you to leave the room for five minutes. That includes all non-police personnel.' He looked pointedly at Grimshaw who was taking off his anorak and tucking into a cup of tea.

A couple of Uniforms walked over and ushered the people out. Once they were gone and with the doors closed, Warlow cleared his throat. 'Thanks for coming in. I don't have a lot to say. Only that I appreciate your efforts and that I've come from interviewing Nia Owen, a little girl who went missing for twenty minutes a couple of weeks ago while on a school nature trail. The one piece of new information I've been able to gather is that she saw, and was beckoned to, by a man she describes as the Green Man. He was dressed in a camouflage jacket and had likely attempted to camouflage his face.'

The crowd murmured.

'Bear in mind, this is from a six-year-old. But she is bright and definite about the jacket. I've given the PolSA details of where this happened. It's within half a mile of Osian Howells' house. It may not be much, but it's something. And we keep it very much to ourselves, understand?'

Nods and murmurs.

'Right, keep it up.' Warlow walked towards the entrance and called to Catrin and Jess while the PolSA stepped forward.

'We not going to wait and hear what he says?' Jess asked.

'No. Let them get on with it. Time we got our heads together. I said we'd meet Gil and Rhys at HQ.'

CHAPTER ELEVEN

Seven hours, ten minutes missing…

WARLOW GOT to the Incident Room just before six. Gil and
Rhys were already back, and the room buzzed with activity
from the indexers and Uniforms manning phones. Most of
them collating and assessing reports of sightings and
curious bits of information sent in by the public. A public
keen to do whatever they could to help Osian Howells.
The police had appealed for anyone with any information
to ring a hotline. Unfortunately, most of this information
ended up being irrelevant or nonsensical to everyone but
the caller.

Still, you never knew.

Rhys stood up immediately as Warlow entered the
room. His fixed grin rang an alarm bell in the DCI's head
on seeing it.

'Hello, sir,' the DC said.

Warlow recognised bad news being delivered when he
saw it. 'What?' he growled, expecting the worst.

'Sergeant Jones said it might be better if I…warned
you, sir.'

'Of what?'

Rhys made a face.

Warlow stepped forward. 'Don't tell me they've found Osian. Don't tell me he's—'

'No, no, sir.' Rhys answered quickly and jerked a thumb over his shoulder 'You have a visitor.'

Since Rhys's head was at least half a foot higher than Warlow's, he had to lean to the side to peer past to the back of the Incident Room. To where, standing in the doorway of the tiny SIO's room, stood the reason for Rhys's warning.

Warlow raised a hand in greeting and saw the movement mirrored by the person standing there before the hand dropped back to clasp its fellow and complete a relaxed military stance. Warlow glanced to his right where Gil sat, the sergeant desperately trying to keep a straight face, before taking a quick step and leaning forward so that his head was down and out of the eyeline of the figure at the back of the room.

'You could have bloody well warned me sooner,' Warlow whispered.

'She got here a minute before you did,' Gil replied in an equally hushed tone. 'She was prowling, watching our every move. If I'd texted, I'd have got detention for sure.'

Warlow shook his head. Having Two-Shoes call was a bit like a visit from the headteacher. 'Hilarious,' he hissed out the word. 'But if I'm not out of there in five minutes, set off the sodding fire alarm.' He pinched the skin on the bridge of his nose, closed his eyes, and took a quiet breath. As he walked towards the SIO room, he pivoted, made his index and middle finger into a V, pointed them at his own eyes and then towards Rhys, before making an exaggerated pouring motion.

'On it,' Rhys said with a nod.

Warlow turned back and composed his face into a

semblance of a cheery greeting for the woman he was about to meet, one Superintendent Pamela Goodey. She had short dark hair, a smile that made her mouth look like it had too many teeth, and a managerial role in the machinery of policing that Warlow could not understand, no matter how hard he tried. In all honesty, he hadn't tried that hard and had no intention of attempting to unless forced. Goodey had risen in the ranks because of her ability to enforce rules and send memos about how modern policing needed to 'comply with societal mores' without throwing up in the back of her throat. And because it took police recruits about ten seconds to think up nicknames, she was known to all and sundry as Goodey Two-Shoes, or in the main, just Two-Shoes.

'Afternoon, ma'am.'

'Not a social call, Evan. I promise I won't keep you long.'

'Things are a bit manic.' He gave a vague wave of his arm in the direction he'd come from.

'I know, I know.' Two-Shoes pushed open the door and ushered Warlow in. She, all pixie hair and no makeup, sat in the seat Warlow normally occupied. The DCI remained standing. He had no intention of making this a sit-down affair. Almost immediately, his phone buzzed. He didn't ask to take the call. Didn't need to. Gil's whispering voice came down the line.

'You really want me to set off the alarm?'

'No, but tell them I'll be…' He looked up at Two-Shoes with his eyebrows raised. She held up one hand with her fingers splayed. 'Five minutes,' Warlow said.

Two-Shoes nodded earnestly and Warlow signed off.

The superintendent pursed her lips and steepled her fingers. 'Evan, as part of my brief in charge of compliance and liaison with the Commissioner, I am charged with ensuring that officers are clear in their duty in cooperating with internal and external investigations.'

Warlow nodded. He knew where this was going. Two-Shoes confirmed it with her next words.

'Sergeant Mel Lewis is, I'm sure, still a raw wound for you.' Her nostrils flared. 'But making life awkward for another force's officers whilst they're looking into corruption and organised crime links will not help. In fact, it does more harm than good.'

The quickest and easiest way to get rid of Two-Shoes, in everyone's opinion, was to let her have her say, nod, take your lumps and move on. But Warlow had never bought in to quick and easy. He tilted his head and felt his lids go to half-mast. Rhys Harries called it the DCI's Clint Eastwood look, though never to his face. All it needed was a cheroot, a hat, and a poncho.

'They suggested I might have had a motive for helping Mel jump off that cliff in Pembrokeshire, ma'am.' The words came out stiff and low.

Two-Shoes flinched, and her eyes narrowed. Her lips parted in what might have been the beginning of a sentence, but nothing emerged.

Warlow took the initiative. 'Oh, didn't they tell you that bit?'

'They did not.' She took out a small notebook, wrote something in it, closed it and put it away. 'That's…regrettable.'

'Not the word I used, ma'am.'

'No, probably not. Am I to take it you will not speak to them again?'

'Not to those two.' The DIs, McGrath and Cheesely, had pitched up in the middle of another investigation trying and failing to catch Warlow unawares. Their investigation into Mel Lewis's death and his involvement in an organised crime gang that the team had helped break up would not go away. And though it might seem that Warlow had been trying to dodge the investigation, he had not. Yet, funnily enough, he took exception to being accused of coercion and conspiracy on his own patch. He wanted to know how deep Mel Lewis's involvement had been as much as the next man. But there were ways and means and so far, West Mids Police, the force tasked with carrying out the investigation, had not covered themselves in glory.

'Fair enough. I'll pass that along. But the investigation is ongoing. Someone will need to talk to you again.'

Warlow nodded, then turned to go.

'One more thing, Evan. Derek and Karen Geoghan. What do those names mean to you?'

Warlow pivoted, a frown crinkling his brow. 'The Geoghans? Don't tell me they've turned up at last?'

Two-Shoes shook her head. 'Unfortunately, not. But we've had a request from a journalist through Freedom of Information to ask if you are involved in investigating their disappearance.'

'Simple answer, no. Last I heard, Owen Tamblin told me they'd gone AWOL after Derek Geoghan's release from prison.' Tamblin was an old colleague of Warlow's and a DCI with South Wales Police.

'I've already spoken to Tamblin, but I want your take.'

Warlow bit back his frustration. If she'd talked to Tamblin, there'd be nothing to add. But he was willing to play the game in order to get Two-Shoes out of the room. 'Putting the Geoghans away was a joint operation between us and them. I worked with Owen on it. The Geoghans were as nasty a pair of parasites as I've ever come across. They sent Derek Geoghan down for manslaughter. Karen did some time, too, but nowhere near enough in my humble. They befriended the vulnerable – older people, challenged people – pretending to be carers. Sometimes moving into people's homes and robbing them blind. And finally, starving and suffocating a victim. Their defence was that their charge had become violent and Geoghan was trying to subdue him. The bastard got out of prison a month or two ago. Medical grounds. He has leukaemia. I said a prayer of thanks to the God of Karma.'

Two-Shoes blinked at that but said nothing.

Warlow continued, 'I'd be delighted if I never saw either one of the bottom-feeders again. Karen Geoghan sent me cards: Christmas, birthday, you know the drill. I won't spoil your dinner by telling you what she said, or what she sent in the envelopes by way of presents. But the short answer is, no, I am not involved in trying to find them.'

'Geoghan's parole officer has officially listed him, or them, as mispers. And now a journalist has hold of it. That's also why I felt we needed to chat.'

Warlow waited. Two-Shoes was persistent, he had to admit.

'Your relationship with the press is also something that might merit a little work, if previous encounters are anything to go by.'

'I have no problem with the press, so long as they stay behind the bars of their cages.' Warlow's answer tripped off his tongue.

Two-Shoes smiled and showed far too much gum. A sight that was neither pleasant nor necessary. 'You see, there. That's your problem. That sort of talk doesn't help.'

Warlow disagreed. That sort of talk helped him enormously. But the sooner he played ball with Two-Shoes, the sooner this little dance would end. 'Ma'am, I haven't been near the Geoghans for years and I have no intention of getting within a hundred miles. And that, if a journalist ever asks me about it, is exactly what I will say.'

'Right. But we also have a press officer and I suggest that if anyone contacts you, deflect them in that direction.

I think that's a far better approach than jousting with someone who can and will manipulate whatever words you choose to use.'

Much as he hated to admit it, Two-Shoes was right. 'I can live with that, ma'am.'

'Good. However, what you do not know, because it has not gone any further yet, is that when the parole officer called on the Geoghans, he found evidence of an altercation. Some broken plates, chairs overturned, some blood which turned out to be Derek Geoghan's on the edge of the sink. I have photographs if you'd like to see them.'

Warlow shook his head. 'What do we make of all that?'

'Tamblin thinks that the Geoghans had a visitor. And that they did not leave their house willingly.'

Warlow thought about this and said the obvious, 'There'd be a long line of aggrieved relatives willing to throw a brick through their windows. But actual GBH? I can't think of anyone.'

Two-Shoes nodded. 'DCI Tamblin said the same. Still, a word to the wise. Stay away from any journalists and be prepared if someone rings you up about the Geoghans. Say nothing but be polite.'

'Piss off and crawl back under the guano-stained rock you came out from under won't do it?'

Two-Shoes kept a straight face. 'We both know it won't. Not even when it's directed at me.'

Warlow grinned. 'I wouldn't dream of doing such a thing, ma'am.'

'Good. Because I don't think I will ever sleep again if I thought I ever featured in one of your dreams, Evan.' She stood up. 'Any news about the boy?'

'Not yet.'

'I'll leave you to it. The rest of this can wait.'

Warlow expected another turn of the screw. An appeal for him to play ball, but, to her credit, Two-Shoes said no more, except, 'Anything I can do to help here, you know where I am.'

Warlow nodded. Even a dyed-in-the-wool manager like Two-Shoes felt the pressure of a case like Osian Howells. You wouldn't be human if you didn't. It was like a festering thorn in your finger, always there, even when you were forced to talk about something else.

Two-Shoes walked through the door, leaving Warlow with his own thoughts. And what a murky whirlpool they were.

CHAPTER TWELVE

Seven hours, twenty-five minutes missing…

WHEN THE DOOR closed behind the superintendent, Warlow's first instinct was to open it and get right back to the fray. But he held back. A visit from her was always fun-packed and brought with it uncomfortable thoughts of responsibility and the consequence of your actions. Mel Lewis and the Geoghans were like the dusty corners of a room he no longer went into. A room that needed a damn good spring clean to make it habitable. The difficulty was finding the time to get the Hoover out. There'd always be an excuse not to. Excuses like Osian Howells, or Jeez bloody Denise.

Warlow walked around the desk, fell into the chair, and took a breather, considering each of those little problems in turn.

As for Mel Lewis… He'd been genuinely clueless about the DS's involvement in anything drug related until he and Jess stumbled on a marijuana farm hidden under an old engine house on the edge of the wild Welsh coast. But Lewis was linked to the death of more than one innocent person, including two walkers on the path whose story had haunted Warlow as missing persons for years. Lewis was unforgivable of that. But West Mids could dig as deep as they wanted to. They'd find nothing linking Warlow to any of that crap. Worse was that he'd liked Mel. At least the Mel that sang in the pub and bought everyone a round. Warlow had to somehow not let the tail-end of that fondness get in the way. He wanted to find out as much as anyone what had turned Mel. Greed? Coercion? There'd be an answer somewhere.

And then his thoughts strayed to Denise. Was it really only a few hours ago that he'd been with the boys at her funeral? He ran a hand through his greying hair and glanced at his watch.

The Geoghans were another story. Incredulous to think that even now, years after he'd been involved in putting them away, they could reach out and involve him in their sordid lives. Thankfully, they were not on his patch, but Two-Shoes was right to assume it would not be the last he'd hear of them. He could feel that certainty stirring in the depths of his soul. He glanced at his watch. She'd been in the room for no more than a few minutes. He could spare two more.

Warlow rang Owen Tamblin's number but got the old 'Leave a message' brush-off.

'Owen, it's Evan. Give me a ring when you can. You know who it's about.'

Phone still in his hand, he gave in to instinct and made a second call. A background murmur of voices told Warlow that his intended target was in a car.

'Hi, Dad.'

'Hi, Tom. You on the way back to London?'

'We are. Me, Jodie and Al.'

'Stay long after I left?'

'Only an hour or so.'

'Yeah, sorry about that.'

Jodie's voice broke in. 'It was on the news, Evan. A minute ago. Police are searching for a six-year-old boy missing since eleven this morning in Carmarthenshire. That is you, isn't it?'

'Yes, that's me,' Warlow admitted. 'I may not have much time over the next few hours, so I thought I'd catch up with you all now.'

'We're all good, Dad.' Alun's voice from the back seat.

'What time is your flight?'

'Midday, tomorrow. I'm crashing at Jodie and Tom's tonight.'

The plan had been for Warlow to go to London with them to see Alun off. But here he was, apologising for being at work. Again.

'I'm sorry I can't be there.'

'Don't be, Dad.' Tom's voice. He'd always been the people pleaser, avoiding confrontation. The human WD40 oiling the friction Warlow and his eldest son always seemed to generate. Warlow waited to hear what Alun had to say.

'Yeah, Dad. We understand. It's a kid for God's sake,' Alun said.

Warlow sighed, wondering not for the first time about the kind of world he lived in where he craved the approval of his sons for hunting a monster who took children. Probably said more about him than the world, he mused. And normally he wasn't needy in any sense of the word. But today these men had cremated their mother. They had a right to expect support from their father.

'I'm still sorry,' Warlow said.

'Are you going to find him, Dad?' Alun again.

For several very long seconds, the only noise on the phone was the hum of the engine and rumble of tyres on the motorway.

'We will. We definitely will.'

No one asked the dead or alive question and for that, Warlow was grateful.

'If I get a chance, I'll ring you at the airport tomorrow morning, Al,' he added.

'Okay,' Alun said. 'Best of luck, Dad.'

Luck. Good word that. And they'd need it. That one little thing that might point them toward a mistake the criminal might have made. He'd spend the next few hours looking for that, digging, thinking, making his own luck. The vague idea he'd had of using this moment to broach the subject of his medical status – he preferred that to using the word illness because he wasn't ill – in one last-ditch effort at honesty, it blew away in a puff of smoke. If there might be a good time and place, this was not it.

'Safe journey boys. Tom, look after Jodie and Alun, give my love to Reba and Leo.'

No sooner had he ended the call though than his phone rang again. This time, Warlow didn't recognise the number. He grunted out his usual greeting in such circumstances.

'Warlow.'

'Evening, sir. This is Ken Morris, the PolSA.'

Warlow's heart rate shot up to a gallop. PolSA's rarely rang the SIO unless they had something significant to say.

'What have you got?' Warlow asked, straining to keep his voice even.

'The weirdest bloody thing, sir. One of your DS's, Richards, is it? She asked us to go back across to the woods where that odd report of a stalker came through from the school.'

'The Green Man business?'

'That's it. Asked us to go over before it got dark and get some photographs taken. Where they found the little girl is less than half a mile from the Reading Room. Nia Owen, wasn't it?'

'That's her.'

'You familiar with the report then, I take it?'

Warlow confirmed it. 'I talked to Nia myself. Bright little thing. Drew me a picture.'

'Well, I couldn't spare anyone, so I walked over myself. I'm on the way into the woods now, crossing the little brook in the field's corner which leads to the stile into the woods itself.'

Warlow felt the hair on his neck stand to attention. 'She said that the Green Man had made a face out of leaves for her there.'

'I know, sir. I read that too. We swept this area two hours ago… I can't believe we wouldn't have seen it.'

'Seen what?' Warlow barked out the question.

'A glove. A bloody Spiderman glove. Inside a ring of leaves.' Morris sounded incredulous. 'I'm sending you the image now. I've already sent it to DS Richards. No way we would have missed it. Impossible in fact. Not where it was, lying on the ground next to the stream.'

Warlow's phone beeped a different tone. He opened the message, hoping that he wasn't cutting Morris off as he did so. He knew it should be possible to multitask on these things, but he didn't trust himself enough. The image formed and Warlow stared at a dark patch of ground with a red glove crisscrossed by dark lines in a web design laying splayed out on the mud surrounded by a rough circle of leaves. 'Are you sure it's his? Osian's?'

'Not yet. It matches the description of what he was wearing, but until we get it looked at, get some DNA… I'm getting a forensic team out here now.'

'Make sure it's Povey,' Warlow said automatically. Alison Povey ran forensics for Dyfed Powys. Warlow wanted to make sure she was in on this. He wanted no cockups. But knowing her, they'd have to set fire to her and beat her with nail-studded clubs to keep her away.

'It's pretty wet ground, you can see the stream is about a foot away,' Morris said, his voice catching as he moved. 'It hasn't rained for a couple of days, so the water is low.'

Warlow blew up the picture. Sure enough, the dark water of a little brook ran close by, no more than a couple of inches deep. 'Any chance the glove was washed down?'

'What, and placed inside a ring of leaves by the fairy folk?' Morris said. 'No bloody chance.'

'So how do you explain this?'

Morris blew out air. 'Two possibilities. Both make my blood boil. First, this could be someone's sick idea of a joke. Osian's description is out there in the world. He's already been on the news. Some idiot might have fished out a Spiderman glove from their toy-box and thought this would be a good way to piss off the police.'

'They succeeded hands-down there,' muttered Warlow.

'Or, and this is the one I can't believe I'm even considering; the abductor has waited until we've been and gone and come back to leave us his calling card.'

Warlow squeezed his eyes shut. There were all kinds of people on this planet, and they included idiots with distorted and misguided senses of humour. Like the twits who quipped about a bomb in their luggage at an airport and ended up shutting the place down. Or broadcasted to the nation that the Martians had landed and triggered widespread panic. But this? To even contemplate that someone was sick enough to prank this... He shook his head. Worse things appeared every day on YouTube, so his sons kept telling him. But Morris was right. If this was not a prank, if this was real and left by the perpetrator, they were looking at something way worse than any prankster. They were looking at a sick tormentor in every sense of the word.

'Any point me coming out there?'

'Not until the crime scene techs have been and gone.

The less clodhopping, the better. Christ, it's doing my head in. I mean, the area is swarming with Uniforms.'

'But no one watching the woods, I assume?'

'No. Why would there be? We'd already searched.'

He was right. 'Okay, can you finish what DS Richards asked you to do? Photos of the woods?'

'Yes, we're securing the scene, so I'll get those to you shortly. Bloody hell, this is a bad one, sir. Have you any idea what the hell is going on?'

'As of this moment, none, Sergeant. I really don't.'

CHAPTER THIRTEEN

Seven hours, thirty minutes missing…

WARLOW WALKED out into the Incident Room to a fresh mug of tea and one of Gil's biscuit arrays. He grabbed a Hobnob and a fig roll and perched on the edge of a desk.

'Did she make you do lines?' Jess asked, eying Warlow warily, weighing up what sort of mood he might be in.

'You mean a hundred "I shall be nice to West Mids CID from now on" in my best handwriting, as opposed to the little white powdery ones you always see idiots separating out with a credit card before snorting up a nostril?' Warlow paused before continuing, assessing the team's expressions as they stopped mid-slurp, or bite, shocked by what he'd just said. 'On TV, I bloody mean.'

'The former,' Jess said, her eyes crinkling.

'No, she did neither. No lines of any kind. Ours not to reason why. In fact, we had a productive meeting, and she's offered us help if we need it.'

'That's nice of her.' Gil nodded.

'You okay, sir?' Rhys asked, summing up the surprise the rest of the team all felt in that one question.

'I will be once we get Osian Howells back to his mother. Did Catrin brief you over the PolSA's find?'

Jess nodded.

Catrin turned from where she was pinning up the image of the Spiderman glove on the Gallery. 'Once I have the nature walk, woods images, I'll print those off, too, sir.'

But Warlow was only half listening. His eyes remained fixed on the image of that glove posted on the board.

'You want me to go out there?' Gil asked.

'No. The PolSA doesn't want us there and neither will Povey. Too many cooks. Let's let her do her stuff.' He turned towards Rhys. 'But you could ring Gina and ask her to talk to Nerys Howells about what clothes Osian was wearing. Where she bought them. That way, we'll get a clearer impression of what they looked like. A clearer impression of whether the glove is kosher without involving Nerys Howells in ID-ing it. I don't want to do that, until I'm sure.'

'On it, sir.' Rhys turned to his desk and picked up the phone.

'And keep it strictly business,' Gil warned.

'Of course, sir,' Rhys replied, then caught the DS's theatrically raised eyebrow and grinned.

Warlow didn't turn from the board. 'Jess, how did it go with the headmaster... Boyce, isn't it?'

'Catrin's run him through the PNC. Nothing at all on record. I think he's the genuine article. Principal of a tiny country school, wife, rose beds, one child. Never had a parking ticket.'

Catrin nodded. 'We can corroborate the story with the other teachers, sir, but it seems genuine enough. A nature trail in the woods and a curious little girl that wandered off. Difficult to believe in this day and age. We're not discounting the faint possibility of an accomplice, so we're keeping an open mind.'

Warlow reached into his jacket pocket for a folded piece of paper. He walked to the Gallery and pinned up Nia's finished drawing. 'This is the little girl's depiction of what she saw. Our Green Man.'

'Looks like a camouflage jacket,' Gil said.

'Agreed. So, we need to input all this on to HOLMES. See what it comes up with.'

'I'll get on with that, sir,' Catrin said.

Warlow knew how it worked. The indexers would punch in details, collate, and compare it with the mass of information already in the major crimes enquiry system. It would spit out something. The key was in ensuring its relevance.

He threw Gil a glance. 'What about your SO?'

Gil wrinkled his nose and sniffed. 'Watching brief, obviously. But his thing, if thing is how you'd describe it, involved distributing images of a minor. Said minor being a fifteen-year-old who lied about her age. Something she admitted to later. Didn't change the facts.

Though according to him, all of it nothing but a huge misunderstanding.'

'Believe him?' Jess asked.

'I don't believe anyone who messes with kids, victim of circumstance or otherwise. She was fifteen, and that's the law. But as for his involvement in this case...' Gil shook his head. 'We're waiting on CCTV to confirm his where-abouts this morning, but I'd be surprised if he was lying. Let's put it that way.'

Catrin walked to a colour printer and came back with the PolSA's images of the woods where Nia Owen saw her Green Man. She stuck the images around the edge and used some twine to link them to marked areas on the map.

'You should think about doing this professionally,' Gil said.

Catrin sent him a look that would have burned through the heat shield of a re-entering spacecraft.

'Only saying,' Gil explained. 'You have a knack.'

'I've got some ointment for that,' Rhys said, having finished his call and joining the others while they waited for Catrin to do her thing.

She did not turn around this time. 'If this is the comedy club, I'm asking for my money back.'

Jess joined her at the Gallery with a pen in hand to use as a pointer. 'This is the school. This is the lane into the woods. This is where Nia Owen's group was when she went missing, and this is where they found her and now the Spiderman glove.'

Rhys's phone pinged. He looked at it, did something with his finger to an image, and stood up to show the others. 'Just had this from Gina. These are the Spiderman gloves on the shop's website. Four quid from H&M. He got them for Halloween last year.'

Catrin peered at the phone and then at the blown-up glove image from the PolSA she had posted. 'Stripes are the same on the fingers and the black spider looks to be the same shape and dimensions. I'd say they're from the same manufacturer.'

'Okay, Rhys, let the PolSA know so he can tell Povey that,' Warlow ordered.

'Yes, sir.'

The DCI followed the lines on the map. 'So, the kids leave the school as a group, cross the road, walk along that lane past the treatment works, cross a field and then cross the stream into the woods. Did they have to stop for traffic?'

Jess tapped the map with her pen. 'Two teachers stood thirty yards up and down the road to flag traffic while they crossed. But only two cars stopped. It's a quiet road.'

'We need to ask the teachers to ID those cars.'

Catrin wrote something on the Job Centre.

'I've walked that lane past the water treatment works. There's a path up towards the Howells' property.' Warlow stepped forward and found it on the map, traced it with his finger. Catrin took out an orange marker and highlighted it.

'Someone on the path could have got there, unseen from the other direction,' Jess said.

'Or followed them along the lane.' Gil stood and pointed to the houses next to the school. 'That's the Caeglas estate. How many houses, twenty-five?'

'About that,' Catrin confirmed.

Gil nodded. 'Anyone in those houses could have seen the kids leave. Heard them even. I can't believe for one minute they wouldn't have been noisy. Anyone could have followed.'

Gil was right. 'Have we knocked on all the doors?' Warlow demanded.

Jess shook her head. 'Last I heard, they were concentrating more on where the dogs had lost Osian's scent. Further out.'

Warlow glanced at his watch. Six fifteen.

'Right. I'm not leaving this to chance. Rhys, Catrin, get someone else on HOLMES. You two go back out there and do the houses directly behind the school. Even if they've been contacted, ask again. Did they see anything last week? You know the drill.'

'Will do, sir.' Catrin turned away from the Gallery.

'Gil, we need that CCTV footage,' Warlow said.

Gil nodded. 'I'll start banging heads.'

'We ought to talk to the other teachers for confirmation of Boyce's story and the cars. I can do that by phone,' Jess suggested.

Warlow wanted to be doing these things himself, but he couldn't. He needed to keep a clear head. And one way to do that would be to get rid of the crap littering it up. And, as if the gods of coincidence had been listening, his phone rang, and Owen Tamblin's name came up.

'I need to take this in the office,' Warlow explained. 'Owen,' he said into the phone ten seconds later as he half shut the door of the SIO's room.

'Evan, sorry to hear about Denise. How are the boys?'

'They're fine. Denise has been a sinking ship for a good couple of years now.'

'Never easy though.'

'No.' Owen was being polite. He'd met Denise and knew exactly what she was like, though he'd been spared the excesses of her deteriorating behaviour over the last decade. But time was short and getting shorter. Warlow got down to business. 'Thanks for coming back to me. I had a chat with one of our superintendents today. Looks like the Geoghans are now officially mispers.'

'Yes, they are,' Tamblin said. 'When I learned of that fact, I have to say I did not shed a tear. I'd like to think that the earth split open, and they buggered off back into the depths they were vomited up from. Unfortunately, the probation officer saw it differently and when he called and got no answer, he got some Uniforms to call.'

'Signs of a struggle, I hear?'

'Definitely. Karen Geoghan's car was still there. They did not leave via the new Merc she'd just bought.'

Warlow hissed. With the luck of the devil, Karen Geoghan had won a scratch card prize on the lottery a few months before. She'd sent him a cutting from the local rag to gloat. 'Has anyone talked to you about that? On the record I mean?'

'As in, where were you on the night of? No. Off the record they have. Did I have a list of scenarios? I gave them the names of all the poor sods the Geoghans had defrauded and given cold baths to.'

'Long list then.'

'The DI I talked to looked like I'd just spat on his grave.'

Warlow snorted. 'What's your gut telling you?'

'Who knows? Perhaps someone else read the article about Karen and her winnings. They were living in Town-hill for Christ's sake. Not exactly a gated community.'

The area had a terrible reputation, having once been the country's car theft capital and recently the scene of riots where anti-establishment temperatures had come to the boil.

'Are we talking home invasion?'

'Possibly,' Tamblin paused. 'But there's been no activity on Karen Geoghan's bank account. No withdrawals. All that cash is just sitting there. Of course, both our names appeared in correspondence from Ms Geoghan. She even had a writing table with cards and letters already written to you and me but not yet posted.'

'They can have the stack I've got at home as well,' Warlow said with feeling.

'Me, too. The only good news, if you can call it that, is that I doubt Derek and Karen are going to turn up on your doorstep with a shotgun.'

It had crossed Warlow's mind that with Derek Geoghan's release from prison and Karen's winnings, their long-festering resentment against the two officers who put them away might manifest into more than threats. Owen was right. If something had happened to them, that threat seemed to be one less thing to worry about. 'Let your DI know I'm happy to chat, but I've got bugger all to add. And I might be busy for the next day or two.'

Owen got it in one. 'You've caught the abduction case?'

'Yes.'

The noise of a long breath being let out came over the phone. 'As they say around here, rather you than me, *mwsh*.

Anything to do with kids sends me up the wall. I'll tell the DI to keep away until you clear this case.'

'Thanks for the vote of confidence.'

Tamblin laughed, but it was tinged with sympathy. 'Ah, come on. If it was my kid, you're the man I'd want on the hunt, Evan. Get the bastard for all of us.'

CHAPTER FOURTEEN

WARLOW STILL HAD the Geoghans on his mind when a knock on the half-open door drew his attention. He looked up into the concerned grey eyes of Jess Allanby.

'Finished your call?'

'All done.'

Jess stepped inside. 'The teachers confirmed Boyce's account of what happened on the nature trail. I also spoke to a Tanya Jenkins. She oversaw Nia Owen's group, and the stories match exactly. One minute Nia was picking flowers and the next, she's done a Houdini. Tanya Jenkins is full of praise for Boyce. Didn't panic, took control. He's well-liked by pupils and staff.'

'Right.'

Jess tilted her head and peered at Warlow. 'Are you really alright, Evan? You seem distracted. Molly would say you're… mithered. And so would I.'

'Mithered just about does it.'

'Two-Shoes' visit upset your apple-cart?'

'In a way. Old ghosts that won't stay laid.' He studied the DI. Her clean white shirt, her stylish suit. She put effort into her appearance, and he knew it to be a matter of pride, not narcissism. He also realised that he hadn't had a normal conversation with another person at all that day. 'And how are you and Molly?'

Jess sat on the other side of Warlow's desk, legs crossed. 'She's missing Cadi. So am I.'

Warlow gave her an apologetic grin. Cadi, Warlow's black lab, had become a firm favourite of Jess and her daughter's. Currently, Cadi was being looked after by the Dawes, a pair of dog-loving neighbours.

'Tell Molly I'm sorry. I've been tied up with the bloody funeral and the boys. But that's done now. Once things settle here, I'll bring Cadi over for her to walk.' At seventeen, Molly had as much energy as the Labrador.

'Mol understands. The good news is she'd been distracted, too.'

'School?'

Jess's eyes went ceiling-wards. 'That and a boy, would you believe.'

Warlow could believe. Molly had the same meld of Celtic and Italian genes in her physiology as her mother. Boys would be queuing up to be beaten away with a stick.

'Does he pass the Jess test?'

Jess snorted. 'He seems nice enough. And he has a car.'

'Ah.' Warlow smiled. 'How are the lessons going?'

'Not fast enough for Molly.'

A brief silence grew between them. Warlow didn't need a degree to work out Jess had something else on her mind. The unaccustomed seriousness of her expression said everything.

'Go on, I'm listening,' Warlow prompted.

'Two-Shoes talked to me, too. I didn't want West Mids coming to the house while I was off sick, so my interview with them is still pending.'

Jess had fractured her wrist doing her job. All healed

now, but she'd been off for a few weeks. 'You hardly knew Mel Lewis.'

'Does that matter? They're digging for dirt.'

'That's their job.'

'But?'

'But McGrath and Cheesely, West Mids answer to Ant and Dec, hinted I might be involved in what happened to Mel.'

'What?' Jess's voice shot up an octave. 'I hope you told them to shove it?'

'I did. Still, it's what someone must be thinking.'

'Well, they can think again, can't they. You came back from retirement; you weren't anywhere near—'

Warlow held up his hands to stop her. 'I know, I know.'

Jess simmered in the chair. She shook her head and sighed. 'You know you can talk to me about this stuff.'

'I do. I'm not very good at it, that's all.'

'You need to work on that, Evan. Talking. People do listen. And you may even find it helps. Over a drink. Away from the madhouse.'

She was right. And Tom would say the same thing. They had that in common, Tom and Jess. Both empaths. Whereas Alun was more like him. Keeping things rolled up in a tight ball inside. 'The same thing applies to you,' Warlow said by way of a riposte.

Jess frowned.

'I appreciate you might want to keep what happened in Manchester between you and Rick separate from work,' Warlow explained. 'That's understandable. In that way, we're alike. But if you ever need to talk...'

Jess smiled. 'Thank you.'

'Not sure how good a listener I'd be, but—'

'There you go again. Underestimating yourself. You are a good listener. You listen to Molly. That's medal worthy for a start. I know she opens up to you. That's a skill set in itself. And she hasn't talked to many people since I left her dad.'

Warlow shook his head. 'That's all down to Cadi therapy.'

'Some of it, yes. But not all of it.'

Warlow cocked an eye. He could have said more. He should have said more. A door had opened, just a couple of inches, but a crack, nevertheless. And something inside him told him he ought to push it open a little wider. But words failed him. Was this how it went? Christ, it had been so long since he'd had a normal conversation with another woman, an attractive woman, he'd forgotten not only the words to the song, but how the bloody tune went as well. He cleared his throat and fell back on his favourite sword, the one with humour stamped on the handle. 'So, want me to run this boy she's found through the PNC?'

Jess laughed. 'No. He's a nice kid. Rugby-playing farmer. I would not have said he'd be Molly's type at all. Besides, I've already run a check on the PNC and Interpol. Just waiting for the FBI to get back to me.'

Warlow's turn to smile.

Another knock on the door. Gil put his head in. 'Is this a bring a bottle party?'

'News?' Warlow asked.

'Just had the CCTV through from Sainsbury's. Pitcher was there when he said he was. That's him off the list.'

'Okay. So, we're back to the Spiderman glove. Let's hope that Povey can find something.'

———

Seven hours fifty minutes missing...

RHYS AND CATRIN stood outside Cwrt Y Waun school. Built in the early part of the last century, the sturdy grey stone and slate-roofed structure had been partly rendered and painted in cream. A high hedge bordered a play area and, with the summer coming, a small marquee stood in the yard with interlinking mats as flooring, all visible through the chain-link fencing.

'How do you want to do this, Sarge?' Rhys asked.

'Gil suggested we start with the house the school backs on to.' Catrin walked up the minor road running to the side of the building. There were open fields opposite and a stone wall with more chain-link fencing bordering the pavement. The school was security conscious, that was obvious. 'There are three properties along this stretch and another two in the cul-de-sac behind the school.' She consulted the map she'd brought inside a transparent plastic envelope. 'Let's start with these…numbers seven to eleven.'

A marked response vehicle sped past. Rhys watched it go before saying, 'Do you think Osian could be this close? I mean, there are blue and whites and Uniforms all over the place.'

Catrin shrugged. 'Who knows? But as Gil says, you won't find treasure unless you dig for it.'

'He also says he's not superstitious, just 'stitious. And he can't count the number of times he failed his maths O-Level. And he told me that his granddaughters are into Frozen, so he bought them a bag of peas for Christmas.'

Catrin's face fell. 'Oh my God, not Gil's dad jokes, please.'

'His wife was furious. Apparently, she still hasn't let it go.'

'Okay, okay. You are spending far too much time with that man. My fault for mentioning him. It's bad enough when I'm out here with him. I can't have you turning into his clone.'

'I've seen you laugh at his jokes.'

Catrin shook her head. 'You are mistaking laughter for wincing with pain.' She started walking towards the first of the houses, but then hesitated and took out her phone and a business card. 'I ought to check in with…' she read the card, 'Grimshaw.'

'Who?'

'The Social Services guy. Some residents here have been rehoused. Relocated here to escape abusive relationships. It's an off-the-radar sort of place. Grimshaw wanted us to liaise with him if we were going to make contact.' Catrin punched in numbers and held the phone to her ear.

Rhys waited, eyeing up the first bungalow – number seven – while Catrin made her call.

'Oh, hi, it's Detective Sergeant Richards. We're about to knock on some doors in the Caeglas estate. You said you wanted to know. Ring me back.'

'No joy?' Rhys asked when she joined him.

Catrin shook her head. 'Answerphone. I'm not waiting. He has my number. Let's get on with it.'

They'd rehearsed a series of questions on the way in the Focus.

Were you at home on the afternoon of Tuesday the 17th?

Did you see or hear the children from the school leave on their nature trail?

Did you see anyone following them?

Did you see anyone in the lane leading to the woods before or after?

Have you searched any outbuildings on your property?

Have you been aware of any unfamiliar people around the area for the last two weeks?

They got the same answer in the first three houses.

Yes, they'd either seen or heard the children on the afternoon of the 17th.

No, no one followed them.

No, no one in the lane.

Yes, sheds checked.

No, definitely no strangers mooching about.

These came from a retired couple, a woman in her seventies living alone and a young couple with a toddler of their own peeping out from between her parents' legs.

Rhys took down names and telephone details while Catrin asked the questions and fended off offers of refreshments.

Then they moved into the cluster of houses in the cul-de-sac known as Beili Road. Number ten and eleven's back garden backed on to the stone school walls, topped off with four feet of chain-link fencing. The houses were small two-up, two-down semis with flat-roof extensions at the rear. An identical box numbered twelve and thirteen stood at right angles to ten and eleven.

A young woman answered the door to number ten when Catrin rang the bell. Small, in her early twenties, in tight jeans and fluffy slippers, orange hair and a nose ring. She opened the door on a safety chain and peered out, her dark eyes under their canopy length lashes, cautious.

Catrin introduced herself and Rhys, asked the same questions, but had to repeat four of the five, as the woman had not understood her. When she answered, it was not with a local accent. Hers was south of London. Another woman, older but dressed in a saggy sweatsuit, appeared in the hallway behind.

The younger woman turned and shooed her off. 'It's okay, Mum. It's the police about the missing boy. It's fine. I'm sorting it.'

Rhys wrote down their names, Pat and Jaydon Munro. Mother and daughter.

Catrin took a step back to look at the upstairs in both houses.

Jaydon Munro caught her disquiet.

'We have the whole house, but they're council flats next door, they are. The upstairs is empty. Trashed by the last owner. She and her four cats and a Pug. I reckon the council is redecorating.'

Catrin smiled, wondering how much of the redecoration comprised disinfecting and discarding.

At number ten, Doris Sibley had bright blue eyes that wobbled over Catrin's features as she peered at the DS, scanning as if they couldn't settle on anything. Catrin put her somewhere around her late seventies. Mrs Sibley listened but didn't answer. Instead, she told them to stay where they were, went back inside and emerged a couple of minutes later with two mugs of tea on a tray and four fingers of Kit Kat as she rode over their protests. 'You must be hungry. My husband always was. He was a sergeant in Swansea.'

Rhys noticed a white stick leaning against the wall inside the door. He nudged Catrin and pointed at it.

'Are you sight impaired, Mrs Sibley?' Catrin asked.

'I have the degeneration, at the back of the eyes. It's the dry type, so injections don't work.' She dropped her voice. 'Bloody nuisance it is. Still, I have my radio.'

That's skewered her as a witness, thought Catrin. But such practical knowledge didn't seem to bother Rhys.

'Are you registered?' he asked.

'I am. But I manage pretty well in my little flat. I know where everything is.'

Once she started talking, they couldn't shut her up. And yes, she, like everyone else, had heard the children as they'd lined up in anticipation of their nature walk, but had seen nothing useful.

'Do you have a key for the flat upstairs?' Catrin asked.

Doris Sibley giggled. 'I do. I should have given it back to the council, but I haven't seen anyone to give it to. There have been decorators, and they're back and forth, but they already have a key. So does the young man who is supposed to be moving in. He's nice, but he wishes the decorators would get a move on, too. She dropped her voice. 'They have their music on loud all day.' She smiled. 'Aren't you two a lovely little couple.'

'We're not,' Catrin said.

'But you look it,' Doris chirped. 'Stay there for a minute.' She trotted off and came back with a Yale key on a piece of grey string. Rhys took it and walked around the side of the house to a separate door and stairs up to the flat.

Jaydon Munro was right about the redecorating. Bedroom, living room and kitchen were all empty, floors covered with paint-stained dust sheets. More heaped dust sheets and paint cans were stacked in one corner of the living room. There were no curtains on the windows and two aluminium step ladders filled the living room space. It looked like they'd finished the kitchen. A wood-effect worktop and a new sink showed through the plastic sheets covering the rest of the units.

Rhys retraced his steps, gave Mrs Sibley her mug back, and joined Catrin to stand once more in the lane outside the school. He quickly confirmed Mrs Sibley's take on the upstairs flat as being empty and full of decorating equipment. 'What now?' he asked when he'd finished.

'We keep knocking on doors until it's done.'

'Keep digging until we find the treasure,' Rhys said, and followed his sergeant as she crossed back towards the rest of the Caeglas estate.

CHAPTER FIFTEEN

Mair Pitcher lit her eighteenth cigarette of the day and sucked in the hot smoke, coughed, then sucked in some more. The late afternoon was cooling rapidly on its downhill slide towards evening. She'd had chips in the oven for fifteen minutes and beans and sausage simmering on the stove. Not that she would be eating any of it. Her appetite, of late, had packed its bags and caught the night-bus to can't be arsed. She preferred a quick ciggie any day of the week or hour of the day.

And maybe a vodka and tonic.

She crossed her right arm over her chest to rub the thin biceps of her left arm in an attempt at warding off the cold that always seemed to seep into her. Mair did not know why she felt cold all the time these days, but she did. That's why she never objected to making Leighton's tea. That meant she'd be by the stove. Even on a sunny day, the cold seemed to live inside her like an icy core that would never melt.

The stove and another ciggie kept her warm and stopped her thinking about the two stone she'd lost over the last three months. She shook her head. After all those years of struggling with her weight, the dieting, and the pills and all that crap. Now she could eat as much chocolate as she wanted and not put on an ounce.

Except she didn't even feel like chocolate anymore.

Mair cursed. She'd already called Leighton for his tea once, but he hadn't replied. Not even when she'd texted him.

She took the cigarette from her mouth and shouted down the garden towards his shed.

'Leighton, your tea is getting cold.'

No answer.

'Leighton!'

Nothing. Probably had his earphones on, playing some stupid bloody game. She turned to face the kitchen and grabbed a fleece from behind the door, stuck the cigarette in her mouth while she fed her arms through the sleeves, and hurried down the garden in her Crocs.

She stood at the door and called out, 'Leighton? Leighton?'

No answer. She rapped on the door. When her knuckles found the wood, the door moved away from her and swung inwards. Leighton was not in his shed. Mair frowned. He'd been silly, messing about with girls too young to be messing with. But he worked hard at his business and what he did brought in some money. He'd explained to her that getting a job at the builder's merchants, or the chicken factory didn't do it for him. He stayed away from people as much as he could. One day all this would blow over, but for now, Leighton preferred his own company than to be called 'Little Paedo' everywhere he went. And Mair didn't mind. He helped her with the shopping and gave her a bit of rent for his upkeep.

They argued. What family didn't? Especially when she

told him how stupid he was for not looking for better paid work. A bright boy like him could do anything. No one cared about minor offences like stupid phone pictures of some tart's tits. Not these days.

He would look at her and shake his head and say, 'You have no bloody idea, Mam.'

But the one thing about Leighton was that he liked to be tidy. He kept his shed clean and organised. So, when the door swung open and Mair saw the chair on its side and papers strewn all over the floor, the little jolt of fear that jerked through her brought her up short. She put her still alight cigarette carefully down on the edge of a flowerpot and stepped inside. Things looked worse once she crossed the threshold. A shelf had been wrenched off a wall and Leighton's collection of old video game discs was scattered underneath, some with the discs spilled out from the plastic casings.

'Leighton?' Mair called again. She hurried back out to the storage shed. It was still padlocked. 'Leighton?'

Mair looked down at the concrete path. At something dark at her feet. A smudged trickle of black against the grey and shaped like a seven-inch-long elongated pear. She knelt and touched it. Her finger came away damp and when she held it up to look at it closely, it wasn't black. It was red.

'No,' she wailed. 'No… Leighton?' Mair looked up and around, but no one answered her. She got up and ran back to the house, her cigarette forgotten. To the phone and the card next to it that big police officer had left her.

He picked up after half a dozen rings. 'Gil Jones.'

'Something's happened to Leighton. Something bad.'

'Who is this?'

'It's me. Mair Pitcher. You came to see my son today. Leighton. Leighton Pitcher.'

'Ah, Mrs Pitcher. I should have recognised the voice. What can I—'

'It's Leighton, I tell you. He didn't come in for his tea. I shouted, but...he's not in his shed. The door is open, and the place is a mess. Something's happened. I know it has.'

Gil's voice remained calm. 'Can Leighton have gone somewhere and left the door open? Maybe the wind—'

'The wind doesn't turn chairs over,' Mair Pitcher shouted down the phone. 'Something's happened. There's blood—'

'Whoa. Back up. Did you say blood?'

'On the path. I saw blood on the floor. I—' Mair Pitcher coughed then. A rasping, wheezing mother of a cough that went on far too long.

When it finally stopped, Gil Jones whispered, 'You okay, Mrs Pitcher?'

'I'm fine,' she gasped. But her voice sounded ragged and anything but fine.

'When was the last time you saw Leighton?'

'After you left. He came in and made himself a cup of tea, then went back out to his work. I called him in five minutes ago. He never leaves his shed door unlocked. Never.'

Gil sighed. 'Right. Stay put. Someone will be with you shortly. Don't touch anything until we get there. Understand?'

'Hurry up,' wheezed Mair.

———

GINA MELLINGS BUSIED herself in the kitchen of the Howells' house. It was just before seven and Fflur had wanted some cereal for supper. Gina, happy for something to do, had put bowl, milk and cereal box on the table and sat with the little girl as she ate. Fflur's parents were in the living room sitting on the sofa staring at their phones and the TV. Gina had warned them to stay away from the news channels. Instead, they'd chosen *Homes under the Hammer*. They watched and let the words and images flow in through their eyes without taking anything in.

Gina had learned a lot about Osian in the twenty minutes it had taken Fflur to eat a bowl of Multigrain Cheerios. She'd learned that his favourite cereal was Rice Krispies, that he hated almost everything except chicken pasta bake and pink ham, that he feared moths and that his favourite book was *The Wild Robot*. The little girl was a real chatterbox.

'Do you think he's scared now?' Fflur asked.

Ten out of ten for the trickiest question of the day, thought Gina. 'No,' she answered. 'I think he's probably missing you and his mam and dad, but he knows we're looking for him. I don't think he is scared.'

'I hope there aren't any moths there,' Fflur said. 'I'm not scared of moths. I'm scared of wasps, though. And big spiders.' She paused and thought. 'Is he in someone's house?'

Gina shrugged. 'I don't know, Fflur. Could be.'

'Or a tent or a car. At school they say never to get into a car with a stranger.'

'I'm sure Osian didn't do that.'

'Have they taken him because they don't have a little boy of their own? I heard someone did that with a baby at the hospital once.'

'It's possible,' Gina said but didn't elaborate. 'Wherever he'll be, I'm sure he's being very brave.'

Fflur thought about this and shook her head. 'He's a scaredy cat. When he goes fishing with Uncle Jim, he won't put the maggots on the hook. If I go, I have to put them on for him.'

'Does Uncle Jim take you fishing often?'

'No, only when it's fine.' Fflur chomped on a mound of cereal and ladled in an extra spoonful of milk. She chewed for a moment and then added, thoughtfully, 'Uncle Jim knows the man who puts the fish in the pools. I like going because Uncle Jim always buys us an ice cream at the post office on the way home.'

'You like Uncle Jim?'

Fflur smiled a sly smile and nodded. 'He sometimes says rude words when he's fishing. When one wriggles off the line when he tries to catch it, he says, "Ya bastard, bastard thing".' She'd dropped her voice. 'But he makes us promise never to tell Mam or Dad.'

Gina, whispering too, said, 'I won't say anything, either.' She took the empty bowl to the sink.

'And today he used a rude word in front of Mam. But he didn't know I was listening. He said that they should string them up by the balls.' Once more, Fflur delivered the word in a whisper.

'Did he now?'

Fflur tilted her head with a wry smile. 'I know balls isn't aways rude. I can say tennis balls and it isn't rude, but it was rude when Uncle Jim said it because he said all six offhanded should be strung up by the balls.'

Gina waited for the inevitable. For Fflur to ask what an offhanded was. But it seemed she'd made her own mind up about that one and Gina felt no inclination to clarify that 'all six offhanders' in reality meant 'all sex offenders'.

'Uncle Jim sounds like quite a character.'

'He's funny,' Fflur said. 'He's—'

The scream from the living room made both Gina and Fflur whip their heads around.

'Stay here,' Gina ordered, and rushed out.

Both Nerys and Lloyd were sitting forwards on the edge of the sofa, staring at a phone. Nerys had a hand over her mouth. Presumably to stifle more of the scream that had already escaped.

'Nerys?' Gina asked. 'What is it?'

Nerys turned up a pale face, owl-eyed from fear. 'It's on Twitter. The Green Man.'

'What?' Gina asked, as something twisted inside her.

Lloyd's breathing sounded heavy. He held the phone up for the FLO to see. 'Here, on bloody Twitter. Look.'

Gina stepped closer and looked at the screen.

Desp007ish @Carnagilous

Is this the kid stealer in Wales? Cops on the lookout for Green camo man #kidnap

#saveosian #eyesopen

Underneath Desp007ish had posted an image of a man in a green camouflaged jacket and hat walking through a wood. A stock photo, not of the actual man they were after, just enough to give a flavour. A string of responses ran underneath. Most of them horrified. Most of them suggesting some kind of terminal punishment for the Green Man.

'I thought your boss didn't want anyone to know.' Lloyd's voice loud and angry brought Gina back into the room. She looked into Osian's father's florid face and read the terror and frustration boiling there.

'He didn't.' Gina held his gaze. 'Let me check this out.'

On the sofa, Nerys reached for the TV remote. 'If it's on Twitter, it'll be on the news, too, I bet.'

'Not a good idea, Nerys,' Gina said. But she had no power to stop the Howells watching TV. Instead, she turned away, walked back through the kitchen, and reached for her phone. Best she found out what was going on from the horse's mouth. She opened the back door and stepped outside into the cool evening air with her phone to her ear.

CHAPTER SIXTEEN

Seven hours, forty-five minutes missing...

IT WASN'T COMPLETELY dark in the room, but the curtains were drawn and what light there was served only to illuminate its strangeness to six-year-old Osian Howells. An unfamiliarity that made him anxious and uncomfortable and added to the fear and loneliness that the day had brought.

He knew he'd done wrong by talking to the man. He knew because in school they were taught all the time not to talk to strangers. But he'd been at home and people came to the house all the time. And this man hadn't seemed strange. He'd stopped at the front gate and looked up and down the road. All smiley. A nice man who'd said hello and asked if this was the way to the school.

Osian knew the way to school because he went there every day with Fflur and Mam, except for the holidays. He knew the answer to the question, and he was a child who liked to please, and so he'd stood in the front garden in his spacesuit and pointed. When the man pointed in a different direction, the wrong way, Osian corrected him.

He'd walked to the gate and pointed to the right way.

That was when everything had gone wrong.

He didn't see the lunge the man made until it was too late. By then he'd been plucked upwards, his head jerking forward so that the helmet fell off. He'd screamed. But the noise came out as nothing but a moan as the man clamped a hand over his mouth.

Then they were moving. The man started running. Osian wriggled and fought, but the man clasped him tight against his body. Osian remembered the roughness of the man's coat against his face, the hot breath against his head. They ran for only a few yards. To a car. To a box in the back that smelled of old clothes. A big hand held him down and put a sticky tape over his mouth and around his hands and then the man ran around, and the car drove away. Osian didn't know how far they drove because he was trying to shout through the tape. Shout for his mother and Fflur from inside the dark box. But nothing came out except a moaning noise.

Osian couldn't remember how long they were in the car before it stopped. Daylight came back and the man appeared, picked him up and carried him through a door and into this room.

To the dim light.

The man took off the tape from Osian's face and from around his hands. But he looped a plastic thing around his wrist like sometimes was on the sticks and plants his mother bought from the nursery. A nylon rope linked the plastic tie to the sofa and the man told Osian that if he made a noise, something terrible would happen. He needed to stay quiet.

There was water and crisps and biscuits, but they weren't Osian's, so the boy left them alone.

When the man left, Osian had lain on the sofa and cried.

He didn't like the room. It was strange, and there were shadows.

At home, in his bedroom, Dad had given him a night light. A 3D astronaut he could change the colour of.

But there was no night light here. And no Fflur. And no stuffed dog by the name of Arth. Thinking of Fflur and Arth brought a fresh bout of tears and so he curled up on the sofa with his lips quivering and the odd ratcheting sob in his breathing.

Until he heard the noise.

A low, groaning, growling noise from beyond another door. Something tied up like he had been. Something with maybe a tape over its face. Something hungry or in pain.

It didn't make a noise all the time. But when it did, Osian shivered and squeezed his eyes shut.

There were no moths. But there was the noise. And he was scared that if the door opened, whatever groaned and moaned in the darkness would come for him.

He shut his eyes and cried as he softly, quietly, called out for his mother.

CHAPTER SEVENTEEN

Eight hours missing…

JESS SENT GIL a wary glance as they stood behind Warlow watching a 7pm bulletin on the news. Gil had his suit jacket on ready to leave to pick up Rhys and drive out to the Pitcher property when the call had come in from Gina Mellings. Jess had immediately searched Twitter and confirmed what Gina had told them. Gil had glanced at his watch and suggested they switch on the news.

It had made top spot.

'POLICE HUNTING for a missing six-year-old have refused to comment on a leaked eyewitness report suggesting they are searching for a man dressed in a camouflage jacket. The leak first appeared on Twitter, saying that a man spotted by a child two weeks before might be responsible for the disappearance of Osian Howells from his front garden in Carmarthenshire earlier today. Our correspondent, Alex Dagnall, is in the village of Cwrt Y Waun, where the boy went missing. Alex, what can you tell us about this development?'

The scene shifted to outside the police cordon leading to Maes Awelon, the Howells' residence. Alex Dagnall stood with his back to a couple of response vehicles and Maes Awelon in the background. 'Well, Alison. This story broke via social media. We already knew that a couple of weeks ago, the local primary school here went on a nature walk to some woods about half a mile away. Reportedly, one pupil was unaccounted for but turned up within minutes, claiming she'd followed a Green Man. The police did not investigate this as the school did not report it to them, but this evening, in an extraordinary twist, the Green Man has resurfaced as possibly someone dressed in an army or camouflage jacket. This person is someone the police would like to speak to in relation to the disappearance of Osian Howells, the six-year-old who went missing earlier today.'

Dagnall half turned. 'As you will see, there is a significant police presence here. More officers and volunteers are combing the surrounding woods and fields and knocking on doors, hoping to find traces or information that might lead to Osian's whereabouts.'

'SHIT,' hissed Warlow. 'Can someone please tell me how these slimy bastards got hold of this?'

'Who knew?' Jess asked.

'Everyone I briefed in the Reading Room and our lot here.'

'Could someone from the press have been in the Reading Room?' Jess asked.

'Not possible,' Warlow muttered. 'I chucked everyone but essential personnel out. Or at least I thought I did.'

'It's also possible one of the coppers there has a big mouth,' Gil said. 'Or kids of his own in the area.'

Warlow let out a sigh that seemed to never end. He pushed himself up out of the chair. 'Well, it's out now. Bugger all we can do about it.'

'Everyone with a camouflage jacket will be fair game for pointing fingers,' Jess said.

'They simply do not give a toss. Did I tell you how much I hated the press?' Warlow shook his head.

'I think you might have mentioned it.' Jess gave him a thin smile.

'They'll probably want a statement from you at some point.' Gil raised an eyebrow.

'Yes, well. They can bloody well wait for that. And why are you still here? I thought you were going up to see Pitcher's mother?'

Gil flinched and hurried for the door. 'I am. Picking Rhys up on the way. Want me to call for some food on the way back?'

'I'm not hungry.' Warlow's appetite was non-existent.

'Me neither,' Jess agreed.

'You might regret that in three hours' time. I'll see what I can do.' Gil picked up his keys and exited.

Warlow watched him go. 'That man cannot take no for an answer.'

'He's probably right, though. The longer this goes on, the more we'll flag. And coffee only delays the crash and makes it a harder one when it comes.'

She was right. So was Gil. He glanced back up at the TV. Dagnall was still talking into his microphone. Warlow picked up the remote, pointed it at the screen and flicked off the picture with a snarl. 'What time is it?'

Jess looked at her watch. 'Just after seven.'

'That gives us what, another two and a half hours of daylight. Catrin rung back yet?'

'Not yet.'

Warlow's insides felt like two cats fighting in a sack. They needed something to happen. They needed a break.

———

IN THE HOWELLS' living room, Gina Mellings handed out the tea in mugs. She knew how Nerys and Lloyd took it. It had been one of the first things she'd made a point of learning. Neither of them objected when she handed over the brew, though Gina would not have blamed either of them had they opted for a slug of whisky each.

In the end, she'd sat and watched the news with them. Watched the reporter speaking from outside the house they were all sitting in only a couple of hundred yards away. The Howells' faces registered the same surreal disbelief as she herself felt. Gina explained how Warlow had most definitely not given permission for the information about the Green Man's camouflage jacket to be released. But she'd also emphasised the fact that now people would be on the lookout for anyone who wore one. What she didn't say was that the same information would now be available to the Green Man. If he was watching, he'd know the police were looking for him. And if he really had a camouflage jacket, he'd more than likely bin it.

'Some of Jim's fishing friends wear those things,' Lloyd said, hunched low over his tea. 'They have guns, too.'

'Jim's friends wouldn't do something like this. They were the first to begin searching.' Nerys gave her husband a pained look.

'That proves nothing,' Lloyd muttered.

Gina stepped in. 'It wouldn't do any harm if you were to make a list of people you might know with a camouflage jacket. It all helps. It'll only take a phone call for us to tick them off the list.' What she didn't add was that the statistic showed that most child abductions were carried out by non-family members known to the child. That Lloyd Howells, despite his wife's protestations, had made an excellent point.

Nerys stared at her, the pained expression a mark of her resistance. But it quickly faded, and she nodded, seeing the sense of it.

'I'll get you a pen and some paper.' Gina stood up and went to the kitchen. She lifted her bag off a kitchen chair and put it on the countertop. The back door was open and Fflur waved to Gina from where she knelt near the vegetable patch.

'What have you got there?' Gina called out.

'A beetle. It's huge.' Fflur held her hands apart by a foot.

Gina smiled and reached into her bag for a pen and a spiral notepad. At first, she took little notice of the buzzing noise in the distance. Common enough in the country at this time of year. An electric lawn mower or a strimmer, maybe? Barely loud enough to register except at the very edge of her hearing.

But Fflur, whose fear of wasps meant that one encroaching anywhere near sent her into a froth of frenzied, flapping hysteria, heard it well enough. She stood up, looking around in panic at the source of the noise. Finding it only when she looked up and behind her from the direction of the fields.

'Mam!'

The shout, high-pitched and fearful, jolted Gina out of her search for a clean page for the Howells to write on. She dropped the pad and saw Fflur running towards the open doorway, eyes wide with terror as the buzzing grew in volume. Gina pulled the door fully open as Fflur leapt across the threshold.

'Wasp, it's a wasp.'

But now it didn't sound like any wasp Gina had ever heard as Fflur hurled herself into the police officer's body, grabbing at her. They stumbled backwards from the momentum. The buzzing flared in volume, but before Gina could step back out to look, her eye was caught by something falling and hitting the ground at the exact spot where Fflur had been kneeling.

It made no sound. Merely fluttered down and settled where it hit.

Something soft and red.

'Go inside, Fflur,' Gina said.

'No…no…it's a wasp.'

'No, it isn't. It's not a wasp. Go on in to your mother.'

'Don't go out there,' Fflur wailed.

But Gina was already peeling away the girl's arms. Once loose, she turned Fflur around and shooed her into the living room before stepping out into the garden and walking slowly across, her mind swirling towards the red… What exactly?

She looked up instinctively, searching for the source of the faint buzz and saw a shape disappear over the trees. A buzzing shape? Too big for a wasp. Had something dropped its prey into the garden?

But no carrion feeder she'd ever seen buzzed like a giant wasp.

And the object looked too flat, and half-folded in on itself to be a vole or a mouse or a…

When she got within a yard, Gina stopped and stared, unable to process what she was seeing at first. Until realisation dawned and she let out a little gasp of disbelief. She didn't touch it. Warlow and forensics would never forgive her if she did. But she didn't need to prod or poke this thing to know what it was. The black hatching and the black insectoid symbol gave it away.

Lying on the grass, deposited from the heavens, Osian

Howells' other spidey-glove lay like the corpse of a broken
bird.

CHAPTER EIGHTEEN

Eight hours, thirty minutes missing…

WARLOW PARKED up inside the police cordon twenty-five yards away from the Howells' property. There were more cars parked up than there had been the last time he'd been here a few hours ago. He recognised the crime scene vans and Catrin Richard's Focus. As he exited the Jeep a volley of questions from the journalists encamped thirty yards away assailed his ears.

'DCI Warlow, have you found something at the house?'

'Any news about the Green Man?'

'Is there a body in the garden, DCI Warlow?'

He didn't turn around to acknowledge them, wary of what he might say or do. He'd been known to favour gestures when some kind of response was called for. But the dignified thing to do was to ignore them and shelve the image that filled his head. That of strafing the bastards with a machine gun.

He had more important things to think about.

Catrin got out of the Focus and met him at the gate.

'Povey here?' Warlow asked.

Catrin nodded. 'They've set up a tent in the garden.'

'Right. There first I think.'

They acknowledged the Uniform guarding the gate and Catrin led him through the little passageway where Osian had built his cardboard spaceship. They'd cleared all that away. The boxes fattened into flat rectangles against the wall.

'What about the parents?' Warlow asked.

'Inside. Waiting for you.'

Warlow grunted. Of course they were.

When he rounded the corner of the house, two white-clad crime scene techs were crouched over a marked-off area. A small tent that reminded Warlow more of a beach hut than camping gear stood half on the grass and half on the vegetable patch. One of the techs stood up and nodded.

Warlow reached her via a laid-down plastic path. He looked at the indicator flag between the tech's feet, marked with a number one.

'This is where it landed?' Warlow asked.

Alison Povey did not have her hood up for once, and her close-cropped hair framed her ruddy face. Her answer, as always, was straight to the point. 'Yep.'

Warlow looked up to the sky above. Thin cloud covering had crept over, and the wind had dropped. No trees or power lines crossed the garden. 'Where is it?'

'In the tent.' Povey led the way. Inside, a small table was set up. Centre piece was the glove in a clear evidence bag. Around it was the accoutrements of Povey's arcane art. A few reagent bottles, a woods lamp, a field microscope, and an open laptop. 'Photos first I think.' She took off her nitrile gloves and crouched over the laptop keypad. The screen filled with thumbnail images. She moved an arrow with her fingers and clicked. An image expanded to show the crumpled glove on the ground.

From behind them, a figure appeared, uniformed and wearing the standard issue DP police baseball-style cap. Warlow glanced back and nodded at Gina Mellings.

'Ah, right,' Povey said. 'We can hear how it got here from the horse's mouth.'

Gina quickly explained about Fflur's fear of wasps and the noise she'd heard in the garden. How the buzz preceded the glove parachuting in.

'Not a giant wasp, then?' Catrin asked.

Gina shook her head. 'I didn't see it, but one of the guys at the end of the road caught a glimpse. Definitely a drone.'

'A drone capable of carrying the glove and depositing it. Which direction is the A40?' Catrin asked.

Gina pointed towards the bottom of the garden. 'That's south. The A40 is five fields away.'

Warlow shook his head, grimacing as if he was in pain. 'How the hell did he do that?'

Catrin shrugged. 'Drones have cameras, sir. They can also carry payloads. Sometimes heavy ones. You know that Amazon has been experimenting. And in some third world countries, they use drones to deliver medical supplies to remote areas.'

Warlow let out a low and barely audible, 'Hmm.' He turned his gaze back to the laptop and Povey. 'I see you've had a poke at it.'

Povey nodded. 'When we examined it, we saw some staining, here and here.' She pointed to two dark, almost purple marks on the palm of the glove.

Warlow's gut churned, but he asked anyway. 'Way too early for DNA, I realise. But it is blood, right?'

'But not Osian's. He may have wanted us to think it was Osian's, but we've run it through Raman spectroscopy and it's actually pig's blood.'

'What?' Catrin said. 'So, are we looking for an anaemic sow? A farm?'

'Maybe,' Warlow muttered, 'it's what he wants us to think.'

'I don't follow, sir,' Gina spoke from behind him.

Warlow stood up from the laptop. 'All this.' He waved a hand. 'It's theatrics. He's trying to make us react. Twisting the knife. Torturing the parents.'

'But we can't simply ignore it, right, sir?' Catrin's expression tightened.

Warlow flicked his gaze up at her but didn't shoot her down. She had the bit between her teeth. Desperate to use this to their advantage. He shot Povey a question. 'It's definitely the other glove?'

'Same manufacturer, same size. We'll confirm with DNA, of course. But for now, I'd say assume yes until proven otherwise.' Povey scrolled through the remainder of the images, but there was little more to be learned and Warlow already had all he needed. Which, when you added it all up, came to bugger all except knowing that whoever had done this was enjoying the thought of them all clustered in this tent scratching their heads.

'Where are the Howells?' He turned and addressed Gina.

'Watching us from the kitchen window.'

Warlow glanced at his watch. Almost seven-thirty. 'Right, get them into the living room. I'll talk to them there.'

———

RHYS AND GIL pulled up in front of the Pitcher's bungalow for the second time that day. This time, the door opened without either of the officers having to knock. Mair Pitcher stood there, one arm across her chest, angled up so that the stained ochre fingers of her left hand were clamped onto her right collarbone. She looked even more hunched in on herself than before.

'You took your time,' she croaked.

'No need to thank us, Mrs Pitcher,' Gil answered and got a filthy stare in response.

'Has Leighton turned up?' Rhys asked.

'Eh?' She cupped a hand around one ear.

Rhys repeated the question with the volume up. 'Has Leighton turned up?'

Mair shook her head. 'He isn't answering his phone, either. Not even when I text him. He always texts me back.'

'And he's not locked himself in his storage shed, has he?' Gil said.

'No. He's particular, is Leighton. He wouldn't leave his shed in a mess. He wouldn't.'

'Best we have a look.' Gil stepped back to allow Mair to step out.

They followed her on the same path Leighton had trodden earlier. She showed them the shed, the overturned chair, and the scattered papers. 'This isn't Leighton,' she said.

Rhys went to the storage shed and hefted the lock, pulled on it to make sure it was locked, rattled it, and then knocked on the door.

No response.

'Do you have a key to the lock?'

Mair scowled.

The DC tried reassuring her. 'Look, it's unlikely he's in there, but we need to check. To be sure.'

Looking even more miserable than she had previously, Mair shuffled off back to the house, leaving Rhys and Gil alone.

'Didn't know you had Irish blood, Rhys,' Gil said

'I don't.'

'You'd better check that, to be sure.'

The joke finally found its target, causing Rhys to nod and smile uncertainly. 'Very good, Sarge. You got me there.'

'Fish in a bloody barrel, Rhys.' Then Gil caught the DC's expression. 'What's the matter with you?'

'Superintendent Goodey sent us a memo about using triggering language. She'd probably call that joke micro-aggressive borderline racism.'

'But she'd still laugh at it, right?'

Rhys's eyebrows went up.

'No, you're right. She wouldn't. But then she wouldn't laugh at a cat seeing a cucumber. But tell me how that's offensive? It's a saying. I have a mate from Limerick whose old dad said it once. I latched on to that. And he says I'm always saying "tidy". He takes the Michael out of me, and I reciprocate. Where is the hate speak in that? Micro-aggression my hairy arse. I mean, anyone can be offended by anything if they want to be. So that makes it victimhood cobblers in my book.' Gil paused and sent Rhys a sideways glance. 'You're not from a shoe-mending family, are you?'

Rhys shook his head but failed to suppress the smile that came with it.

'And I know where to draw the line with the Irish. Never wear a leprechaun hat and remember, them and their shillelaghs are only sixty miles away across the sea.'

'What do you reckon to Leighton Pitcher, Sarge?'

Gil blew air out of the side of his mouth. 'If he's buggered off, he's not been subtle about it. I mean, why not leave things tidy.' He nodded towards the house. 'And tell Miss Congeniality in there he was going out for the night.'

'Fair point, Sarge.' The same thought had occurred to Rhys. Leighton Pitcher came across as a clean freak. Not quite full-on OCD, but…tidy. The office smacked of someone leaving in a hurry and not of his own volition. 'Maybe he had some encouragement to leave.'

Gil agreed. 'We'll get the VISOR team out here.'

'VISOR is…?'

'Violent Offender and Sex Offender Register. Let them have a peep at his hard drive. I doubt there'll be anything, but you never know.'

'But Leighton understands they can call at any time, right?'

'He does.'

Both officers looked up as Mair Pitcher returned, wheezing along the path, holding one key of a bunch between her fingers. Rhys took it, undid the lock, and opened the door. Apart from the neatly stacked and arranged shelves, it was empty.

'Right,' Gil said, taking out his pocketbook and addressing the woman. 'When was the last time you saw or spoke to Leighton?'

Mair had gained a shoulder bag on her return to the house. From it, she took a pack of cigarettes and a lighter.

The lighting up ritual had always fascinated Rhys as a non-smoker. And though Mair's hand trembled through-out, within fifteen seconds, she had a cigarette lit and puffed upon.

'Five minutes after you left, Leighton came up to the house to make a cup of tea for me and him. He's good like that. Always polite. He took his back out to the office.' She nodded towards the shed.

'So that would be, what, around five fifteen?' Rhys asked.

Mair shrugged.

'And you haven't seen or spoken to him until you fetched him for his supper?'

Mair sucked on her cigarette, blew the smoke away from the officers, and nodded her head.

'And no one came to the house after us?'

'Not that I know of. I'm a bit deaf, so Leighton's put this special doorbell thing up for me. It's extra loud. It also tells Leighton someone's there. Internet thingummyjig.'

Rhys sent Gil a glance and walked back into the office. He came back half a minute later clutching a black iPhone. 'This Leighton's?'

Mair's face stiffened. 'Where was that? He don't go nowhere without his phone. No wonder he isn't answering.'

'On the desk.'

Gil still had his notebook open. 'Okay, so where could he be? At a mates? The pub?'

Mair shook her head with a sour expression. 'He don't go nowhere since you bastards made him a paedo.'

'Right.' Gil snapped his book shut. 'We'd better get the crime scene lot up here.' He took out his phone.

'Hang on a sec, Sarge.' Rhys held up his hand and trotted back up the path and around to the front door. He peered at the black box where a doorbell should have been. It was almost as big as his own phone with a shiny lens. He ran back to Gil and Mair, looking pleased.

'Feeling better?' Gil asked.

'It's a camera doorbell security system. Let me look at Leighton's phone. Unless it's password protected.'

'Shouldn't be. VISOR insisted that any device isn't encrypted in any way.'

Sure enough, when Rhys swiped the surface, the phone came on immediately to a home screen. Rhys scrolled through the apps, not sure of what he was looking for but letting out a satisfied, 'Ah,' when he saw the NOCK app. He opened it to a menu page with headings like 'alarm', 'chimes', 'history'. He clicked on the latter and a new menu appeared with a list of entries under either 'detected' or 'rung bell'.

Rhys scrolled to the entry for 4.05pm. A mini video appeared of him and Gil Jones standing at the front door. He held the screen up for Gil to see.

'Bloody hell. Clever stuff.'

Then Rhys looked for later entries and found one under 'Detected' at 4.50pm. He found the video and pressed play, again holding it up for Gil to watch with him. On the screen, a man hurried through the gate but did not go to the front door. Instead, he turned along the path that led to the rear.

'Who is that?' Gil said.

But Rhys said nothing. The niggling memory of something he'd seen at the post office while he waited to be picked up by his DS on their first visit to the Pitcher house came back to him. A mud-spattered pick-up idling in a parking bay, the driver watching him.

That same man was on-screen now, sneaking into the Pitcher property but not going anywhere near the front door. Unaware that the motion sensor on the bell had been triggered and picked him up.

'Rhys?' Gil demanded. 'You know who this is?'

'I do, Sarge. That's James Ryan. Osian Howells' uncle.'

CHAPTER NINETEEN

Nine hours missing…

WARLOW SAT on the same sofa he'd used the first time he'd called in to speak to the Howells, fighting the feeling he had that he and they were like rodents on a hamster wheel.

He'd already promised these people he'd find their son and that had been hours ago. If he was honest with them and himself, he had sod all to tell them except that someone was enjoying seeing him run around, chasing his tail. He'd give anything not to be on that sofa, but the job made it his responsibility.

Nerys and Lloyd Howells sat, like before, waiting for him to give them something. A morsel of hope to chew on. Yet, all he could do was be honest with them.

'We think it is Osian's glove in the garden. Our forensic colleagues will do tests to confirm that.'

'But how…?' Nerys breathed out the question.

Warlow glanced at Gina, and she gave a little shake of her head. She hadn't told them.

'We think a drone delivered it,' Warlow said.

Nerys frowned. 'Drone?'

'Someone flew a drone over your house and dropped the glove.'

'Why?'

'That I can't answer. Not yet. Just like I can't answer who left the other glove at the stream near the edge of the woods.'

'It's sick.' Lloyd glared back at Warlow. 'Whoever is doing this wants us to suffer.'

Warlow didn't deny it. There was no point.

'Either of you seen any drones around before? Over the fields or the woods?'

Lloyd shook his head. Nerys let hers drop without looking at Warlow, and asked in a whisper, 'Is this the Green Man?'

'We don't know, Nerys. But we're doing everything we can to find out. This is hard. It's torture. But I need you two to stay strong. I'm still not ruling out the possibility that whoever has Osian will try to contact you. If he does, we need to be prepared. Gina will stay with you.'

Nerys looked up and smiled wanly at the FLO.

'Nerys and Lloyd were about to make a list of people who might wear camouflage jackets,' Gina said.

'Good idea.' Warlow nodded. 'And add to that anything you can think of regarding van drivers, delivery men. Anyone you've seen near the house over the last few weeks.'

'You think he's been here?' Nerys asked, shooting Warlow a look of horror.

'He knew the lie of the land. The field, the garden. You can't get all that from Google.' Warlow pressed the point home. He couldn't do much to ease the Howells' pain, only make them feel like they were helping.

A noise broke the tense silence in the room as Catrin's phone buzzed. She glanced at the screen and walked out of the room to take the call.

'Who told the press about the Green Man?' Lloyd demanded.

'We don't know yet. But when we find out, I will deal with them, believe me.'

Lloyd shook his head. 'The press. They're like…'

'I have a long list of choice words you could pick from, Mr Howells. But don't let them get to you. They want to provoke a response. They're magpies, looking for the next shiny thing. It's sometimes better that they have something like the Green Man to concentrate on. That way they don't make things up.'

Catrin re-entered the room and her expression and the way she held up the phone told Warlow he needed to speak with her.

'Excuse me,' he said to the Howells.

Catrin walked him out of the house and into the garden. 'It's Gil, sir. They're at the Pitcher's property. Leighton Pitcher is AWOL, and they have CCTV video of a caller.' She held out the phone. Warlow took it.

'Gil? What have you got?'

He listened in silence for a full two minutes while Gil spoke. Finally, he said, 'Good idea. I'll meet you there.' He handed the phone back to Catrin.

'Tell Gina to give the Howells my apologies. You and I need to get back to HQ. Rhys and Gil are bringing James Ryan in for questioning.'

———

HALF AN HOUR LATER, Warlow stood staring at the video screen showing a bird's-eye view of James Ryan sitting in the interview room alone. Gil came in, a carrier bag in one meaty hand, a tray of tea in the other.

'What do you think?' Warlow asked.

Gil glanced at the screen. 'It's a voluntary interview.

We told him there'd been some recent developments and his cooperation would be appreciated. He gave Rhys a bit of a look, but then agreed to come in.'

'How could he not?' Warlow said. 'It's his own nephew, after all. Solicitor?'

'He laughed and said something like, "Why? You're not charging me, are you?"' Gil smiled wryly. 'I hate the cocky ones.' He held up the carrier bag. 'Picnic. I got Anwen to sort something out for all of us. Fresh rolls. She does a load for the WI on Fridays. Dab hand, she is. There's ham and mustard, tuna mayonnaise, turkey with hot mango chutney or halloumi with dried tomato.'

'Who's that for?'

'Jess and Catrin. You know what they're like. Oh, and there are crisps. Ideally, she would have sorted something hot, but circumstances being what they are...'

'So, no wagyu beef or caviar? What sort of catering establishment is your wife running, Gil?'

The DS swung the carrier bag away. 'Plenty of uniformed gannets in there who would strip this bag to the handles in three minutes.'

Warlow blinked. He had not allowed the idea of food to impinge on his thoughts too much, but at the mention of the goodies in the bag, his mouth flooded with saliva. 'No need to be hasty.' He grinned.

'I made the tea, too, so it'll be stronger than something that has passed through a cat, which is Rhys's usual blend.'

Warlow took his mug. 'Thanks, Gil.'

'Needless to say, our resident food taster has sampled all but the halloumi. He'd have had seconds had Jess not told him to stay at James Ryan's place for a proper look around.' Gil put the bag on a table.

Warlow nodded. Jess had shot off to meet the DC and see what they could find.

'You happy for me and Catrin to have a go at Ryan first?' Gil asked.

'I'd be delighted.'

'Give you a chance to grab a bite.'

'I might have a quick roll.' Warlow smiled. 'You're a good man, Sergeant Jones.'

'Thank the lady Anwen for this. She doesn't want to see me wasting away on the job.'

Gil wasting away seemed about as likely as a hen with premolars and chances were the statement had been delivered in jest. For once Warlow reined back the sarcasm. The food would do wonders for his flagging energy and as an old boss of his used to say, never look a gift horse in the mouth, ear or any other orifice. You'll inevitably be disappointed.

Gil exited as Warlow reached into the carrier bag and took out a soft roll wrapped in cling film. Anwen had even labelled them. He went for the turkey and mango chutney, unwrapped it and bit in.

It tasted…bloody wonderful. On-screen, the door opened and Catrin Richards walked in and held the door open for her fellow detective sergeant and his tray of tea. Warlow found a chair, opened a bag of crisps, and settled himself in for the show.

CHAPTER TWENTY

JAMES RYAN LOOKED DOWN at the table as DS Gil Jones pushed a mug of tea towards him.

'Splash of milk and three sugars, as ordered,' Gil said.

Ryan nodded.

'Tidy.' Gil smiled. He'd taken the lead here with Catrin riding shotgun next to him, sitting back, listening, ready to come in with a question or comment if and when. Gil had been the one to knock on Ryan's door and knew all about the Pitcher situation, so it made sense that he conducted the band. And he hadn't needed to convince Warlow of his keenness to nab whoever was involved in Osian Howells' abduction.

Ryan picked up the mug and cupped his hands around it, sipped and nodded. 'Good cuppa.'

'Years of practise.' Gil nodded.

Catrin, unsmiling, gave Ryan one steady look before dropping her eyes back to the file she had on the desk and an open notebook she was scribbling in.

Gil opened proceedings. 'We know one another by now, James. Don't mind if I call you Jim, do you? That's what Osian knows you as, am I right?'

Ryan slurped his tea. 'No problem.'

'Good. And this one next to me, the talkative one with a speck of halloumi at the corner of her mouth, is Detective Sergeant Catrin Richards.'

Catrin sent fingers to her lips but came away empty-handed. She scowled at Gil, who'd adopted a butter-would-not-melt expression, leaned forward, and placed a phone midway between her and Ryan. 'Don't mind if we record this, do you? Saves on a lot of paperwork.'

'Go ahead.' Ryan shrugged.

Gil, all smiles, said, 'And thanks for coming in. Things are moving quickly. We appreciate your cooperation.'

Ryan looked interested. 'I'll do anything to help. Have you found something?'

Catrin answered, 'There have been some developments, but we're not at liberty to discuss details, Mr Ryan.'

'Oh, come on,' Ryan protested. 'He's my nephew.'

'What about you though, Jim?' Gil asked. 'I'm assuming you've been busy on Osian's trail.'

Ryan considered Gil with suspicion. 'I've been out searching with some of the boys, yeah.'

'Whereabouts?'

Another shrug. 'More than one place. Woods, mainly. Over towards Capel Isaac.'

Gil sipped his tea, but his gaze never left Ryan's face. He put the mug back down. 'And how about this morning at around 11am? Where were you?'

Ryan frowned, as if he hadn't heard properly. 'This morning? Why are you asking that?'

Gil sighed. 'An investigation like this is all about elimination. Think of it like setting up the pieces on a chessboard and then knocking them down. Taking them off the board if you like.'

'This morning I was up near Llandysul. We're building an extension up there.'

'You run a small construction company, am I right?'

'Building and general maintenance.'

'And if we contact the address, they'll vouch for you?' Catrin asked.

'Yes, and two other men who work for me.' Ryan bristled. 'What is this?'

'Routine, Jim. That's all.' Gil schmoozed out the words. 'You must be familiar with the area, then? Builders are all over the place, aren't they?'

Ryan's belligerent expression softened. 'We get about.'

'So where are your crew working this afternoon?' Catrin asked.

'Still Llandysul.'

'But not you?'

'No, not me. I've been looking for Osh. I came to my sister's place as soon as I heard. Been out since then.'

'Searching?' Catrin said.

'That's right.' Irritation clouded Ryan's features once more. 'Like you two should be. What the fuck is this? What am I doing here?'

'Helping us,' Gil said.

'How is telling you about an extension in Llandysul helping exactly?'

Catrin leaned forward and rotated a laptop so Ryan could see the scene as she replayed the clip showing him arriving at Pitcher's house. She let it play through. Ryan watched it in silence.

'Is this where you were searching, Mr Ryan?' Catrin said.

Ryan put the mug down with a clatter, his eyes darting from Gil's face to Catrin's and back again. A movement both police officers had seen in the interview room many times. The look of a man facing a deep dilemma. Whether to carry on lying or face the truth. In the end, Catrin let him off the hook with a question.

'Okay, Mr Ryan. Let's start again. How long have you known Leighton Pitcher?'

Panic flared in Ryan's face. 'It's not like that. I don't… Shit.' His hand came up to the back of his neck and stayed there, moving back and forth as if he could rub an answer into his brain.

Catrin drove the point home. 'We have you on camera at Pitcher's house. His mother tells us he's missing. Are you and he in this together, Mr Ryan?'

'Together?' Ryan made an ugly high-pitched laughing sound. 'No way. I didn't even know his name until…' He shook his head.

'Then what were you doing at his place?' Catrin glared at him.

A great deal was happening behind Ryan's eyes. He swallowed loudly. You could almost see the survival mechanism kick in. In the end, he opted for a cliche as his best line of defence and uttered a monosyllabic, 'No comment.'

Gil looked perplexed. 'No comment? Is that the best you can do, Jim? No comment?'

'No comment,' Ryan said.

'You're not under arrest,' Gil explained.

Ryan thought and then said, 'So I can leave?'

Catrin shook her head. 'Well, you could have.'

'Right then, I'll be off—'

'I said you could have.' She didn't move. 'If you told us what you were doing at Leighton Pitcher's house.'

'No comment.' Ryan stood up.

Gil sighed. 'Oh, Jim, Jim, Jim.'

'Can I go now?'

Catrin sat back and folded her arms. 'No, you can't. James Ryan, I am arresting you on suspicion of conspiracy to obstruct the course of justice. You do not have to say anything. But it may harm your defence if you do not mention when questioned something which you later rely on in court. Anything you say may be given in evidence.'

'You can't do this. Osh is… This is wrong.' He sat back down, breathing fast. 'Right. I want a solicitor.'

'Of course.' Gil studied the man in front of him and shook his head. 'What do you think your sister is going to say when we tell her?'

'No comment.'

———

DC Rhys Harries stood outside James Ryan's house, staring up at the dark windows and closed doors. Ryan had locked up when he'd left with Gil. He'd taken his own car with the DS following. And now Rhys and Jess were left outside without a warrant. Jess's phone buzzed. She glanced at it and then at Rhys.

'They've arrested Ryan for obstruction. They showed him the CCTV, and he's clammed up.'

'Does arresting him help us, ma'am?'

'Not one bit. Now there'll be a solicitor. Catrin's getting a warrant, but it's damned paperwork and we'll need to track down a magistrate…'

Rhys nodded. It all took time. 'We could look outside.'

The house stood on a couple of acres off a B road that led to the A48. A renovated farmhouse with outbuildings that Ryan had converted into storage units for his business. Unmarried, Nerys Howells' younger brother had no family of his own. He still played the field, according to some people Jess had spoken to. The house itself looked like a child's drawing. A square two-storey structure: three windows on the first floor, two beneath it on either side of the front door. A classic vernacular Welsh farmhouse. An entrance drive ran into a yard and the half-dozen outbuildings beyond.

The five-bar gate leading into the yard stood open. A couple of vans with Ryan Roofing and Repair in a circular logo stamped on their side panels stood parked up next to an open barn with a corrugated iron roof full of stacked wooden battens.

Beyond that, whitewashed low stone buildings that once might have been animal sheds or even milking parlours led towards a track to an open field and more storage sheds.

'What do we know about this place, Rhys?'

'Ryan and his sister grew up here.'

'Parents still around?'

'No, ma'am. The mother is in residential care. The father died several years ago.'

Jess looked surprised. 'How do you know so much about them?'

'Gina, ma'am. She's the FLO at the Howells' place.'

'Of course.' Jess smiled. 'The lovely Gina. And doing an excellent job, I hear.'

Rhys nodded. 'She is good at it. People talk to her and she's a good listener.'

They walked along the drive past the vans to the open door of the next barn. Inside were a trailer and two cement mixers. Bags of sand and a variety of other materials had been stacked at the rear.

'Being a good listener is a great trait in a FLO,' Jess said. 'It takes a lot of guts to go into someone's home like that. It's never easy.'

Rhys walked into the barn and around the machines, looking under them, and inspecting the materials at the rear. 'Can't see the attraction myself,' he said loudly to continue the conversation. 'I don't think I'd know what to say.' He came back out to join Jess, grinning. 'We're completely different in that way.'

'Opposites attract, Rhys.'

'Sergeant Jones says opposites don't attract. It's only that if you're too like someone, you end up seeing how much of a berk you really are. Best to stay on the other side of the fence.'

Jess shook her head. 'That sounds like a Gil-ism.'

'He's always telling me how glad he is that he isn't starting out on the dating game. He said he'd rather be dead than be on Tender.'

'He actually said that? Tender?'

'Yes, ma'am. But then he says the one he really likes is Tandoor where you swipe right on your favourite curry.'

Jess let the smile come. 'What about you, Rhys? Have you tried apps? Before Gina, I mean?'

'Once or twice. I didn't like it. Too many unknowns. What about Molly? I mean, it's second nature for kids, isn't it?'

'Molly says they're for losers.'

That earned a snort from Rhys, who'd already met Molly and knew she looked at the world through black and white, as opposed to rose-tinted, glasses.

'Still, it's academic for you now that you have Gina.'

Rhys's silence and slightly confused expression made Jess stop walking and tilt her head. 'I'm not committing the faux of all pas here, am I? You are still with Gina, aren't you?'

'Yes, ma'am. She's…amazing. She's…so amazing that I…I only wish I knew what she wanted. What any girl wanted.'

Jess's mouth flattened. 'That's easy. What any woman wants is to feel safe. And I don't mean physically. You treat her like an equal, don't you?'

'She beats me at most things.'

'You have a plan for your life, right?'

'Yes.'

'Good. Look after her and yourself and make her laugh now and again. It's that easy.'

'Is it? Sounds like a lot of stuff to get right.'

Jess laughed. 'My God, Rhys. Don't overthink it. Gina already knows what you're about.'

Rhys nodded. 'Thanks, ma'am.'

'I don't think you need to worry. Now, I see another five buildings down there.'

'Should we split up, ma'am?'

'No. Let's stick together.'

Rhys thought about objecting but remembered that the DI had only recently returned after fracturing her wrist while searching a property very much like this one. She'd been alone on that call. Alone and surprised by an attacker. No point testing fate a second time.

'Got you, ma'am,' he said.

'See, that's exactly the sort of thing Gina wants to hear.'

CHAPTER TWENTY-ONE

Nine hours forty-five minutes missing…

WARLOW TOOK the printouts from the hand of a Uniform tasked with helping in the Incident Room as Gil and Catrin came back in. He handed one to each of the interviewing officers.

'What's this?' Gil asked.

'Ryan's record.'

'Anything?' Catrin asked, a tinge of desperation in her hopeful expression.

Warlow shook his head. 'Looks like he's a bit of a hothead, especially after a couple of drinks. Drunk in charge, drunk and disorderly, one arrest for assault, but that never went to court.'

Catrin glanced at the sheet. 'Not much for the last five years. Looks like he sorted himself out after Osian was born. Took on the responsible uncle role.'

'Where are we with the solicitor?' Warlow asked.

'On his way in, sir,' Catrin replied.

Warlow looked at his watch and then at Gil and Catrin. 'Honest opinions, please. Think Ryan's our man?'

'The footage of him at Pitcher's place threw him completely, sir,' Catrin said.

Warlow nodded.

Gil pursed his lips. 'I'd say no, except I've been caught out before. It's possible the two of them were working together.'

'As in a ring, you mean?' Catrin asked.

Gil nodded. 'If they are, then they won't be in it alone. And these sods can be resourceful and dangerous.' Something clouded the sergeant's face. 'I got involved in a case when I was with Op Alice. The crimes were all committed in East Anglia but one of the ring members lived on the outskirts of Machynlleth. Pillar of the community, local councillor, you know the type. He was also a pharmacist. He'd do locums for some of the supermarkets and local chemists. So, he was the one supplying the sedatives.'

'Sedatives?' Catrin asked. And by the look on her face, she immediately wished she hadn't.

All three of them were standing in front of the Gallery with Osian Howells' face staring out at them.

Gil's voice dropped to a level that ensured no one overheard. 'The place in East Anglia was in an old mansion. They'd even had a grant to renovate it so that they could offer residential music courses to kids. The peripatetic music teachers in schools would recommend the most talented kids and they'd go over half term to get tutored. Play together in an orchestra. Except that the tutors weren't only interested in music.'

Warlow studied Gil. The funny, warm joker had gone. In his place was a serious man full of steely fury.

'The kids were in dorms. Three or four to a room. The highlight of the night was hot chocolate. The pharmacist supposedly taught timpani. But what he really did was lace the drinks so that the kids in that room didn't remember what happened to them once they were drugged. They posted videos. That's how we caught the bastards.'

'Oh my God, Gil.' Catrin put the tips of her fingers over her mouth.

Warlow grimaced. 'Christ. If anyone ever invites you to be their motivational speaker, say no for God's sake.'

The DS looked at them both as if he'd only that minute noticed they were there. But his expression softened. 'Sorry. Didn't mean to go there. It's a recollection guaranteed to suck the atmosphere out of the room. My point is you can never be sure with these sods. Ryan could be in cahoots with Pitcher who is tech savvy. He had a drone in his office. Just a toy, but he knows how to fly the bloody things, obviously.'

These were unpleasant thoughts. Warlow had Ryan pegged more as a vigilante than a groomer. But how would he have found Pitcher otherwise?

'Right. Then we need another crack at Ryan sooner rather than later.' Warlow glanced at his watch again. 'I want to know as soon as that solicitor walks through the door. Now, I need to speak to Buchanan.'

Catrin walked to her desk. 'It'll give me a chance to see what's come in regarding the Green Man.'

'Nothing on your house to house?' Warlow asked.

'We didn't get very far. The drone incident put the kibosh on it. Or as Rhys said, kaboosh.'

'I'll give the PolSA a ring. See how they're getting on with that,' Gil offered.

Warlow nodded. He knew how they felt. He wanted to keep busy, too. 'Right, let's get on with it.' Then another thought struck him. 'Any more of those rolls left?'

Gil smiled. 'Anwen's made enough for a small army. Fancy a ham and mustard?'

———

IN THE SIO'S ROOM, Warlow set the phone up to lean against the bottom of his monitor. He held on to it while he navigated WhatsApp to Sion Buchanan's number. He'd tried doing this before without stabilising the phone and the bloody thing would inevitably fall over several times. Why they had to make the buggers so shiny and slippery he'd never know. Some people had gizmos; little stands to keep the phone upright that folded away neatly when not in use. But Warlow was not a gizmo kind of bloke.

The Buccaneer was expecting his call.

'Evan. Anything to report?'

Warlow briefed the senior officer. He stuck to the known facts: the gloves, the main leads including Pitcher and Ryan and his plan of action. He'd done this tens of times before as the SIO. But still, it never got any easier. Then he went on to what the team was currently engaged in and what he wanted to do next, which was to have a crack at James Ryan himself, solicitor, or no solicitor.

Buchannan had his phone arranged much like Warlow's, looking up from below, which gave his long face an even longer appearance.

'The Assistant Chief Constable wants me to issue a press statement. Any suggestions?'

'How about, haven't you all got nice stones to crawl back under?'

Buchanan snorted. 'The voicing the thoughts thing never works well. It'll be a standard appeal for help. We'll flood social media, too. You know the drill. We're concerned about Osian's welfare. Detail what he's wearing. Give out the hotline number again.'

'Be good if you can get them to tell you who released the information on the camouflage jacket.'

Buchannan shook his head. 'We've tried. Of course, some concerned parents put the Green Man warning out as soon as it happened a couple of weeks ago.'

'But the camouflage jacket only came to light today.'

'You think we have a mole?'

'The only people who knew were the little girl who drew the thing, her parents, and the officers I briefed in the Reading Room. And I can put money on it not being the parents.'

Buchannan sighed. 'It's out there now so no point worrying about things we can't change. How are you for staff?'

'We're okay. Once you put out the appeal, the phone lines will be on fire. I'll keep you posted.'

Buchannan signed off and Warlow unwrapped another of Anwen Jones's rolls and took a bite. It tasted so good he even forgot to look at his watch for all of three minutes.

―――――

'IT'S ON THE NEWS AGAIN,' Pat Munro called from the living room of number ten Beili Road.

In the kitchen, butter-smeared knife in hand, Jaydon made eyes to the ceiling. 'Stop watching it, Mum. Put something else on. Look on catch-up for that thing on wossername, that flaky actress. You like things like that.'

'How do you say his name, that missing boy? Ocean is it?'

Jaydon stopped buttering the sliced bread and, knife in hand, walked into the living room. Her mother sat on the sofa, legs up on a covered stool, feet in striped socks that looked the worse for wear. A plate that had contained four biscuits now sat empty on the side table next to her.

'Have you got the remote?' Jaydon asked.

'No, don't change it. I want to see. That poor little kid.' Pat looked across at her daughter and Jaydon knew what was coming. Knew and felt her irritation bubble to the surface even before her mother had uttered a single word.

'We ought to—'

Jaydon made a frustrated growling noise. 'Stop it, Mum. Please. We are not going to the police. If they call again, we say nothing, okay?'

'Yeah, but—'

'Oh my God, how many times have we got to go through this?'

Pat held up a phone. 'It's even on Facebook. They know about the camouflage jacket.'

Jaydon shut her eyes and huffed out a sigh 'Have you read it properly?'

'It's this Green Man—'

'Have you read it?'

Pat blinked and shook her head.

'No. I didn't think you had.'

'I can't concentrate because of my medication,' Pat snapped back.

'I know, Mum. I know. That's why you shouldn't read just the headlines. It's clickbait.'

Pat stared at her daughter; her mouth turned down.

She needs her roots done, thought Jaydon, glancing at the dark line that ran from crown to fringe like the parting of the seas in her mother's otherwise bleached hair. And she needed to lay off the biscuits, judging by the extra chin that wobbled under her once pretty face.

Pat's eyes drifted to the knife in Jaydon's hands. Shaking her head, Jaydon walked back into the kitchen and threw it down on the countertop before walking back in to her mother.

'We can't say anything to the police. You know what will happen. You've seen it on TV. Like that making a murderer stuff. The police just want someone to blame. And once they find out who we are, we'll need to move again. Because you know who will come looking. So yeah, it was stupid of T to go out in his jacket, but that's all he did, Mum. Went out for a walk. My fault as much as his. I didn't twig them kids would be out too. Otherwise, I'd of stopped him.'

'But what if it was him who took this Ocean? What if it was?'

'It wasn't, Mum. Simple as that, okay?' Jaydon walked over and sat next to her mother on the sofa and held her hand. 'With a bit of luck, this will all blow over. They'll find this kid hiding in a barn or something and it'll be okay.' She took the remote and found the programme about an actor who claimed to have discussed her role in a BBC TV series about the Royals with the Duchess she was playing. The kicker being said Duchess had been dead for fifteen years.

'There you go. Stark raving.'

'Are you making his supper?' Pat asked.

'I am.'

'Tell him they were out of those biscuits he likes. Tesco delivered something else, but I don't think he likes them.'

'I'll tell him, Mum. Don't you worry. Fancy a cup of tea?'

'Nah. Must be wine o'clock, isn't it?'

Jaydon shook her head. 'No. Not until nine. Like we agreed.'

Pat's face fell, but then gave in. 'Go on then. I'll have a cuppa if you're having one.'

'I'll get the kettle on.'

CHAPTER TWENTY-TWO

THE WIND HAD PICKED up as the evening wore on at Ryan's property. They were trying to be methodical about it, looking around, behind and inside the buildings and piles of materials where they could. Where the doors were locked, Rhys would try to find a window to shine his torch through and cast a little light on dark interiors.

'Much quicker if we had the dogs here, ma'am,' Rhys said, brushing cobwebs from his coat after clambering up on an upturned plastic container to stare into an outhouse.

'It will be. They'll double check everything we've already looked at.' Jess regarded the jumble of buildings ahead of them. Three stone sheds and a larger barn at the very end. This one had black plastic-wrapped bales. It looked like Ryan had some fields that he grew for silage or hay. She was never sure which. Someone even said it had a name – haylage – though that might have been a Gil-ism. She had seen no animals in the immediate fields, though the sound of sheep and cows was never far from the ear in this neighbourhood. You grew used to it. And perhaps Ryan merely stored the animal feed for a friend.

Jess waited for Rhys to join her, weighing up his

words about the dogs. He was right. They could abandon this and wait for the paperwork to arrive, let the dogs and the professional searchers do their thing. But they were here and while the light still held, she'd feel better if they had a look. You never knew. Besides, Warlow would want them to at least check the obvious.

'Let's keep going for another half an hour. What do you say, Rhys?'

'I'm game, ma'am.'

The sun, dipping lower, now cast long shadows on the west of all the buildings in the yard. Out of the sun, the temperature dropped sharply, and Jess wished she'd brought a thicker coat.

'If you wanted to hide someone, how would you go about it in a place like this, Rhys?'

The question brought the DC to a halt. He'd been on the way to inspect a pile of railway sleepers. But he stopped and swivelled around to consider Jess's question.

'I don't know, ma'am. I've never thought about it.'

'Neither have I. But I'm asking you now.'

'Lots of places to hide things. Not so sure about a person. It depends on…' The thought of what he was about to say stopped him dead.

'Go on,' Jess ordered.

'Well, I meant it depends on whether I was trying to hide a person or a body.'

Jess read his discomfort. He didn't want to consider the possibility, yet they had to.

'Do both,' she suggested.

'Okay, so a body I'd be looking to hide permanently, or at least well enough so that I'd have time to destroy it properly. Burn it or bury it.'

Jess glanced at the furthest barn and the small tractor with a backhoe attachment lying unattached next to the bales. The tractor had two prongs sticking out of the front, like a forklift truck.

'And if I wanted to hide someone who was alive, I'd need a building,' Rhys continued. 'Somewhere quiet. I expect they'd be gagged, but I'd choose somewhere no one might hear anything at all.'

'So, we search buildings and look for any sign that perhaps the ground has been disturbed. Or where there's been a recent fire. In the time we've got available, maybe we should be a little more targeted in our approach.'

Rhys nodded but looked uncomfortable.

Jess eased his conscience. 'It's not like being one of them, Rhys. More like letting your imagination roam a little. Don't feel bad about it.'

Rhys nodded and produced a wan smile. 'There's always a chance they'd be in the house, ma'am.'

'True. But why would you choose that when you've got all this to play with?'

Rhys turned and surveyed the area and pointed towards a breeze-block building. 'That looks like some kind of feed store, ma'am.'

'Let us do that one next.' Jess led the way.

———

ON ENDING the call with Buchannan, Warlow leant back in his chair and shut his eyes. There was no chance of him napping, not with his head buzzing with all the unanswerable questions flying around in there like an aviary full of budgies on amphetamines. He wished he could. It would probably do him a power of good. Instead, with his eyes closed, he searched for a place to go to in his head where everything didn't end in catastrophe. Of late, when he woke up in the dark between three and four in the morning, his mind churning, every problem seemed insurmountable. He'd read that the way the brain processed its thinking changed in the darkness. Nothing ever seemed so bad in the light of day. Logic and context lent illumination to any problem.

Indeed, they said that if you wrote down what was worrying you, however trivial, before you went to sleep, that cathartic manoeuvre worked wonders.

Warlow opened his eyes, reached for his phone, and typed out a list in his notes app.

VISIT ALUN in Australia
  Tell the boys about HIV
  Get James Ryan to come clean.
  Find Osian

HE HESITATED, then wrote down another word – *Jess*.

He looked at that last entry, grimaced and scrubbed it out while muttering, 'Get a bloody grip, man.'

There were other issues, but those were the big four. The fuel that powered the cement mixer of his troubled ruminations. He usually countered the demons by thinking about taking a walk with Cadi. But he couldn't do that now. He looked at the phone in his hand.

9. 05pm. Osian had been missing for ten hours.

He put the thing face down on the desk, leaned back, shut his eyes again and did the next best thing. Warlow imagined walking out of the front door of his cottage in Nevern. Walking up the lane and along the road for a couple of hundred yards until the little gap in the fence led to a field…

A knock on the door brought him back. He opened his eyes in panic but didn't move, thinking that sudden movement and the squeak of the chair might give the game away. Instead, he stayed where he was, fingers intertwined over his abdomen, legs out in front of him, chin on his chest, and said, 'Come in.'

The door opened and Gil put his head around it, his eyebrows going skywards at the sight of Warlow…wallowing. 'Meditation, is it?'

'Kind of,' Warlow answered in a low growl.

'You look like Buddha.'

'As in wouldn't melt in your mouth?'

'Oh, very good. And quick considering your age and groggy state.'

'I resent that.'

'Doesn't make it any the less true. Thought you'd want to know that Ryan's solicitor is here.'

Warlow shifted his weight forwards, and the chair shot backwards and thumped against the wall behind. 'Shit.'

'That meditation can take it out of you. Better than forty winks, they say. But I wouldn't rush. The solicitor says he wants twenty minutes with his client.'

'We'll give him ten.'

'That's what I said. Ryan wants to prepare a written statement.'

Warlow frowned. 'Is he delivering a bloody budget? What's that all about?'

'No idea.' Gil opened the door fully to reveal a mug of tea in his other hand.

'You could have told me about the tea,' Warlow protested.

'Wasn't sure you'd want it. I kept on hearing this odd sound when I got to the door. Could have sworn it was snoring. Must have been the pipes.' Gil put the mug on the table.

Warlow affected a wry smile. 'It was the pipes. Well, my pipes.' He reached for the mug. 'Thanks. What did the PolSA say?'

'Not much. They've found nothing so far. But I'll tell you who is in the building. Ryan's ex. I thought we might get some background on him while we waited for his masterpiece.'

Warlow took a sip of tea and smacked his lips. 'Good idea.'

'She's in the conference room.'

'Name?'

'Heidi Ryan.'

Warlow stood up and hoped no one heard his joints creaking. 'Lead on. I'm right behind you.'

———

SERGEANT CATRIN RICHARDS stared at the screen in front of her, waiting for a page to load. An indexer had brought it to her attention. A cross-reference that had come up with something that might, just might, be of interest. A report going back a couple of years of a pair of kids going missing from a park. Two ten-year-old boys. It had never appeared on anyone's radar because they had found the kids safe and well. A little scared, but unharmed after being accosted – not attacked, the report was keen to point out – by an older boy of sixteen and forced into a war game.

The older boy had a fake gun and had made the younger boys follow him as he tracked down the imaginary enemy. They'd ended up in a makeshift bivouac where the older boy had clearly been living rough.

When he'd heard shouts from searchers, the older boy ran off only to be found by police and arrested. When the police interviewed him, it soon became clear that Thomas Voden was a troubled individual.

The intriguing aspect that brought all this to the index-er's attention was Thomas's insistence on wearing a camouflage jacket. So much so that he became aggressive and angry when it was taken from him.

He'd been given a label of Asperger's with stress-induced psychosis in a pervasive development disorder. All this had taken place somewhere in the New Forest, a long way away in Hampshire. Still, worth a quick call to the reporting officer, a fellow sergeant based in Southampton.

'Yeah, I remember Thomas. Always do when it's one of your own, don't you?'

'Do you?' Catrin asked, when she got through.

'Yeah. Thomas was Geoff Voden's lad. He was one of our DS's. In fact, it all started to go south for Thomas and Geoff when all this blew up. Puts a strain on families, something like that, doesn't it?'

'What happened to him? Thomas?'

'Geoff knew there was something up with the lad from the get-go. Didn't make much eye-contact, fights with other kids, that sort of thing. He became threatening at home, too. That's where the conflict was. Geoff used to say that there wasn't enough support at school. They need consistency, do kids with Asperger's. Changing classes and teachers always buggered it up. Anyway, Thomas had run off from home and gone to the forest. He was into military stuff. Geoff used to say the best way to keep him quiet was to take him to the war museum. He'd read everything and remember everything there was to remember. No interest in things other kids his age were in to. Just before the forest incident, he'd started to imagine things in his room. Voices and that. Geoff said that was tough.'

'So, what happened to him? Is he still living with his parents?'

'Nah. After he was caught, he ended up being sectioned. Went to Alburton House. A low secure unit for youngsters in Tatchbury. Why are you asking?'

'It's probably nothing. I'm following up on leads.

Thomas's obsession with camouflage jackets lit up on HOLMES.'

The Hants officer snorted. 'Yeah, it would. Obsessed with that, he was. So much so they let him have it in the hospital for a while. My understanding was they were going to wean him off it.'

'Must be tough for the dad, your sergeant?'

'Yeah, it was. Still is I suppose.'

'What's the name of that unit, again?'

She'd taken down the number and was trying to look it up, but the page was taking forever. All she really needed was a phone number. A quick call so that she could tick another box. She was still waiting when Gil and Warlow appeared from the SIO room.

Gil waved. 'We're off to see Ryan's ex.'

'I thought for a minute you were going to say the Wizard of Oz. You look a bit like the cowardly lion.'

'Everyone's a comedian,' Gil said to Warlow. 'Have you noticed?'

'I know there are a few clowns in this building,' Warlow muttered.

'Need me?' Catrin asked.

'No. We'll catch up after this,' Warlow told her.

Catrin nodded and turned back to the screen, cursing silently to herself as the little blue progress bar at the top inched slowly across at a speed that would make a snail look supersonic.

CHAPTER TWENTY-THREE

RHYS HARRIS WALKED around the circumference of the field next to the black barn. It had been his suggestion and DI Allanby had agreed it would probably be a good idea. The grass was long, and his shoes were now soaking wet. But he'd seen no disturbance in the soil in the field he'd walked around, nor the adjacent fields. Of course, that meant little. Ryan could have chosen anywhere, and the canine squads would find whatever there was to find. He'd seen cadaver dogs at work. They were always impressive. Amazing to think they detected buried remains six feet down.

Rhys paused and looked back towards the DI standing at the gate, hands in her coat pockets, looking up and around at the landscape. Ryan's property stood on high flat ground, unusual for this normally undulating landscape. To the east, the rolling lines of hills led the eye to the escarpment at Llyn y Fan and the Beacons beyond. They'd driven past signs for villages with names that hinted at the revivalist nature of this rural community. Capel Isaac was nearby and Salem not too far away. Pockets of habitation were clustered up and down the steep hills and valleys, usually at the deeper points near the rivers. Even so, it remained a sparsely populated area dotted with farms and conifer forests on the higher ground at Abergorlech and Brechfa, sparser still further north towards the university enclave of Lampeter, and eventually to the great curve of Cardigan Bay.

He'd go out on his bike sometimes, pleasant weather permitting; he wasn't a masochist. Often, he'd find himself on the high moors with no living soul or dwelling in sight. Some people might find it a little scary. How often in a city could you ever honestly say that you were alone? A twenty-foot square room didn't count. Alone in the great outdoors had a different feeling about it. Humbling in a way.

When he'd said all of this to DCI Warlow once, he'd received a wry smile and a nod in reply. 'It's a rare thing, Rhys. The world looks altogether different when you're alone. It looks neater somehow. Fields, trees, rivers, all the right size and shape and all quietly doing what they were meant to do. And would carry on doing just that until the sun goes out if it wasn't for the sodding people.'

He remembered that sort of thing word for word. Replayed it all in his head as he headed back to where he started. When he got to a point close enough not to have to shout to be heard, he said, 'Not a blade of grass out of place ma'am.'

The detective inspector nodded but said nothing. She didn't move either. She simply stood still and waited for him to arrive; her gaze distant.

'Everything alright, ma'am? You look…thoughtful.'

'Good,' Jess said. 'Better than fed up.'

'Right. So, are we off?'

'Five minutes ago, I'd have said yes, most definitely. No more for us to do here. But when you were at the end of the field, I thought I heard something.'

'Heard what, ma'am?'

'That's the trouble. I haven't heard it since, so I'm left wondering if it was purely my imagination, or wishful thinking playing silly beggars.'

'We could stand here and listen, ma'am.'

'We could. But that wind is bitter.' She half turned as another gust proved her point and blew the collar of her coat up.

'So, back to HQ then?'

The DI made a face that depicted the little skirmish going on inside her head. She looked up at the sky once more and turned her back to the wind. 'No,' she said eventually. 'The sound I thought I heard came from inside the barn and…oh, shit. It sounded like someone groaning.'

Rhys took a step back. 'Groaning?'

They both turned to peer at the barn and the stocked bales. 'How are we going to get past them, ma'am?'

'Use your initiative, Rhys.'

'Thanks, ma'am.' He stepped towards the building.

'Don't bother going around the back. I've looked. There is a door, but it's locked.'

Rhys nodded and stood staring. Though Allanby hadn't said it, they both knew that there could be only one way in. Up and over the stacked wall of bales. Rhys wasn't particularly fond of heights and didn't list climbing as one of his hobbies. But then no one said this job would be easy.

———

HEIDI RYAN WAS small and neat. She wore her hair short and didn't wear the kind of makeup that ended at her chin. From the way she was dressed, in a fleece and a T-shirt, Warlow guessed that her colouring might have come from the great outdoors.

Gil had offered her a cup of tea, but she'd declined and sipped from her own metal drinks bottle now and again.

'Thanks for coming in, Mrs Ryan,' Gil began.

'It's Heidi. And I've gone back to using my maiden name. Green.'

'Okay, Heidi, it is.'

Heidi smiled her agreement.

A good smile, thought Warlow. Good teeth, in an attractive face. An active lady who looks after herself. Why did Ryan let this one go? he wondered. 'We've asked you here to chat about your ex-husband, James.'

'What's he done?' If Heidi had any inclination that her presence had something to do with a missing child, she showed no sign.

'We have James in custody, Heidi.' The slightly amused resignation of earlier dissolved into concern.

'He's been arrested?' There was more inquisitiveness than surprise in her tone still.

Warlow nodded.

'How long have you been separated if you don't mind me asking?' Gil was all smiles.

'Three years. We divorced two years ago, but I moved out before that.'

'But he's still at the house?'

'He bought me out. My share, I mean. I didn't mind. It was more than enough for a deposit on a rundown property in Whitemill. My dad's handy. He's been helping me work on it.'

A woman after his own heart, thought Warlow, who'd spent the best part of two years converting a shepherd's hut into a bijou residence for him and one other occupant – Cadi the Labrador – in Nevern.

He nodded to show his understanding, too, of post-separation marital arrangements. He came well-versed in that subject as well. Qualified in that with distinction, he had. He gave Heidi a reassuring smile to let her know she wasn't the one in trouble here.

'Some questions we want to ask might seem a little personal.'

Heidi gave up a nervous little titter. 'Now you've got me worried.'

'Was your married life…normal?'

Heidi pulled back, her already large eyes suddenly much bigger. 'Normal? I would not say normal, because we are divorced. If it had been normal, we'd still be married.'

Warlow waited, letting the question stand.

'Do you mean in the bedroom?' Heidi glared at him.

'Yes,' Warlow said.

'I suppose. We all have our quirks, don't we? Jim liked to drink. It made him amorous. But it turned me off. That's one reason we drifted apart.'

'You don't have any children, Heidi?' Gil asked.

She shook her head. 'That's another reason. We couldn't have children. Jim can't. Obviously, there were other routes. Surrogacy, sperm donor, even adoption. But Jim wasn't… He didn't know if he could bring up another man's child. That's what he said to me, anyway. That and making me promise never to tell anyone.'

Warlow nodded. 'But he is very fond of his nephew and niece, isn't he?'

'That's why I found it odd. They're not his kids, but he adores them. You'd think…' Her words dwindled into silence, fed by a sudden awareness of why she might be there. 'Oh my God, is this about Osian? Is that why he's here?'

'No.' Warlow wanted to be certain that Heidi understood this. 'Not directly. I don't want you thinking that.'

'Look, Jim can be a real pain. I've never met such a stubborn, bull-headed, argumentative man. But—'

Gil stepped in with the question she was really there to

answer. 'No sign of him having any tendencies towards pornography.'

This time Heidi's brows crumpled. 'No, my God, no. I mean, people do, don't they? Look, I mean. Well, men, anyway. Don't they? These days, you need to go out of your way to avoid it. But nothing like that. Nothing with children. I wouldn't have stayed a minute with him if I thought…that's not Jim. I know we've split, and I think I've spoken to him twice in the last six months, but Jim is…he's not like that.'

Gil looked at her directly. 'Sometimes we think we know people, Heidi. But we really don't.'

'Well, I lived with him for seven years, so I know him a lot better than you. I hate the sod, but he's no monster. I know that.'

———

CATRIN FINALLY GOT through to someone at Alburton Hospital who was willing to talk to her. She'd had the runaround from the switchboard and a duty doctor who'd sounded so far up his own backside he'd need a proctoscope to lever himself out and up in the morning. But finally, she got through to a nurse manager. Even then she'd had to wait for said manager to return her call just to make sure she was who she said she was.

Her phone rang five minutes later. She answered, giving her name and rank.

'I'm returning your call.' An English accent, not officious exactly, but if Catrin was forced to describe it, warm was not the adjective of choice. If asked, she'd have plumped for borderline hostile.

'Thanks for ringing me back. We appreciate it.' Catrin deliberately used the plural pronoun, informing the nurse that this was official and not a personal call.

'If it's information about a patient you're after, I'm bound to not reveal any details.'

'That's fine. If we need anything specific, I'll go through the proper channels. This is a general enquiry.'

'Good. It's not the first time we've had calls from the police or prison service, and it has to all go through lawyers, I'm afraid.'

'I understand. This is a simple question about a patient, Thomas Voden.'

'Ah, right.'

Catrin noticed the knowing tone and the hint of relief. 'Sounds as if you've been expecting my call?'

'Hoping, certainly.'

Catrin paused and let the little tingle of suspicion she felt finish its wriggly dance. 'Hoping how, exactly?'

'That you'd be in touch as soon as you found him, obviously.'

Catrin's pulse did a drum solo. But she knew when to shut up and let the cat crawl out of its bag.

The nurse obliged. 'As we say in the report, Thomas was out on unsupervised day release and should have been back by six o'clock. All very odd because he'd been out a dozen times before. He'd shown no tendency to want to abscond.'

'When was it he went AWOL again?'

'Three weeks ago, now.'

'And he wasn't tagged?'

'No. That's not our policy. We prefer a structured rehabilitation into the community. We're trying to instil trust.'

'Sounds like that was a one-way street here, then.'

'We'd rather look at it as more like a bump in a long road.'

'Would you say Thomas is a danger to himself or others?'

'He was in our care because of a Section Three order.

But he'd shown no violent behaviour during his time with us.'

Catrin knew what a Section Three order was. She had it written up on the screen in front of her. 'For the health or safety of the patient or for the protection of other persons that he should receive such treatment and it cannot be provided unless he is detained under this section.'

The DS's loaded silence triggered a moment of doubt in the nurse manager's voice. 'You have found him, haven't you?'

'No, we haven't. But we will keep an eye open.'

CHAPTER TWENTY-FOUR

THE THING in the room next door was waking up. Grunts and groans and thumping noises had grown steadily louder as the light through the curtains had gradually dimmed. Shadows in the room's corner seemed to grow darker and bigger. Osian knew that night was coming. He didn't like the dark. He'd tried to get to the door and the light switch, but the rope around his leg only let him move a few feet. Not far enough for the door or the switch.

He wished for the hundredth time he had his astronaut light.

But it was only one of a hundred things Osian wanted to happen as he sat, frightened and alone.

But most of all, he did not want what was in the next room to wake up. He didn't want to see the door open and for it to come in. He wanted to go home. He wanted Arth and Fflur and Mam and Dad.

Dad would be angry if he did come because he'd eaten the crisps even though they weren't his. But Dad would have money to pay for them. He would, he always did. And his mother would have a Hoover to get rid of the crumbs. He hadn't wanted to eat the crisps, but he'd been hungry and…

Thud.

Another noise. Like someone, or something, falling. Or someone, or something, banging their legs against the wall.

Thud.

Osian jumped. Was it trying to make a hole to crawl through?

Thud.

He held his breath. He wished Fflur was here. She'd know what to do. She was always telling him what to do, but now he wouldn't mind if she did. He'd listen, he'd—

'Mmm…Aah…Ah…shit.'

It had a voice, the thing next door. A loud voice.

'Can anyone hear me? Can anyone help?'

But then another noise, one that Osian hadn't heard before. The sound of a key in a lock and then a voice he knew. The voice of the man who had taken him from his garden.

'Shut up!'

'No, please, no… Christ, urgh.'

Sounds of something hard hitting something soft. Many times. Each time with a groan to follow. Each groan growing fainter until it ended in an unfamiliar noise that, though he didn't recognise it, sounded bad.

Osian had heard his mother crying when his grandmother, his mamgu, had been in hospital. He didn't like her crying, though she did it softly and quietly, trying not to let others hear. But Osian and Fflur had heard. And the noise he heard from the room next door, now, was like that. A soft noise, a whimpering. Like their old dog had done when his back legs gave way.

Osian could tell that someone was sad or hurting. Perhaps both.

Then another key in another door. This one closer. The door between him and the room where the thing was now crying.

A face appeared around the door. The man who'd taken him. He looked in. Not sad, not happy.

'No more noises.' He threw a bag towards the sofa. It landed on the floor with a clunk. 'You want the light on?'

Osian nodded. 'I want to go home. Please?'

'Not now. There are people after you. We're safe here. But it's almost time.'

He saw the lie. He could tell in the man's voice. Sometimes Fflur would tell him lies to get him to do things. He was getting better at knowing.

'I'll put a light on.' The man stepped in and switched on a lamp next to a small table. 'There are more crisps and biscuits in the bag, too.'

'I don't want…' Osian sucked in air and felt the cry coming. A wail of desperation. 'I wa…want to…to…to go…ho…home.'

'Eat the food. Stay quiet or I'll turn the light off and you'll be in the dark. Understand?'

Osian nodded miserably.

The door shut, leaving him alone again. At least now there was light. But he was beyond consolation. He threw himself down on the sofa and let the sobs come. When, sometime later, they stopped, he couldn't hear the thing next door anymore. Maybe the man had fed it to keep it quiet. But Osian didn't care.

All he wanted was to go home.

CHAPTER TWENTY-FIVE

Ten hours forty-five minutes missing…

WARLOW AND GIL went to the observation room and looked in on Ryan. His solicitor, a lanky, fair-haired man in a wrinkled suit by the name of Izzard, sat next to him. Warlow wasn't sure what made him instantly take a dislike to the bloke. Perhaps it was the way he'd clapped Ryan on the shoulder. Perhaps it was the fact that he had a briefcase with a red leather handle. But no, though they were good enough reasons, it was the stupid quiff he affected that really got Warlow's goat. The sort of hairstyle that might work on a youngster like Rhys Harries, but not on a forty-something lawyer with a face like a racehorse.

'Right,' Warlow said to Gil, 'We're going in. There's no more time for this crap.'

'He'll make some noise.'

'Let him. The clock is ticking.'

Which is exactly what Warlow said to Izzard when the man stood up as the officers entered the interview room.

'I appreciate that time is a factor here, even so, my client—'

'Your client has had ample time for a break and to talk to you. Now we need to press on.' Warlow sat down and opened the cardboard file on the desk. Izzard remained standing in an attempt at looming over the DCI. But Warlow was having none of it. He'd been loomed over by better men than this beanpole.

Eventually, Izzard sat down. 'We have a prepared state- ment which Mr Ryan wants to read.'

'We're still doing this under caution,' Gil said.

Izzard nodded. Gil did the necessary, cautioning Ryan once again, recorder on. Once they'd done that, both he and Warlow sat back and listened.

It didn't take long. Warlow kept his eyes glued on Ryan, who wilted a little under the intensity of the glare. In his hand was a single sheet of paper upon which a scrawled paragraph in black ink vibrated as it shook in the man's trembling hands.

'I am James Ryan, Osian Howells' uncle. I want to make it clear that I had nothing to do with Osian going missing. When I heard about what happened, I immedi- ately volunteered for the search. I also need to clarify that I had no previous knowledge of Leighton Pitcher, having only learnt his name when I visited him today.'

Ryan looked up at the two police officers as if he were waiting for approval. Warlow looked at Gil, who sent him a side-eyed glance in return.

'Is that it?' Warlow asked.

'Yes.'

'And you needed help to write that? Who ties your shoelaces of a morning?'

'You don't need to answer that,' Izzard said, returning Warlow's stare with one of his own.

'Okay, so you've written a statement. Though I'd hardly call it a statement,' Warlow told him. 'More a stut- tering paragraph, wouldn't you say, DS Jones?'

'Definitely,' Gil said.

Warlow dropped his voice. He had a vague idea that he sounded a bit more intimate that way. Most people told him it simply made the words exponentially more menacing. 'Nothing has changed because you've written down that disclaimer, James. Osian is still missing. And whether you knew Pitcher's name or not is irrelevant. Often the people, and I use the term loosely because animals might be a closer match, who band together on websites and chatrooms and show an interest in little kids, rarely use their real names.'

Ryan swallowed loudly. 'No comment.'

Warlow shot Izzard a glance. 'Is that your advice? Say nothing?'

'My client is within his rights.'

'Yes, of course he is. Well within his rights to issue a statement denying any involvement when he's involved up to his ears.' Warlow glared at Ryan afresh. 'I'm sure your sister is going to read that paragraph and think, ah, well, *that's* alright then. James says he didn't do it. That's set my mind at rest.'

Ryan squirmed a little in his chair and glanced at Izzard, who simply shook his head, his expression dismissive.

'Come on, James,' Gil said. 'We know you were with Pitcher. Was it him who took Osian?'

'No comment.'

'Where is he, Jim?' Warlow asked. 'Where is Osian? Think of your sister, for God's sake. What do you think she's going to say when she finds out you wouldn't help us? Your no comments are going to go down a storm with her, I bet.'

'I resent your tone, Detective Chief Inspector,' Izzard said.

'Resent it as much as you want. We have a missing

child to find, and we've been waiting for Mr Ryan's cooperation for far too long. I can live with a little resentment. But I can't live with any more time-wasting.'

For a moment it looked like Izzard wanted to say something but weighing up Warlow's words made him bite back whatever witty gem he had lined up.

'Why did you take Osian, Jim?' Gil asked.

Warlow followed up without waiting for an answer. 'You can't have kids of your own, can you, James? Are you jealous of your sister, is that it?'

Ryan flushed bright red as the barb pricked his thick skin at last. His eyes widened. 'Jealous? What are you talking about? Jesus Christ. Osian's a great kid. I wouldn't harm him. I wouldn't…'

'But maybe you'd let Pitcher do it, right?' Warlow leaned in again. 'One step removed from the act. Let someone else do the dirty work? Is that it?'

'No. It isn't like that.'

'You do not need to say anything else,' Izzard warned.

'That's right, Jim.' Warlow nodded, and his grin was mirthless. 'Keep quiet and let everyone else make their minds up about you. Including your sister, your brother-in-law and your niece.'

Ryan's head fell forward slowly and shook from side to side. 'It isn't like that,' he whispered.

'Then what is it like?' Gil asked. 'Because from where I'm sitting, you are looking at charges, court and prison time. And everything you've read about the way child molesters and kidnappers get treated inside is bang on, Ryan. Fun it is not.'

'Do not listen—' Izzard began, but Ryan shut him up with a dismissive wave of his hand.

'I don't know where Osian is. I don't… But I know where Leighton Pitcher is.'

Warlow sat forward. 'At last. Okay, James, in your own

time. You're in a deep hole here. But let's see if you can climb out because this is the last time that we're throwing you any rope.'

———

THE BALES, wrapped in shiny plastic, were squat cylinders and whoever had stacked them knew what he, or she, was doing. Or it appeared so to Rhys. At the ends, four bales stood end to end in a tower formation, but in between they'd been laid flatter, like bricks in a wall, canting slightly backwards as the wall went upwards in four layers, leaving a four-foot gap between the top layer and the roof.

Rhys contemplated the task. Impossible to know if there were other bales behind this outer wall to provide support. He walked forward and peered through the small gaps between. Beyond was nothing but the faint greyness accompanying the oncoming dusk and a suggestion of space.

'Hello? Anyone there?'

They waited. Jess standing next to Rhys as the wind rattled the wood of the barn walls.

'Hello, Osian? Are you there?' Jess called out.

Nothing, until…yes, a noise, muffled, but a noise that sounded much like a moan or a groan.

'There is someone there, ma'am.' Rhys turned troubled eyes to Jess.

'I'm calling for an ambulance,' Jess said.

'The sensible thing to do would be to get a tractor driver here to remove the bales. But who? And from where?'

'It could be done, but how long would it all take?'

'I'm going to climb this wall,' Rhys said.

'Is that wise?' Jess asked. 'It doesn't look all that safe.'

But Rhys was already taking off his coat. They both

realised that the only way to get to whoever was on the other side was to climb up and over. Both officers knew the stakes were too high not to try.

The plastic wrapping of the bale felt slick but not slippery under Rhys's hands as he reached out for the lower layer.

'Be careful,' Jess said from behind him.

Rhys took a breath and climbed up. It made for awkward manoeuvring. There were no footholds on the plastic and dragging himself up each bale one at a time involved using his knees and planting his face flat against the material, blindly reaching with his foot until it found a gap between one bale and the next.

A heady, not unpleasant, tobacco-like aroma filled his head as he climbed. But he made slow progress. One, two, then three bales conquered. When he got to the third, he stopped. The entire structure seemed to sway a little as he shifted his weight.

Sweat ran down the inside of his arms.

'Was this in the job description, ma'am?' He didn't look down as he spoke and wasn't sure if the DI had heard him as he'd delivered the words. His face was side-on to the bale, his cheek mashed against the plastic.

'I doubt it,' Jess replied. 'But then it didn't say you'd never have to clamber up a wall of stacked bales, did it?'

'Fair enough.'

With a final grunt of effort, Rhys reached up and felt for the top of the uppermost bale, got his hand on it, and hauled himself up to lie belly-first on its surface. Inching forward, he wriggled along its length to get a look at what lay on the opposite side.

Three things became quickly apparent.

The first was that there were no bales behind. This was a single-thickness construct.

The second was that the DI had been correct. She had

heard a groaning noise. Because Rhys heard it now too as his face reached the edge of the bale and he peered down towards the dim floor beyond. The only light came from a high window at the far end and the little that filtered through between the bales and the roof where Rhys now lay. But it was enough to show him what he wanted to see.

'There's something there, ma'am. Difficult to see. It's not moving much. I think I'll need to climb down. I'm going to—'

It was at this point that Rhys realised the third thing. As his weight on the top bale shifted when he tried to get his legs around to climb down, momentum and gravity, those co-conspirators of inevitability, did the rest.

The bale toppled. He felt the shift and tilt, scrabbled for a handhold, and succeeded only in his palm sliding against the upright bale stacked next to him.

'Rhys,' Jess yelled.

But all he could do was hang on for dear life, his hands clutching at the taut plastic beneath him as the bale fell through twenty feet of air. It wasn't so much the distance that flashed through his mind, more the fact that he lay fully splayed open, face down, ripe for injury.

A phone rang somewhere as he braced himself for impact.

He hoped to God it wasn't Gina.

The bale hit with a thump and didn't roll. Rhys, attached limpet-like to it, sank into its surface, nose and face compressed into the plastic.

But as landings went, it ended quickly, softly, and with Rhys, the attached limpet, completely unharmed.

'Rhys?' Jess yelled, high-pitched from panic.

'I'm fine ma'am. I'm fine.' He slid off the bale, dusted himself off and reached for his own phone, still thankfully safe in his pocket. He switched on the torch just as he heard another groan.

The light picked out the source of the noise. A trussed-up body, gaffer-taped from head to foot.

'Rhys, what's happening?' Jess called out.

'I found him, ma'am. I found Osian.'

Yet even as he spoke the words, a sliver of doubt snagged in his head. Osian was six. This body looked longer than a six-year-old's.

'It isn't the boy, Rhys,' Jess said.

'What? How do you know that n—'

'I have Gil on the phone. Ryan has just confessed to what he's been doing all day. Your groaning man is Leighton Pitcher.'

CHAPTER TWENTY-SIX

RHYS UNBOLTED the locked door at the back of the barn and dragged the bound figure of Leighton Pitcher out into the fading light of day as carefully as he could. Which, from the moans of pain that accompanied it, wasn't anywhere near careful enough. Pitcher's swollen eyes stared up at the DC accusingly. With the tape across his mouth removed, a cut lip, as well as a bloodied nose, added to the visible damage. When he expectorated a bloody wodge of spit, it didn't take a genius to realise he'd been worked over thoroughly.

'Are you okay, Leighton?' Not the most subtle of questions, and yet Rhys realised it needed asking.

With most of the tape undone and a tissue from Rhys's pocket as a wipe, Pitcher dabbed at his nose with a hand that had a finger pointing in an odd direction. Dislocated, it looked like to Rhys.

'Okay? What does it fucking look like?' Pitcher said in a nasal whine. 'You bastards.'

'This wasn't us, Leighton,' Rhys argued. 'This was a man called James Ryan. He's in custody.'

'Of course it was you,' Pitcher squeezed the words out

through gritted teeth in a quavering voice. He took a swallow of water from the bottle Rhys had retrieved from Jess's car. Both officers watched as the man felt around the inside of his mouth with his tongue, checking out the other damage that no one could see and only he could feel.

'Leighton, if you know anything—' Rhys began.

'Fuck right off,' Pitcher yelled. 'How many times. I don't know anything. Why would I know anything? I hate kids. I keep telling you this, but no. I'm on your poxy list, so I'm the first one you call on, right?'

Jess shook her head. 'Just doing our job, Mr Pitch—'

'Great fucking job. He followed you. That's what he told me. He followed you and asked a mate of his from the village about me. The paedo at the address you led him to. I'm the village perv, do not forget. So, Ryan calls on me because there's no fucking smoke without a fire, right?' He squeezed his one open eye shut and turned away, sobbing.

Rhys had his hands on his hips. 'Shit,' he whispered.

'If that is what happened, then we're sorry,' Jess said.

'No, you're not,' Pitcher muttered, not looking at them. 'You're never sorry. They're just words. He was going to kill me. But you don't give a shit, do you? I can't wait to see what excuse you're going to use to let Ryan off the hook for doing this. Because we both know that deep down you think I deserve it.' He swung his damaged face back to them, looking first at Rhys and then at Jess.

'If what you say is true, then Ryan will pay. He assaulted you,' Jess said.

'You don't say.'

'I promise you—'

'Keep your shitty promises.'

The paramedics came and decided that Pitcher needed x-rays and obs for a head injury, so they whisked him off to hospital.

In the car on the way back to HQ, Rhys was quiet.

'You feel sorry for him?' Jess asked.

'No one deserves that. Tied up and beaten like that.'

'No one? Probably not. But there'll be people you come across who might test that sentiment.'

'Really, ma'am?'

'Really. But then punishment is not our job, is it? We find the bad guys and let the courts deal with them.'

'But are we any closer to finding Osian, ma'am?'

Jess sighed. 'Doesn't seem like it, does it? If Ryan got something out of Pitcher, I hope he'll have the sense to let us use it. But my gut tells me that Pitcher is telling the truth. He's no predator.'

'No. I don't think so either.'

They drove on for a few minutes in silence until Jess turned again to the DC. 'By the way, I saw you fall.'

Rhys frowned. 'When ma'am?'

'On the bales. I saw it topple. I ran forward. Used my phone as a torch. There were a few gaps at the bottom level, and I saw you plummet.'

Rhys flushed. 'Not my best moment, ma'am.'

Jess raised her eyebrows. 'Nines for effort, a poor five for style, I'd say.'

'Knocked the wind out of me, ma'am.' What he didn't add was, that during the descent, another kind of wind had almost escaped his control. This one accompanied by the contents of his large intestine. Thankfully, he'd hung on to both his breath and his sphincter control.

Jess grinned. 'I have to say, it looked bloody funny. Thank God hay is soft. You could get a job as a stuntman.'

'Thank you, ma'am. Do Sergeant Jones and Sergeant Richards need to know about this?'

'Your secret is safe with me, Rhys.' Jess grinned. 'Of course, I'm going to have to write up a report…'

Rhys smiled back at her. It had the nature and appearance of a condemned man's rictus grin.

———

GIL HADN'T SEEN Warlow in the Incident Room for almost twenty minutes, but he doubted the DCI was having a cheeky nap this time. When Ryan had finally 'confessed' his big secret, both he and Warlow had sat, motionless and momentarily speechless.

It had not been what they'd expected to hear, but Gil had been around long enough to twig that Warlow's silence had little to do with surprise and a great deal to do with a barely restrained, volcanic anger. Gil had the sense to call for a couple of Uniforms to take Ryan and Izzard out and get the former back to his cell before Vesuvius blew.

It almost did when Izzard turned at the door to deliver another supercilious smirk. 'I hope you'll give my client's cooperation due credit, gentleman.'

Warlow didn't lift his eyes from the table, so it had been Gil who'd nodded and said that he'd be sure to take everything that happened into account. Izzard could bet on that. He'd motioned to the Uniform to get a move on because he'd seen the knuckles on Warlow's hand clenching the table turn white as the solicitor's words elicited another spasm of anger. With the room empty, the sergeant turned off all the recording equipment and nodded to the obs room camera with a finger-across-the-throat gesture to make sure all were closed down before he ventured a word.

'You alright, Evan?'

'Thanks,' Warlow muttered.

'What for?'

'For getting those two bottom feeders out of my sight before I said something…regrettable. Because if I'd said something I would have followed it up by wringing that waste of bloody space's scrawny neck.'

'Are we talking about Ryan or the solicitor?'

Warlow sent Gil a side-eyed glance under lowered brows. 'I was going to leave the weasel solicitor to you.'

'Fair enough.' Gil grinned.

'How long?'

Gil paused, wondering how far he ought to push things. Decided a leopard could not change its spots and opted for trademark flippancy. 'Is a piece of string?'

'How long,' Warlow growled, 'did we wait for that bloody idiot to tell us precisely nothing about Osian's whereabouts?'

'I'd say about an hour and a half.'

'Christ!' Warlow let go of the edge of the table and brought his palm down on the top, once, twice, three times.

Though Gil had been expecting something, the force of the blows made him flinch each time. 'Better?'

'A bit,' Warlow said with a long sigh. 'Do you sometimes feel we're rowing upstream without a bloody paddle?'

Gil turned back to answer. 'All the time. But I bring my granddaughter's water wings to work in case I fall in. She tells me they're guaranteed to stop me drowning.'

Warlow nodded and looked up. 'She got a spare pair?'

'Always. Do you want the pink ones with giant inflatable unicorns on them or the ones with a Batwoman logo?'

Warlow cocked an eyebrow. 'Is that the red-on-black job that looks a bit more menacing than the Batman one?'

'You got it,' Gil said.

'Then you already know the answer to that, Sergeant.'

Gil nodded. 'Unicorns it is for you, then. Tidy. I'll even get Izzard to blow them up. He's got enough hot air to inflate the bloody Hindenburg.'

Warlow shook his head, but one corner of his mouth flickered with the beginning of a smile. 'You realise that you and I are the only people on this team, Christ, maybe in the entire building, who have even heard of airships?'

Gil shrugged. 'The one thing you can't get on a course or sit an exam for is experience, Evan. So, when we have these exchanges, I prefer to call it plumbing the deep well of professional wisdom. We'll catch this *cachgu*, don't worry. Once we get those water wings on.'

By the time Gil had confirmed that Rhys had indeed now found Pitcher and put his head back around the interview room door to inform Warlow, the DCI had gone.

The word in the Incident Room was that he'd walked through with a face like thunder and retired to the SIO office. He'd spoken to no one.

Gil shared the senior officer's frustration. Ryan was an idiot who realised he'd done something stupid but who'd also only been interested in damage limitation for himself. In so doing he'd caused a barrel-load of collateral damage and forgotten about the hunt for his nephew in the process.

A second phone call to Jess had yielded no further news, other than the fact that they were on the way back in, and Catrin seemed absorbed by whatever computer-based angle she was working on. Gil's experience told him to expect lulls in any investigation. The difference here was the very loud ticking of a clock in everyone's head. A metronome that counted out the agonising beats like a club playing drums on your marrow bones.

And, in his experience, there was only one answer.

He picked up the phone and dialled Rhys's number, spoke briefly to the DC, and then sat back and waited.

CHAPTER TWENTY-SEVEN

Eleven hours fifteen minutes missing…

FIFTEEN MINUTES after he'd rung Rhys on the mobile, Gil knocked on Warlow's door.

'Yes?'

The burly sergeant pushed the door open. 'You're still alive, then? Not spontaneously combusted?'

'Not yet.' Warlow locked the fingers of both hands behind his head and stretched his neck. 'But I have drawn up a list of things I'd like to do to James Ryan short of actual murder. Many of them do, however, involve a loss of blood.'

Gil glanced at the list on the DCI's desk. Not actually a list of torture methods as suggested, but a scribbled time-line with lots of crossings out.

'Catrin's better at that,' Gil said.

'I know. This is for my benefit because I've got bugger all else.'

'Right, well, I have something.' Gil pushed the door fully open to reveal the rest of the team filing in behind him.

The SIO's room was not big and with all five investigating team members inside, it was standing room only.

'What the hell is this?' Warlow frowned. 'Did I miss someone's birthday?'

'No. It's an intervention,' Jess said.

Catrin removed all the files from Warlow's desk and Jess unfolded some sheets of newspaper.

'What is that smell?' Warlow sniffed the air.

Rhys stepped forwards and removed five paper-wrapped packages from the plastic bag he was carrying and put them on the newspaper-covered desk. 'Em's fish and chips, sir. Award-winning. From Water Street in town, direct to your door. Courtesy of Sergeant Jones.'

'What, are you working for Deliveroo, now?' Warlow muttered.

'You can pretend to be the miserable curmudgeon,' Gil said. 'But the saliva drooling down your chin speaks otherwise.'

Warlow, genuinely taken by surprise, sent a flummoxed glance towards Jess. 'This room is going to stink.'

'I've got news for you. It stinks already,' Jess said.

'No problem then,' Warlow grunted and, for the first time in a while, cracked a smile.

Rhys had a second bag with a variety of soft drinks. Catrin opted for a Diet Pepsi, much to Gil's disgust. 'How can you count calories when you're eating chips?'

'This is an emergency. One that only chips can resolve,' Catrin said. 'But one does what one can.'

'Agreed,' Jess said with her mouth full.

The room descended into silence. Well, silence except for the sound of Rhys's masticating jaws that made a noise like Red Rum in a feeding frenzy, even with his mouth shut. But banished hunger smoothed away the irritation. Gil had brought a black refuse bag and when they'd finished and Rhys had polished off whatever scraps anyone had left, the chip papers were balled up and binned.

'Good shout, Gil,' Warlow said, dabbing a little grease from his lips. 'We'll call that Em's emergency protocol. Make a note of that, Rhys. For future reference.'

The team nodded.

Warlow refolded the newspapers on his desk and shoved them into the bin bag. Then he stood up. 'Right. Much as I hate to admit it, that's made me feel a lot better. Let's get back out there and see what we can salvage from this bloody mess.'

———

Doris Sibley's eyesight may not have been twenty-twenty, but her hearing more than made up for that. She was putting down food for Rollo, her marmalade Tom, in the kitchen at the rear of her ground-floor flat with the back kitchen door open. Usually, the sound of the kibble hitting the metal bowl was all the signal the cat needed, so Doris always left the door open six inches. She should have had a cat flap fitted, but one of her friends, Carol at number nineteen, had told her that when the wind blew, the draft through the flap went all the way into the lounge. When the nice Care and Repair people had offered to put one in for her, Doris had politely declined.

The little garden beyond the door had become a shapeless square of indigo with the arrival of dusk, but the sound of Rollo's mewing reassured her the cat was on his way. But then the sound of a footstep on the gravelled area outside the separate entrance to the first floor flat drew her attention just as Rollo, tail up, scampered in.

Doris went to the back door and peered out and around the corner where a figure stood hunched and silhouetted against the streetlight behind. 'Mrs Munro? Is that you?' Doris asked.

'No, it's me, Dave. Just going to check on progress in the flat.' The voice that answered sounded oddly stilted and lacking in any colour.

'Hello, Dave,' Doris said. She couldn't really make out his face. Her maculas were that atrophied. All she could see was his shape. Tallish, his figure top-heavy under the bulky coat he always wore. Perhaps he was rake-thin under all that. There was no way of knowing. 'They clocked off at just after five. I heard them leave.'

'Yeah, I…wanted to check on progress, you know.'

'Best you do. I don't hear them breaking any speed records up there during the day. Though they both sing along to the radio a lot. One day they'll sing the right tune, too.'

'Thank you, Mrs Sibley.'

A key slid into the lock.

'Oh, by the way, the police were here earlier. Checking for that little boy, Osian.'

'Yeah?'

'I lent them my key, the one you borrowed to copy, so they popped upstairs to look, too. I don't think they found much because they were out of there in double-quick time. Good that they are checking though, isn't it?'

'It is.' The door to the upstairs flat swung inwards to open and Doris saw Dave mount the steps.

'Right, see you then,' she said.

'See you.'

She waited until the door shut and listened to his footsteps on the bare stair before stepping back in and closing the kitchen door. She didn't think she'd mind Dave as an upstairs neighbour. He was quiet and kept himself to himself. Funny thing, she rarely heard him coming down after his visits. But then she was always falling asleep in front of the telly these days. And once she was asleep, the gas mains could blow up and she wouldn't hear it.

Rollo was purring at the bowl. He was marmalade in colouring, though he was nothing more than an orange blob to Doris. One that was still happy to rub against her legs and sit on her lap of an evening, but no longer light and dark. The stripes had long since ceased to register in Doris's eyes. All she saw were shapes and overall colour. For the same reason, Dave's coat appeared a uniform, drab, olive jacket with no sign of the brown, light-green and black stippling that made it difficult to see in all sorts of terrain. Not that it mattered, because she was not to know the police were looking for someone wearing a camouflage jacket.

And even if she had, it would have made absolutely no difference to her.

———

THE TEAM GATHERED around the Gallery and the Job Centre, both plastered with images and notes in sharp contrast to their appearance that morning.

Christ, thought Warlow. Was that only a few hours ago?

The DCI took the lead.

'I don't think I need to tell you we've been led up the garden path on this one. We've wasted too much time with James Ryan, but I'm quite sure now that he's just a hothead who took things into his own hands. Jess?'

'CID are out at Ryan's place doing a thorough search. We have a dog team, too. But I agree. From what Pitcher told us, Ryan wanted to get information from him. That is the only reason they were together.'

'I should have realised,' Rhys said, looking as miserable as a scolded cur. 'I saw him parked at the post office while I waited to be picked up by DS Jones on our way to Pitcher's place. I should have known.'

Warlow was having none of it. 'That's self-flagellating crap, Rhys. You couldn't have known. He's followed two detectives to see where it led him. I should have realised he'd do something stupid when I spoke to him earlier. But we're not bloody mind readers, are we?' He looked at his team. All of them nodded. Consensus on no blame for Rhys.

'What is Pitcher's story, then?' Gil asked.

Jess answered this one. 'Ryan appeared, stormed into Pitcher's 'office' and demanded to know why the police had called. He already knew Pitcher was on the SO register because he'd asked around. When Pitcher tried to get him to leave, things turned nasty. Pitcher is not a big man, nowhere near as big and strong as Ryan, who man-handled him out to his pick-up and drove him to his small-holding. Ryan tied him up and tried to beat the non-existent information out of him. Even threatened to set fire to him if he didn't tell him where Osian was.'

'Bloody idiot,' Gil tutted.

'Did he say anything?' Warlow asked.

'Pitcher has no idea about Osian,' Jess answered.

'Ryan said the same,' Gil agreed.

'We'll get a formal statement from Pitcher once he's deemed fit, but I don't think he's involved,' Jess said. 'The VISOR team has checked Pitcher's computers. No sign of any illegal downloads.'

Warlow nodded. 'As I say, a dead end.' He turned to Rhys. 'Once we're done here, I want you out at the Howells' property. They need to know about Ryan before his ex starts blabbing on social media. Think you and Gina can handle that?'

Rhys nodded.

'It's not an excuse for you two to get cosy, so get that idea out of your filthy mind right now,' Gil added.

Rhys held his hands up and sighed.

Warlow moved to a desk and perched his hip on the edge. 'Catrin, what have you got?'

'I've been chasing up a lead on our Green Man.' Quickly, she filled them in on her enquiry into Thomas Voden. When she'd finished, both Gil and Warlow had questions.

'So, this kid is on the spectrum and is still missing?'

'As far as I know,' Catrin answered.

Gil looked dubious. 'And this low secure unit, it's in Kent?'

Catrin nodded.

'What possible reason could he have for being here?'

'I have no idea.'

'If he's challenged, like with Asperger's or whatever, would he have access to a drone?' Rhys asked, further deflating Catrin's theory.

'I wouldn't dismiss that as a possibility because of the Asperger's,' Gil said. 'I met a kid in a case once who couldn't concentrate for more than one minute in a classroom but who could strip a motorbike to pieces and put it back together without one page of a manual.'

Catrin shrugged. 'As I say, I need to ask more questions.'

Warlow turned to Jess. 'PolSA?'

'They've stood down the search for the night,' Jess said. 'Nothing to report so far.'

'What about the door to door?'

Gil shook his head. 'As I say, nothing to report yet.'

Warlow summarised, letting his thinking emerge as words. 'Okay. We know it isn't Ryan. Some other bugger snatched Osian.'

'Using the fire and the chickens as a distraction,' Catrin added.

'In one fell swoop,' Rhys muttered. It earned him a couple of nods from the others.

'More one fowl swoop,' Gil said.

'Is that fowl with a "w" as per the chickens or with a "u" for disgusting?' Jess asked.

'Take your pick. Works both ways, I think.' Gil bent his knees out in a mini curtsy.

Catrin shook her head. Jess raised one neatly plucked eyebrow. All Rhys could do was blink with a slightly bemused expression, as if he was silently replaying what he'd just heard.

Warlow snorted softly and nodded. 'One of your better ones, Sergeant.'

'Had to be said, sir.' Gil shrugged.

Warlow folded his arms across his chest and sighed. 'Right. I need to talk to Superintendent Buchannan. I know it's late, I know we're all tired, but he's been missing for eleven hours so I'm not going to call this a night just yet.'

Everyone nodded.

'Rhys, on your way. Jess, can you double check with Povey re the drone? Let's see if anyone else saw where the thing came down. Someone must have seen something.' He pushed off the desk, unable to sit still for any longer. 'Okay, we've all got jobs. Let's do them.'

CHAPTER TWENTY-EIGHT

Eleven hours, thirty minutes missing…

RHYS TEXTED Gina when he got to the Howells' property, and she met him on the path by the front gate.

'All right?' Rhys beamed at her.

'As well as can be expected under the circumstances.' She took him around the outside, through the passageway where Osian had made his den. By now it was fully dark and halfway along where light from the front and the rear of the property did not reach, Gina stopped.

'What's up?'

'Nothing,' she said and pulled him close and held onto him. 'It's just nice to be able to hold on to something good and real in the middle of all this awfulness.'

Rhys squeezed her back but threw a quick glance over his shoulder to make sure they were not being observed.

'You're twitchy,' Gina said.

Rhys gave up a throaty laugh. 'Maybe I am. DS Jones told me to be sure not to make this an excuse to get too cosy with you.'

'Cheek,' Gina said and hugged him a little tighter.

Rhys buried his head in her neck. She smelled good, a lot better than he did after his climb up the north face of bale mountain and his rapid descent. 'Sorry if I'm sweaty. I've been running around.'

'It's okay, I'm used to it. Sometimes I like it when you meet me right after rugby training.'

'That's sick.' Rhys pulled back, but he grinned at her. 'You make up for it, anyway. You always smell good.'

She lifted her eyebrows in mock challenge but didn't move away.

'Has it been bad here, then?' Rhys asked, glad he'd had the sense to chew some gum on the way over in the car.

Gina flattened her mouth. 'About as bad as you can imagine. Except neither of us can imagine what it's like for Nerys and Lloyd.'

Rhys breathed in her hair. Was that aroma strawberry? Or melon? 'I don't know how you do it. But if it had happened to me, I'd count myself lucky to have you as my FLO.'

She laughed softly. 'You say the nicest things, Rhys Harries.'

'It's a gift.'

'Have you got something nice to say to the parents?'

Rhys signed. 'I expect they're not going to like it much. But DCI Warlow's given me the job.'

'Okay, let's do it. Tea?'

'You already know how I like it.'

She let go of him and started walking ahead, speaking without turning around. 'I do. But what about the tea?'

Once again, Rhys stopped, wondering at how a bit of flirting and a few words could get his heart pumping so fast. What had DI Allanby said? She's a keeper. It certainly felt like it at that moment. It wasn't at all the right place or the right time to have grabbed a quick kiss, but then what was the right time in this job? And why not take a second to reaffirm a morsel of joy and bliss in the middle of all this misery?

Oh, yes. Gina Mellings was a keeper alright.

With a fresh cup of tea on the coffee table and with Gina next to him, all eyes were on Rhys five minutes later. Warlow had spoken to him before he left, told him that this part of the job was even more difficult than falling off a twenty-foot-tall wall on a tumbling straw bale.

It took a different kind of guts, that was all. And he wouldn't be there if the DCI didn't have every confidence in his ability to get the job done. Even if he was smart enough to realise that everyone else was too snowed under to get this job done. Rhys had taken all this in good grace. All part of the training. But a step up for him. Knowing all that didn't stop his insides churning, though.

He cleared his throat. 'There have been some developments in the case since DCI Warlow spoke to you. He felt it only right that you are kept informed.'

Nerys's face began to hollow out, her eyes widening with fear of what was coming next.

'No, it's not Osian. Not directly. It's your brother James.' Rhys looked directly at Nerys. 'He's been arrested.'

'Arrested? Why?'

Lloyd Howells sat up. 'If he has anything to do with what's happened to Osian…'

Rhys answered quickly, wanting to reassure them. 'No, it's not that. It's complicated, but Mr Ryan attempted to take the law into his own hands. He abducted and assaulted someone who we had shown some interest in.'

'Oh my God,' Nerys said. 'He hasn't killed anyone, has he?'

'No, not quite. Though the victim is in hospital with severe, but thankfully not life-threatening, injuries.'

'Who was it? Who did he attack?' Lloyd demanded.

'I'm not at liberty to say, Mr Lloyd. But we think that

Mr Ryan was mistaken in targeting this person. We don't think he had anything to do with happened to Osian.'

'So why did James attack him?'

Rhys resisted the urge to tell them all about Leighton Pitcher who remained an innocent victim in all of this. And he was not obliged to tell these people everything related to the case. Warlow had made that clear. 'Let's just say that Mr Ryan has jumped to the wrong conclusion in this instance.'

'Typical.' Lloyd shook his head. 'He's a bloody liability.'

Rhys nodded. 'We wanted you to be aware before the press got word.'

Lloyd bristled at this. 'Not the bloody press again. How the hell are they getting this information?'

Good question, thought Rhys. But of course, it could be more than one person. Ryan's ex, Heidi for example. Though what she'd gain by telling the world her ex was a violent hothead who'd committed grievous bodily harm was anyone's guess. Or Izzard, Ryan's solicitor, might want to apply some leverage by making sure the press knew what had happened to get the story spun from the outset. He might even want to stir up sympathy for a wrongful arrest scenario. Though Rhys couldn't see any way out for Ryan as a serious crime had been committed. The abduction and torture of Leighton Pitcher would not go unpunished. Of that, there'd be no doubt. There could be no doubt either that Ryan's actions had muddied the waters. Still, those were not the words the Howells neither needed nor deserved to hear.

Instead, Rhys said, 'We're doing our best to find out exactly that, Mr Lloyd, believe me.'

From behind Osian's parents, Gina Mellings gave Rhys a double thumbs up.

———

WARLOW WAS ABOUT to ring the Buccaneer when a knock on the SIO office door made him pause.

'Come in.'

The door opened to reveal the towering figure of the man himself.

'Christ, are you psychic?' Warlow asked.

Buchannan stepped inside and closed the door. He levered his long frame into a chair with an apologetic look. 'I don't want to get under anyone's feet, but I'm being chucked out of the house.'

Warlow raised his eyebrows.

'Nothing permanent,' Buchanan explained. 'Caroline said I might as well come in because even though I was at home, I was at work in my head. I need to prep for the press conference tomorrow. You may need to be there, Evan.'

Warlow nodded and felt his toes curl. A necessary evil, but still not something he relished. 'No plans to involve the parents in an appeal, yet?'

'Not yet. That'll take some organising if and when. What about you?'

Quickly, Warlow summarised what had happened over the last few hours. Some of it, Buchanan already knew. Some he did not.

'Jess is looking into the drones and Gil is tying up the loose ends around James Ryan.'

'But you think he's only a loose cannon?'

'I do. I could throttle the sod for wasting all that time though.' Warlow recalled how the last conversation he'd had with Buchanan had ended. 'Did you get any joy with your press connections? You were going to find out who gave them the Green Man information.'

Buchanan nodded. 'Yes, I spoke with the BBC correspondent and someone from the Western Mail. They both said the call had come in anonymously and separately. As if the caller wanted it known by as many people as possible.'

Warlow glowered. 'Making mischief then.'

'It sounds like it.'

Both men sat in silence, contemplating the information they'd provided for one another, but it was Buchanan that asked the next question.

'Next steps for you?'

'I've sent Rhys out to talk to the Howells about James Ryan. I'm worried the press will get hold of that, too.'

'That's wise.'

There was another knock on the door. This time, Catrin put her head around. 'Sorry, sir. You said you wanted to be kept informed if anything developed.'

Buchanan got up. 'No, Sergeant, I'm on my way. He's all yours.' The superintendent paused at the door and turned back to Warlow. 'Sorry this had to happen today of all days, Evan.'

'You mean Denise?'

Buchanan nodded.

'Not much I can do for her, Sion. It's Osian we should worry about now.'

Buchanan sighed. 'Yes, well, you know where I am.' He ducked his head as he walked through the door. Force of habit.

Warlow summoned Catrin in. 'Right, what have you got?'

'I've just had a remarkably interesting conversation with the social housing officer, sir. It's about the Green Man.'

Warlow sat up. 'I'm listening.'

'You remember Thomas Voden? He's the patient that's gone AWOL, the one obsessed with camouflage jackets.'

'I remember. But it was a long way from here.'

'Yes, sir. But something bothered me about that. Remember this morning in the Reading Room, you introduced me to someone from the council, a social housing liaison officer?'

'Beard and glasses?'

Catrin nodded. 'Grimshaw, sir. He was there because of vulnerable families in the Caeglas estate. And when Rhys and I began our house to house, we met people who weren't local. I started thinking about whether someone with a link to Voden could live in that estate.'

Despite the little tingle that worried at Warlow's scalp, he realised this was a straw clutching exercise on his DS's part and said as much. 'That's a stretch, isn't it?'

'We met a mother and daughter living close to the school. The Munros. English accents and obviously not local. So, I rang Grimshaw. Aka the Scarlet Pimpernel, as Gil said. I had to look that one up. Grimshaw isn't the easiest of people to track down. He somehow managed to lose his phone.'

'What?'

'Yeah. The PolSA found it eventually.'

'The PolSA?'

'Yes, and they didn't need sniffer dogs. It was in the Reading Room all along. But Grimshaw got back to me eventually, and though he didn't give me any details, he said that families seconded to the Caeglas estate often revert to their maiden names when they move. To make it that much more difficult for them to be found. I looked up the arrest details for Thomas Voden, our camo-jacket-fetish misper. The listed next of kin for him was a Patricia Voden. I know how much of a reach this is, sir, but the mother and daughter Rhys and I spoke to on the estate…' Catrin hesitated and then shrugged. 'Rhys took down the details, but I seem to remember that the mother was called Pat.'

The tingle in his scalp morphed into a full-blown itch. Warlow was up and out of his chair in a heartbeat. 'You're thinking that the family may have moved to get away from Thomas Voden?'

'It's possible.'

'And now Voden has found them?'

'I've asked Grimshaw to meet me there, sir. He said he'd bring the case files with him.'

Warlow ran a hand through his hair, his brain fizzing. 'This is bloody good work, Catrin.'

The DS nodded her appreciation. 'We know nothing for certain yet, sir.'

'No, we don't. But I will not hang around here waiting to find out. Grab your coat. I'm coming with you to meet Grimshaw. If there is a link, we can speak to the Munros directly.'

CHAPTER TWENTY-NINE

J$_{ESS}$ RANG P$_{OVEY}$'S NUMBER, and the forensic manager picked up after three rings. They'd worked on enough cases together in Jess's brief time with Dyfed Powys Police for them to be on first-name terms.

'Alison, any news on the drone or the glove?'

'Honest answer? Zilch so far. The glove has nothing but Osian's DNA and pig's blood. No fibres or alternative DNA to be of any use.'

'What about the drone?'

'We've done a directional analysis based on reports from a couple of people living close to the A40. But then we had another report of someone seeing the drone take off again and flying back up towards the abduction site, or at least somewhere near to Cwrt Y Waun. These things can be flown with pre-programmed waypoints. That way the user can operate the camera and time the drop.'

Jess knew all about payload drones since they'd become the bane of prison officers, providing a quick and straight-forward way to get illicit items over prison walls and into exercise yards, sometimes even up to barred prison windows. 'Sounds like the drone was always part of the plan.'

'I'd say so,' Povey said. 'I doubt this was a spontaneous act. This was all carefully thought out. The take-off and landing points will have been reconnoitred and set up. Maybe that drone is sitting in a wheelie bin somewhere out of sight awaiting collection.'

'You know how to cheer a girl up, Alison.'

Povey snorted. 'Evan isn't going to like this a lot, is he?'

'He'll be doing back-flips.'

'How is he? I heard his ex-wife passed away.'

'We were at the funeral this morning,' Jess confirmed, and followed it up with a sigh. 'Seems like days ago.'

'They weren't close though, from what I can remember,' Povey said.

'No. It didn't look like it.' Jess recalled Warlow's keenness to get away from the post-service melee. 'But his sons were there.'

'Couldn't have been easy.'

'You know Evan. Keeps his emotions concealed.'

Povey laughed. 'He does, but you'd be surprised. He has his moments.'

'How long have you known him?'

'Since he was a DI, and I got promoted from South Wales Police. I couldn't believe he'd retired when he gave it all up a couple of years ago. When I heard he was coming back, it was my turn for a backflip. He's one of the good ones. You need to scratch the surface to get to the gold, but I wouldn't have it any other way.'

'It does make life interesting,' Jess agreed. And how ironic that scratching Warlow's surface was the very thing he was most afraid of, she thought. In his mind, what lay beneath was not gold, but something poisonous; a risk of infection to others from the HIV he carried. Not a death sentence in these days of mind-bending medical advances, but enough to make anyone bitter. Yet that was not how she would describe the DCI. Cynical, sometimes blunt, but he aimed his vitriol towards the criminals who deserved it. Used it like a sharpened tool. And underneath the hood was another man. A father, a grieving husband – even if the grief seemed buried deep – and someone she enjoyed the company of. In another life, they might have enjoyed something more. A life where her own baggage hadn't fallen off the train and spilled her dirty washing over the tracks for all to see. Washing with labels like 'separated' and 'single mother.' Jess frowned. Where was all this coming from? Was this self-pity? Or something else? Something she hadn't felt in a long while.

Povey's promise to get back in touch as soon as they had something worth passing on brought her back to earth. Jess thanked the scientist, said her goodbyes, and texted Molly to ask if she'd eaten a proper dinner that evening.

———

Josh Stebbings followed Ben, keeping low along the side of the darkened lane where they'd been bollocked by the cops earlier that day. He'd wanted to go back to Cross Hands and grab a Big Mac, but Ben was having none of it.

Instead, they'd gone to a pub in Llandeilo to lie low for a couple of hours.

'Until it gets dark,' Ben had explained over a pint of Bow.

'What's the point?' Josh had argued. 'You said you wanted photos. It's too dark now.'

Ben shook his head. 'Night mode on the iPhone. We can get snaps of the cops outside the house and shit. It'll be good.'

'It won't be good if they catch us.'

'What's the big deal?' Ben taunted his younger friend. 'We did nothing. We've got sod all to do with the kid.'

'They could still take us in. Question us and that. My dad'll go spare if I get into any more trouble. If he…' Josh didn't finish. No point letting Ben know that Josh's old man had warned him off hanging around with Ben who was, in his father's words, 'A waste of bloody good air.' Ben would only get pissed off and sulky.

And so, they'd waited it out in the pub. Josh had half a pint and then a coke. Ben, three pints of cider.

Josh had driven the car back along the quiet lanes and parked far away from the spot where they'd encountered the cop who'd called himself Warlow. They'd walked the rest of the way, hiding in the shadows, and ducking whenever they saw someone. Ben had to stop to empty his bladder. Twice. When they got to the little copse, it was pitch black under the trees, so Ben switched his phone torch on and climbed the bank.

Josh followed up the slope in Ben's wake, but his foot slipped on something slimy, and he stumbled. On reaching out to steady himself, he heard the branch he'd grasped snap under his fingers. He ended up on all fours, hoping that whatever he'd stepped in had not come out of a dog or a fox. His trainers were new, and his mother would kill him.

'The fuck you doing?' Ben demanded in a harsh whisper.

'It's too dark. I slipped.'

'Use your phone, you twat.'

'I thought we were trying to do this without getting seen?' Josh got up unsteadily, irked at Ben's anger.

'Yeah, we are. But falling on your arse and snapping branches isn't exactly being careful, is it? Come on. Over the fence, you dick. It's up there.'

Josh took out his phone and found the torch. Even with

it, the copse beyond the light was a black space with branches hanging down, ready to snag a hoodie or scratch your skin. He glanced up, hoping not to see any weird-shaped bits of twig tied with string. Josh had already begun channelling his inner Blair Witch. He shivered. This was the stupidest idea ever.

'Here,' Ben called, and there was no mistaking the glee in his voice. 'They even left the bloody ladder for us. Not expecting us to come back, were they? Didn't think we had the balls.'

Josh said nothing, but he climbed the ladder after Ben and got down carefully on the other side. Ben had already taken a dozen steps along the hedge boundary of the field when Josh caught sight of the branches.

'Ben,' he called out in as loud a whisper as he dared. 'Ben.'

'What?' the older boy called back, irritation clipping his voice short.

'Something's here. Under the branches. A bag or some shit.'

Josh walked away from the hedge and out from under the trees to where a pile of branches lay heaped next to a fence. But the torchlight had reflected off something shiny and caught Josh's eye. When he got nearer, he saw beyond the collected pile an open bulk bag, the kind his dad some-times got eight-hundred kilos of sand delivered in. It looked dark, with a shiny surface and a big TP logo on the side. But it was what sat at the bottom of the open bag that kept Josh staring until Ben arrived at his side.

'What the fuck, Josh? We could have been there and b
—' Ben's whining voice cut off when he saw what Josh was looking at. 'Shit the bed, is that a drone?'

It wasn't big, ten inches long and a little less wide. But the four arms with blades on the top confirmed what Ben had asked.

'Wow,' Ben said. 'That is lush. What is it doing here?' He leant forward to reach in, but Josh smacked his arm away.

'What are you doing?'

'Only looking. Jesus.'

'You touch that, and your prints and DNA are all over it.'

Ben laughed. 'What are you talking about? If someone left this here, it's their loss. Finders' keepers, man.'

Josh shook his head in warning. 'No way. This might be something to do with the cops. Surveillance and that.'

Ben's face fell. That this might not be a treasure for plundering had, amongst a slew of other sensible thoughts, not occurred to him. He stopped and looked around, as if trying to convince himself that Josh's suggestion held no water. 'They're not going to fly it now, are they?' he countered.

'That's not the point, is it?' Josh was breathing hard.

'I only want one little look.' Ben reached in again.

'Oi!' yelled a voice.

Ben jerked his hand back, and both boys looked up, searching for the source. They found it in the shape of a light hurrying towards them across the field.

'Shit,' hissed Josh.

Ben was already making the ladder, stooped over, the drone forgotten. Josh hurried after him, jumping down onto the soft earth on the other side and almost losing his footing for a second time. They ran down the bank and on to the road, killing their torchlights and only looking back once they were a good seventy yards up the road. Ben called a halt, hands on his knees, lungs straining from lack of exercise and the roll-ups he smoked. Josh was fitter. He didn't smoke. His mother would smell it on his clothes, so what was the point.

'Anyone coming?' Ben asked, without looking up from staring at the floor and vacuuming in the air.

Josh glanced back. 'No.'

'Shit. That was close,' Ben said.

'Now, can we go back to MacDonalds?' Josh asked.

Ben nodded, too out of breath to make the words into a complete sentence. 'Fucking cops. That would have been a cool photo. The drone, I mean.'

'What drone? I'm not telling anyone. I was never there.'

'C'mon Josh. Don't be a prat.'

'If we tell someone, they'll know we were here. Sod that.' Josh turned and strode back to where they'd parked the car.

'Hang on,' Ben said with wheezy effort.

'No. I'm off. You can come if you want, but I am not hanging about for the cops to come. And you need to swear you won't say anything about a fucking drone.'

'What?' Ben objected in a falsetto whine.

'I mean it, Ben. This is it. You can forget me chauffeuring you about unless you zip it. I don't want to be in the pub with you blabbing on about finding a drone and photos of the kidnapped kid's house. I'm fed up with it.'

'Alright. Jesus. Talk about having a cob on.' Ben straightened and followed Josh. 'It's just a laugh, man.'

Josh pivoted. 'No. It's not. It's not a laugh. I haven't seen anyone laughing because the kid is still missing and us pissing about here is asking for trouble.'

'Okay, okay.' Ben held up his hands. 'All I'm saying is that Insta would've gone ballistic for them photos.'

But Josh didn't answer. He didn't think for one moment of ringing the police and telling them what they'd found. They already knew, obviously. No, his mind was fixed on getting away as soon as possible and the gastronomic pleasures to be found underneath those golden arches.

CHAPTER THIRTY

Doris Sibley liked Coronation Street more than any of
the other soaps. Because it had been running for so long,
she didn't need to see the characters' faces to visualise
them. Her memory brought to mind what they looked like
when she heard the voices. That they probably bore no
resemblance to the images in her head bothered her not at
all. Some new actors had appeared on the scene, but
enough old stagers remained for the programme to keep a
sense of familiarity that Doris enjoyed. Tonight's episode
had been delayed because of some football game and then
the news. But it was on now and she settled into it, late
though it was.

Rollo sat on his cushion on the sofa, and Doris had laid
a tray containing a sandwich, a packet of crisps – prawn
cocktail tonight – and a cup of tea for her supper.

Someone in the Street, a voice she was not familiar
with, had won money on the scratch cards and was buying
everyone a drink in the Rovers Return. But one or two
members of the cast were suspicious that the money had
come from a different source. A criminal source.

'Yes, don't you trust the bugger,' she said aloud. Rollo

opened one eye and promptly shut it again. One-way conversations were something he was very used to.

The sound of loud voices and banging from next door made Doris sit up. The Munros must be watching a Netflux film again. She liked Jaydon but had spoken little to her mother. The young girl had even offered to share her Netflux subscription with Doris, whatever that was, but the old woman was quite content with her little set-top box, and the few dozen channels available to her were more than enough.

In the daytime, she preferred listening to the radio. She'd even bought a DAB set for Christmas and with the extra BBC channels she could listen to, there were plays and old comedy shows galore. But at night, she fell into her old habits, and supper in front of Corrie was a tradition she didn't want to give up. Even if she couldn't see the picture that well and even if it was ridiculously late tonight.

Another shout, followed by a muffled scream, came through the wall. It was all kicking off on Netflux. Doris reached for the TV remote and upped the volume. Just as well she hadn't accepted Jaydon's offer. It sounded a bit too energetic for Doris's tastes.

———

CATRIN DROVE and parked in the lane outside the Caeglas estate in Cwrt Y Waun, where she and Rhys had parked previously. She pulled up and looked around for signs of another car.

'What does Grimshaw drive, sir?'

'No idea,' Warlow said. 'Probably one of those VW campers.'

'Yes,' Catrin agreed, and the corner of her mouth curled. 'He does give off a bit of a hippie vibe.'

'I wouldn't be surprised if he turned up with bloody

Scooby-Doo.'

They sat for a while, listening to the car engine thrum as it idled.

'Did you get any more information on how Voden managed to do a runner?' Warlow asked his sergeant.

'Not much. When a patient does this, it's usual to alert the next of kin. Especially where there is a physical threat involved.'

'So why haven't they found him?'

'Delays and miscommunication. Like everything, they're stretched thinly. The probation service was working on rehabilitating Voden. The thinking is that he's now living rough somewhere. Theoretically, he should not know where his sister and mother are.'

'But they'd know where he was, wouldn't they? And he could probably get a phone.'

Catrin frowned. 'I assume so.'

The two officers sat in silence for a while, mulling over the thoughts that were streaming through their heads. They had little or no leads in this complicated case. But the Green Man and Voden's obsessive behaviour – an obsession which included a camouflage jacket – was something that needed to be followed up. Grimshaw could save them a lot of work by confirming whether the Munros had any connection with Voden. That would have taken two minutes. But he hadn't done that and, as always, the seconds were ticking by. Warlow glanced at his watch for the tenth time since they'd arrived. Five minutes had already passed. 'Where is this Grimshaw bloke?'

'I have rung and texted him, sir. I know it's been delivered, too, but so far he's not replied.'

'Right, sod it.' A fresh blast of cool night air filled the car as Warlow thrust the passenger door open. 'No time like the present, Sergeant. Let's see what we can find out by a little subtle questioning, shall we?'

Catrin turned off the car's engine and decided it might be wise not to comment. She'd worked with the DCI long enough to know when to keep quiet.

She led the way through to the Beili Road cul-de-sac. Warlow followed, glancing right and left at the access ways and paths leading off into the rest of the estate.

'See any rabbits when you were here earlier?' Warlow muttered.

'It is a bit of a warren, agreed.'

The only lights in the three semi-detached houses that closed off the blind street came from number eleven, Mrs Sibley's ground-floor flat. Everywhere else, the windows were dark.

'Where the hell is everyone?' Warlow asked.

'Probably up near where the press is,' Catrin answered. 'All those police cars and media vans. Better than anything on TV.'

'Hmmm,' Warlow grunted his disapproval.

'Live entertainment, sir. Can't beat it.'

'It may be where the Munros are, too. I can't see any lights on.'

They had to cross the street at an angle, and Warlow pointed at their target. 'Number ten you said?'

'Yes, sir, it's—'

Warlow came to an abrupt halt and held up a hand to call a halt to Catrin's progress. He stood, peering at the front of number ten, some twenty yards away. 'Door's open,' he breathed out the words, his senses alert.

Catrin glanced up at the other houses. No curtains twitched.

Warlow walked forward, more slowly this time, eyeing the half-open door. From two yards away, he took out a torch and shone the beam inside the hallway. A coat rack hung drunkenly from one screw. Two anoraks and a padded jacket lay strewn across the floor.

'What do I not like more than anything else in the world, Catrin?' Warlow asked, not taking his eyes off the coats.

'Things that begin with "c", sir.'

'Top of the list?'

'Coincidences, sir.'

'Exactly. Like us turning up on the off chance and finding this.'

'I'll go around the back, sir,' whispered Catrin.

She jogged along a walkway that led off back towards the road next to the school. The gate leading into number ten's garden was a rustic wooden affair held in place by a galvanised thumb latch. She depressed the metal bar and heard it click open just as Warlow's voice announced his presence at the front.

'Police, hello? Is there anyone here?'

Catrin swung the gate open. The garden beyond appeared as a dark and shapeless void. She took out a torch and felt the little spark of anxiety that made her hesitate. Switching it on would give her position away. She trod on the thought and depressed the switch. The beam picked out another gate across from her leading into the next garden behind Mrs Sibley's flat at number eleven.

That gate stood open.

So did the back door to number ten.

She took three steps towards it, angled the torch-beam in and gasped as she got a face-full of something cold and wet. The shock and surprise pole-axed her. She dropped the torch, staggered back, sucking in air in a reflex response, as if she'd just plunged into a bath of water. She lost her footing and fell back into the garden onto wet grass. In front of her, a figure leaped out of the house and hurried away. Dark, big, and carrying something on its shoulder.

Catrin tried to shout, but all that came out was a

garbled scream. She couldn't see through the liquid. All she could do was blink it away, wiping it frantically off with her hands.

It was then that the pain started.

A stinging, burning sensation when she opened her eyes. A pain that persisted when she shut them. Panic seized her. Her imagination took hold and threw her into a nightmare of possibilities.

Soap, acid, bleach. None of them were good. Some were devastating.

She needed to get to some water, fast. Through the pain and mist, she reached out, felt the ground, and pushed up. Catrin opened her eyes and promptly shut them again as a searing jolt of stabbing agony made her wince and crouch down. She reached out, groping for something, anything. The door frame would do. That would lead inside and to a kitchen and tap.

Her groping hand waved right and left; fingers spread in a blind lunge. She hit brickwork and tried to stand. A hand on her arm made her recoil in fear. She yelled and struck out, hit something soft. The material of a coat.

'Get off me, you bastard.'

'Catrin. Catrin, it's me.'

Warlow's voice. She half collapsed as his arm reached around her.

'My eyes, sir. He threw something. I can't open them.'

She felt herself moving, half carried, the air changing, the noise contained by a roof and walls.

'Into the kitchen,' Warlow said.

She didn't argue. She couldn't. A chair scraped on hard flooring, and then she was being pushed down into it. Somewhere close by, a tap ran, the sound of something filling up.

Another hand on her arm and Warlow's voice once more.

'We need to irrigate, wash this stuff off.'

'What is it?'

His warm breath near her neck, the sound of sniffing. 'Can't be sure. It's not bleach though.'

She sucked in air, fear cog-wheeling it through her throat on hearing the word.

'You're going to get wet. I'm doing up your coat.'

A zip moved and then water splashed onto her face. She still couldn't open her eyes. Her breath heaved in and out, her brain catapulting from horror to what this all might mean. No vision. No job. Her life in a spin.

She tried to grab Warlow, but the pain made it too difficult. His thumb and forefinger had to prise the squeezing lids apart.

'Don't fight me, Catrin. Got to be done.'

She flinched when the water hit her face a second time, the world a blur of shapes as she desperately tried to open her eyes, the liquid running in and over, right then left. Again. Then again.

Still, her eyes burned and stung. Pinpricks of pain like ground glass, sometimes sharp and causing her lids to spasm, the water seeping under the collar of her coat, cold on her neck.

'I'm filling the sink. Best you put your head in and try to open your eyes, okay?'

She nodded.

More gushing water from the tap. Warlow's voice on the phone, calling it in, demanding an ambulance and more bodies. The call ended, and the water stopped. Warlow's hand was on her arm again.

'I'm going to pull you up to the edge of the sink, okay?'

'Okay.'

She stood, one hand on the sink's rim, the other groping, getting a feel for the space and the water it contained.

'Don't hesitate,' Warlow ordered.

Catrin didn't. She thrust her face in, the water cold on her skin, her eyes tight shut as her brain screamed at her to open them. She'd never been able to do it underwater. Never been one of those people who swam wide-eyed. Always a goggles girl in the swimming pool.

But this was no swimming pool.

Shaking, she opened her eyes and felt the chilly water over her corneas, blinking and straining to keep them open, knowing that this volume of water would dilute and reduce whatever effect the chemical was having on the delicate tissues. She held her breath, kept the lids apart for a count of twenty before pulling back out and sucking in air.

'Good. Well done. Help is coming.'

Another hand guided her back to the chair.

'If it's any consolation, I reckon it's vinegar.'

'Vinegar?'

'That's what I smelled.'

'It's an acid, right?'

'Yes, but not a strong acid.'

'Sir, my face…is it…?'

'It's fine. Couple of red blotches where you've rubbed, that's all.'

'Is that meant to make me feel better?'

'It should. I remember—'

Catrin still had her eyes shut. Warlow's sudden silence sent a fresh surge of fear. An unfamiliar noise, movement and steps. What if the acid attacker was back?

'Where the hell have you been?' Warlow demanded.

'I didn't know where you were. I was parked near the school.'

She tried to place the voice. Familiar but…

'What happened here?' The voice again.

'Someone threw vinegar in my sergeant's face is what happened.' Warlow sounded strained and angry. 'And maybe if we'd had some information from you, it might not have.'

'I came to meet you. It's not my fault—'

'Right, fine,' Warlow again, irritated. 'Tell us now. The Munros, do they have any link with Thomas Voden?'

'I'm not sure I'm supposed to—'

'Christ, man. There is a dangerous, violent bastard out there. Don't come the bloody jobsworth with me.'

'Yes, they are. Thomas Voden is Patricia Munro's son.'

And then she placed the voice. Grimshaw, the social care guy.

She heard Warlow lean in again. 'You were right, Catrin.' Then he heaved out a breath, and she saw his blurry shape stand up. 'Okay. Ambulance is on its way. I want you to fill this jug with room temp water and hand it to DS Richards, who will irrigate her own eyes until the paramedics get here. You understand?'

'Room temperature water. Right,' Grimshaw said.

Catrin heard the tap running again.

'Head back, pour it on the bridge of your nose and let it trickle into your eyes,' Warlow said, his voice softer now, his mouth close to her ear. 'How's the pain?'

'A bit better.'

'Stay with her,' Warlow told Grimshaw, his voice full of authority once more.

'I will,' Grimshaw said.

'You better. You've got a lot to make up for, sonny.'

'I didn't know—'

'Just look after her until the ambulance arrives.'

'He went right, sir. Through next door's garden,' Catrin said.

'Then that's where I'm going, too.'

CHAPTER THIRTY-ONE

WARLOW RAN through to the back of the house and out to where he'd found Catrin screaming. He turned right through the gate to the garden next door. His torch picked out a bird table, flowerbeds and a square of lawn, before illuminating another gate that exited. It, too, stood open. On the other side, another tarmac path snaked off. In his mind, Warlow tried to envisage the whole estate. He imagined radiating cul-de-sacs extending out from the back of the school like an unfurled fan.

The attacker could be anywhere. Hiding in a garden, or already heading off into the fields beyond. They'd get the dogs in, knock on every door if they had to. But it wouldn't help now. Not right this minute.

That all took human resources and organisation, and time was slipping away. No sooner had the next minute arrived than it was gone. The future was nothing but a slippery eel you could never quite get a grip on.

Parked cars lined the streets. Few of the houses had garages or off-road parking. The bastard could be in one of these vehicles, ducking low out of Warlow's sight. He couldn't look in all of them. A man appeared walking his dog. The DCI pounced on him, wanting to know if he'd seen or heard anything strange.

'Not unless a TV crew asking me where the nearest bloody Pret a Manger is counts, no.'

The reply did nothing to help Warlow's mood. In the end, he gave up and retraced his steps to the Munro property. Blue lights were already flashing there. Warlow hurried around the side of the house to find two Uniforms guarding the door.

'Ambulance?' Warlow asked.

'Been and gone, sir. Couple of minutes ago.'

'Where's Grimshaw?'

'Who?'

'Tall, thick glasses, ponytail, beard.'

'Oh, he went as soon as the ambulance arrived. Said he had a thing about eyes. Looked green around the gills.'

Warlow shook his head.

'Okay. This whole block is a crime scene. No one gets in or out until the crime scene crew gets here. Got it?'

Both officers nodded.

A van moved into the cul-de-sac. The satellite dish on its roof made Warlow growl. 'And you can keep those buggers away. We need access. That's the line to take.'

'Right you are, sir.' One of the Uniforms marched smartly towards the van, waving his hand, and shaking his head. The jauntiness of his walk suggested he might be relishing the task.

Warlow turned back towards the house and stepped towards the still-open front door. 'If anyone wants me, I'll be in here.'

He slid on some nitriles and stepped inside the front door for the second time in twenty minutes, this time taking care not to disturb anything instead of barrelling through like the last time. He used the tip of a finger at the very edge of the light switch to get some kind of illumination going. What he saw under the 100-watt bulb was a scene of utter disruption. Anything that wasn't bolted down or was too heavy to shift had been upended. The hallway had the strewn coats, the living room had one mock-leather armchair on its side, the TV lay face down on the floor surrounded by magazines and channel changers scattered like a massacred wagon train. Someone had been in here and had not minded one bit as to the consequences of their actions.

He stepped inside and did a quick sweep, looking for any sign of blood. He found none and took a tiny iota of consolation from that. He went into the kitchen. Not as much disarray, but enough to tell him that the broken cups and overturned toaster were not the normal state of affairs.

He retraced his steps and took the stairs, flicking on the light as he did so. The first thing he clocked when he reached the top was the loft ladder, fully extended to the landing. Warlow stepped under it and across to the first of the two bedrooms and opened the door. In stark contrast to the downstairs situation, he took in a fairly organised room. The bed had been made, some clothes folded over a chair in front of a dresser, the wardrobe doors closed. On a table next to the bed were a glass of water and a face-down paperback, open a third of the way through, next to some glasses.

He had to negotiate the bottom of the ladder to step into the bathroom. Seat down, folded towels on a heated rail. Nothing strange here.

The other bedroom told a similar story, except for the fact that this one had a framed poster dominating one wall. A Festival in Leeds, complete with line-ups and stuck on tickets. There were clothes on the bed here, too, neatly laid out. No book on the bedside table here, but a little hand-held console that, Warlow suspected, played games. So, a younger person's room. And one, like the other, with not much in the way to suggest that any violent act took place here.

Next, Warlow turned to the loft ladder. Above, the space looked unlit. He called out the usual warning. 'Police. Make yourself known.'

No answer. He grabbed the rail and started up, torch in hand. Poking his head through, he took in a dark space with a couple of lagged water tanks under a single naked bulb above, worked by a switch stuck to one rafter. He flicked it on and stark light filled the void, revealing wool fibre insulation stuffed between the four by twos lining the ceiling above. His gaze swept the room in a three-sixty arc. There was nothing of any note. Not even a rat dropping.

Until his eye caught the large piece of chipboard lying half across a black space at the far end of the loft. Someone had laid the same sort of chipboard across the joists underfoot to make a safe passage. On his knees, Warlow made his way across and pulled the chipboard cover completely free. A large square of plaster and insulation had been removed from the wall, the remnants of it scattered in the spaces between the joists below. Warlow aimed his torch through and whispered under his breath. 'Bingo.'

He crawled through on the equivalent chipboard path into the other half of the semi and found himself in a room with a camp-bed, next to a makeshift kitchen with a kettle and microwave on some upturned plastic crates. Clothes and books spilled out from a holdall but lying next to the bed was the item that convinced Warlow that Catrin Richards had hit the jackpot with this one.

There, lying spread out, was a green, black, and brown camouflage jacket.

Warlow took out his phone and photographed the lot before turning his attention to a square of wood in the middle of the floor. A loft door hinged on one side. Lying next to it was a telescoping ladder. Not the automatic extending type that slid down once the door opened, as in the Munro's house. This one needed to be extended manually and had been brought up into the loft by whoever had come through last.

With the door lifted, Warlow knelt and stuck his head through to find dust sheets and cans of paint on the landing and no lights on. He slid the ladder down and descended, remembering Rhys's report of an empty flat being redecorated. A quick search confirmed all of that. A narrow passage led to some stairs and down towards an outside door. The empty flat meant that there'd be no one around at night. But during the day, with the decorators around, it would have been possible for whoever had lived in the attic to move across to access the Munro flat.

Warlow took the stair down and opened the outside door. The cool night air bathed his face, and he stepped down and walked to the front of the property where the Uniform he'd set to guard the Munro's smashed open door did a double take on seeing him.

As he walked across in front of the door to number eleven, it opened to reveal Mrs Sibley on the threshold. 'David, is that you?' she called out.

Warlow turned to reveal himself. The old woman peered at him for several seconds. 'Oh, I am so sorry. I thought you were someone else. I thought I heard someone on the stairs.'

'You did,' Warlow replied. 'That was me.'

'Yes, but you're not David.'

'No, I'm Detective Chief Inspector Warlow.' He flashed his warrant card.

Mrs Sibley lifted her head up to peer through the bottom of her glasses. They made her pupils and irises look huge. 'Another police officer. How many of you are out here?'

'Too many. But none in the right place,' Warlow growled. 'It's Mrs Siddle, isn't it?' He dredged up some vague memory of a name from Rhys and Catrin's report.

'Sibley.' The woman corrected him.

'Who is David, Mrs Sibley?'

Mrs Sibley smiled. 'He's moving into the flat when it's finished. He went up earlier. He likes to check on progress. I thought you were him. A nice boy. He carried my shopping in once.'

'Did he, now? Mind if I come in Mrs Sibley? I have a few questions I'd like to ask you.'

'Of course you can. Tea?'

Warlow's head buzzed with what he'd found in the Munro's house and in the attic above Mrs Sibley's property. It all hummed with implications. But Catrin was on the way to the hospital and reinforcements were arriving. Though he didn't have time to hang around, the crime scene was secure with two Uniforms repelling all borders outside. He could squeeze in a cheeky cuppa.

'Kettle's just boiled,' Mrs Sibley said.

'Go on then. It'll have to be a quickie. Milk and one,' Warlow's reply was automatic.

He followed her through to her kitchen and while she poured boiling water over a tea bag in a cup, Warlow asked the questions.

'This David, he been calling in on the flat long?'

'Nearly two weeks. Poor man turned up one day expecting the decorators to still be there, but they'd gone on the stroke of half past four. I lent him my key. He brought it straight back the next day.'

'And what does David look like?'

'Young. Mind you, everyone does these days. His voice is young, anyway. My eyes aren't so good now.' Mrs Sibley stirred in the milk.

'So, he just turns up and says he's moving into the flat above you and wanted to see it? Have I got that right?'

'You have. He told me he wanted to see how the decorators were getting on. Slowly, is what I said.' Mrs Sibley's eyes sparkled as she cackled at her own little joke. 'I felt sorry for him. Young people don't have it easy these days, you know.'

'And you've seen him regularly since?'

'Ye-es. Heard him, too. Most often I hear him go up, but sometimes it's too late when he comes down because I can't hear him then. Not always.' She squeezed the tea bag in the cup with the flat end of the spoon.

'Remember what he was wearing when you first met him?'

'I do. A big coat. Too big for this time of year if you ask me. Green and a bit blotchy is how I would describe it. But then my eyes are not the best.'

'Did he say anything to you? About where he was from or why he was moving here?'

Mrs Sibley paused in her tea preparations to think. 'No. Quiet he was. Nice and polite, too. Don't get much of that these days.'

'What about the Munros? Did they ever see or speak to David?'

'Not that I can remember. I only used to hear him after dark, going up the stairs. As I say, I expect I was in bed when he came down because he never disturbed me.'

No, thought Warlow. You never heard him come down because he was kipping in the attic.

Mrs Sibley went to a little pantry off the kitchen and came back with an empty plastic pot with Co-Op strawberry yoghurt written on the side. She poured the tea from the mug into the cup, adding a spoonful of sugar.

'There.' She handed Warlow the yoghurt pot. 'You can

take it with you now. My Gethin was always in a rush. And don't worry, don't need the pot back.'

Warlow took it and promptly put it down to avoid burning his fingers. Yoghurt pots, as disposable as they were, were not designed to hold hot tea. 'One last thing, Mrs Sibley.'

'Call me Doris, please.'

'Okay, Doris, anything strange happened this evening. Did you see or hear anything?'

'Only that blasted telly next door. She has a Netflux subscription you know. Makes an awful racket does that Netflux.'

'What kind of noise?'

'Shouting and screaming and banging about half an hour ago. One of those violent films. But not much after that, come to think of it. The programme must have ended.'

Warlow picked up the yoghurt pot and sipped. Boiling hot and sweet. Just as he liked it.

'Is David in any trouble?' Doris asked.

'Not yet. But we need to find him. And you've been a great help.'

'Don't mention it. As my late husband used to say, every bugger is guilty of something and you're a liar if you say anything different.'

Warlow glanced around and noted a photographic collage of a man in a police uniform progressing through the ranks over the years in a frame on a little dresser.

'That him?'

Mrs Sibley nodded. 'Gethin. Gone these fifteen years. But not forgotten.'

'Obviously married the right woman. Right, well, I'm in the middle of it here. Thanks for the chat and the tea. Extremely helpful.'

'Nothing changes, does it?' Mrs Sibley smiled. 'What

should I do if David turns back up? Belt him with Gethin's truncheon.'

For a moment, Warlow panicked. Would she? But then the enormous eyes behind the glasses glinted again, and he smiled.

'No, give him a chance.' Warlow handed over a card. 'Be nice and polite and then ring me instead. Can you see the number?'

'I've got a thing that reads it for me. Deal,' Mrs Sibley said, and followed Warlow to the front door and saw him out, yoghurt pot in hand.

CHAPTER THIRTY-TWO

JESS SAT OUTSIDE in a waiting area on the eye unit at Glangwili Hospital. Catrin was in an examination room full of all kinds of equipment with a doctor and a nurse. A couple of people wearing white eye pads held in place by bits of tape were also in the waiting area. One of them sat forward, holding her hand over the pad, and moaning softly.

Jess spent the time texting Molly and Warlow alternately.

Neither of the sods had answered her yet, and she'd resorted to tapping her feet. But not, as yet, to Candy Crush.

Catrin had been in there for about twenty minutes when, finally, the nurse emerged and walked over, smiling wanly. Jess's pulse did a hop, skip and jump. She hated anything to do with eyes. She'd tried contact lenses once, and they lasted only the time it took for the optometrist to put them in and take them back out again. Even thinking about someone touching her eyes, let alone putting sharp objects near them, which happened every day in this unit, made her shudder.

'DI Allanby?'

Jess stood up.

'Catrin said she'd like you to come into the examination room.'

Suppressing the little flutter in her gut, Jess followed the nurse.

Inside, the room looked even more cluttered than the glance she'd had before suggested. Catrin sat in a black chair opposite a young doctor who must have been all of twelve, in Jess's estimation. The DI flicked Catrin a glance. She wore a pad over one eye, the other blinked up at her, a little red-rimmed but otherwise okay. As was the skin on her face.

A surge of relief washed through Jess. She reached out a hand and grabbed the sergeant's arm. 'You're alright?'

Catrin nodded. 'Diluted vinegar.'

Jess turned her gaze towards the doctor. Her name badge read Hopton.

'Definitely an acid, but not strong. The Ph got back to neutral quickly. The right eye has some superficial changes but no ulcer. We've padded it overnight to help with discomfort, dilated the pupil and put in some antibiotic, but it should recover fully. The left eye has minimal damage.'

'How do you know it's vinegar?' Jess asked.

Catrin answered, 'The fish and chip shop smell.'

'But you're okay? No permanent damage?'

Dr Hopton shook her head. 'I'd say back to normal in a couple of days. Drops only for the left eye so that Catrin can see to get around. We need to check things over in three days.'

'Thank you, Lydia,' Catrin said. The nurse handed her a plastic bag with her meds and instructions.

Jess led the way along the corridor to the stairs that led

down to the main A&E. When they got to the bottom and the larger waiting area, Catrin stopped.

'Are you really okay?' Jess turned to her, concerned.

'I'm fine. It's just…vinegar? I mean, he must have prepared that.'

'You think he might have used it on the Munros?'

Catrin shrugged. 'It floored me, ma'am. Not so much the pain, just the shock of having something thrown in my face and the terror of not knowing if it might have been…' Catrin stopped, the memory of those awful few moments making her blanch.

Both women had inside knowledge of how powerful incapacitant sprays to the face and eyes were in subduing violent individuals. The police no longer used MACE, the standard issue was now PAVA, much more akin to pepper spray. But a homemade version using vinegar implied someone had done their research.

'I can run you home,' Jess said.

'Thank you, ma'am.'

'You've rung Craig?'

'Not yet. I wanted to see what the doctor said.'

'He doesn't know!?' Jess said, failing to hide the surprise in her voice.

'I needed to know if…if there'd be scarring, I wanted to know before telling him. Besides, he's at work. What can he do? I…' She broke down then, a trembling hand covering her face.

Jess stepped forward and hugged the younger officer, feeling the silent sobs jerking her body.

'It's okay, Catrin. It's okay. I'll tell him.'

After a couple of minutes, Catrin pulled back, excused herself, and made for the toilet. 'I must look a mess.'

'Take your time,' Jess said. Catrin's hair, where the irrigation fluid had been poured over her face, looked flat and lifeless. She'd feel better once she'd brushed it out. But, Jess suspected, she also needed a few minutes alone so that she could see herself in the mirror. To make sure that what everyone told her was true, and that there was no damage. It would also give her time for a mental reset. In all the time they'd worked together, Jess had never seen Catrin lose control. The simple spontaneous hug they'd exchanged moments ago was a natural act of consolation, the kind of thing Jess would have done for anyone. But for Catrin, Jess sensed it was an unaccustomed admission of vulnerability. She needed to process that.

While the sergeant freshened up, Jess texted Gil to update him on his fellow officer and get Craig Peters's number. Gil rang her back immediately and demanded more details. His anger positively throbbed out of the phone.

'Bloody coward,' he fumed. 'Throwing anything in someone's face is…the bloody *pwrs.*'

'Do I get a translation?'

'Better you don't, ma'am. It's not a word I'd normally use in anyone's company, but especially yours or Catrin's. So, excuse my Welsh.'

Jess smiled. Gil Jones was the newest recruit to Warlow's team, but she felt she'd known him for years.

'But she's alright? In herself, I mean?' Gil persisted.

'You know Catrin. It's been a shock, but she'll get over it. Will you tell Warlow?'

'I will. He's on the bloody warpath, but he'll want this intel. I'll text you Craig's number.'

She rang off and waited for the chirp that showed a message coming through a few moments later.

While Catrin came to terms with the fact that she would need to play pirate for the rest of the night and make herself as presentable as wearing a bloody great white pad over half her face allowed, Jess phoned Craig, Catrin's partner and a traffic officer. He picked up after four rings. The hum of an engine in the background told her he was driving.

'Craig, this is Jess Allanby. You on duty?'

'I am ma'am. How are you?'

'I'm fine, but I'm in A&E with Catrin.'

The line hummed with expectation. She could almost hear Craig's heart thudding.

'On a case, or is someone injured?'

'Catrin is, but she's fine,' Jess explained quickly. 'A little shaken and wearing an eye pad, but fine. I'm taking her home, but I thought you'd want to know.'

Another pause.

'What happened?' Craig's voice sounded thick.

Jess glanced around. She stood in the A&E waiting area. About a third of the chairs were occupied by people either suffering with something or waiting for the sick to re-emerge from the bowels of the emergency room. Every one of them looked like they wished they could be some-where else. Hospitals were amazing places, but never in anyone's top hundred fun destinations. No one was talking. In fact, her conversation with Craig had become the centre of most people's attention.

'Hang on,' she said and strode to the exit and walked out into the evening air. No need for everyone to hear what she was going to say. Besides, attacking a police officer was a serious crime. This was nobody's business but theirs.

———

Thirteen hours missing…

By MIDNIGHT, number ten Beili Road became a lit-up circus. Rhys joined Warlow from the Howells' property and the two men tip-toed around the crime scene techs as they dusted for prints and circled any stain remotely red, ochre, black or purple, looking ready for swabbing.

Warlow picked up on one particularly lurid-looking blob on the floor of the kitchen under a dining table. His money was on it being tomato ketchup, but he resisted an urge to dip his finger in it and taste the damned thing.

The dog team used the scent from the loft and picked up a trace that flowed out of the back of the house and through the back gate of number eleven but petered out along the snaky passages through the estate. Much as Warlow's hurried expedition of earlier had.

A quick search of the kitchen revealed no sign of anything suspicious. In fact, though the contents of the kitchen table were now on the floor, a couple of plates remained. A half-eaten congealed spaghetti bolognese provided evidence of the Munro's interrupted supper.

There were no drugs anywhere. Minimal booze. Nothing to suggest that whatever happened here had anything to do with the usual causes of crime. In fact, it betrayed all the hallmarks of a domestic incident. Something or someone had triggered a violent reaction which must have led to either the Munros fleeing or being taken.

And knowing what they did about Thomas Voden, the most likely suspect was the young man, now eighteen years old. What Warlow needed to find out was if there was any clue where Voden might have gone after whatever took place here. Exactly how this domestic incident was linked to the disappearance of Osian Howells, Warlow could only guess. But the fact that it took place just a few hundred yards from where the kidnapping occurred set off all Warlow's alarm bells. If Thomas had taken the Munros with him, there was a strong possibility he'd taken them to wherever he kept Osian Howells hidden.

Little point in Rhys going up to the loft. The DC's lanky frame often ducked to get into normal-sized rooms.

Up there, he'd be severely restricted. But it was the room Warlow felt there'd be the most to learn from. When one tech emerged holding a travel pass with Thomas Voden's name on it, any doubts Warlow harboured that their Green Man had been hiding out there disappeared.

There were some anomalies. The kettle and tea-making facilities were the extent of his provisions. Which begged the great big question of what he'd been surviving on. A search of the flat above Mrs Sibley's revealed empty kitchen units and a fridge, also empty. Which meant Voden must have been eating elsewhere.

'You don't think the cat lady—' Rhys had gone for the derogatory cliche, but the warning look from Warlow stopped him dead. Warlow'd warmed to the old woman. No need to caricature her. But Rhys saw the signs and recovered well. 'The uh, lady in the flat below might have been feeding him, do you, sir?'

'Doris? No chance. She'd have told me right off. Voden was stealthy in his comings and goings. He must have a stash of food hidden somewhere. We need to find out if there are any other empty houses around. Airbnbs, houses for sale, that sort of thing. There will be. Maybe not in this village, but in the surrounding area.'

The Towy Valley, apart from its own stunning natural beauty, had a few visitor attractions. Aberglasney Gardens was a stone's throw away, as was the National Botanical Gardens. And Llandeilo had become a trendy destination for city dwellers as far away as London. People came and stayed a few nights, walked, ate, breathed in the pleasant, clean air, sucked in a bit of culture and went away again. For that, they needed accommodation.

Rhys wrote it down in his notebook.

Another CID officer was in with Doris Sibley, quizzing her about any and all details she could provide about the supposed new tenant's movements over the last few days.

That he'd been in the area for a much longer period argued that he'd had plenty of opportunity to scope out the village and the surrounding land.

But after half an hour, the place became too crowded for Warlow. He needed space to think and take stock. The Incident Room provided that. And with all the support and facilities there, it now seemed inevitable that he would need to return.

'Right, Rhys, I'm heading back. No point in me being here. But I need to talk to that bloody idiot Grimshaw.'

'Is he still not answering his phone, sir?'

'Probably got his head down a toilet somewhere.' Warlow recalled the green around the gills comment the paramedic mentioned.

'I could swing by the Reading Room in case he went back there. It's the nearest toilet for the PolSA team.'

Warlow nodded. 'Good idea. But don't waste any time. The fragile bugger might well have shot off home to lie down. Who knows? But what you can do is call in on the Howells on your way back. Best they're kept up to speed on what's happening from you. They'll have seen all the activity and must be wondering.'

Rhys nodded. A little too enthusiastically. But Warlow let it go with just a minor jibe. 'You don't need to look so bloody pleased about it.'

Rhys opened and shut his mouth without saying anything.

'I'm only kidding. Just be straight with them.'

Rhys gave him a relieved, boyish smile that won the hearts of almost everyone he came across, shrugged, and hurried off. 'I'll let you know if I find Grimshaw, sir.'

CHAPTER THIRTY-THREE

WARLOW MADE his way towards the knot of press and onlookers at the edge of the cul-de-sac, pausing only to fire off a text to Gil to tell him he was on the way back and read the one he received in reply explaining that Catrin was fine and had suffered no permanent damage. He huffed out a lungful of relief on reading that.

Then he texted Jess to ask Catrin for the name and contact numbers of the officer she'd been in touch with about the Voden case and sent that off with a thumbs up. He was thinking of it in those terms now, since the missing Munros were all Vodens, really. Simpler, in his mind, to give them a single label. The cat was well and truly out of the bag there. Out and sitting on top of a rooftop somewhere howling like a bloody banshee.

He lifted the cordon tape with a nod to the Uniform guarding it and pressed the button on his key to unlock the Jeep. This triggered the alarm to chirp and the indicator's to flash twice.

Unfortunately, the lights drew the attention of a reporter armed with what looked like a blow-dried rat on the end of a stick. Warlow knew this was a windscreen microphone muff, but he preferred the rat analogy. In his head, he sometimes imagined the buggers eating one when they were bored, like peasants in some Pythonesque medieval market. Next to the rat wielder, a girl carrying a shoulder camera turned the lens towards him and its bright light made him scowl. Warlow had no idea who these people were, but they obviously knew him.

'DCI Warlow?' The shout made half a dozen other people turn towards him.

Warlow didn't stop. He walked purposefully towards his car as the reporter and camera operator hurried towards him and matched his stride.

'DCI Warlow, have you made any progress in finding Osian Howells?'

His immediate notion was to say, 'No, of course not. We've shelved all that for the night. We're all out here running around like guillotined chickens just to take in the air and enjoy a walk in the woods.' But he had enough sense not to voice his thoughts, though it ended up being a close thing. Instead, he fell back on that old standard of good police work. 'We have. But I can't comment further,' delivered with a nod that meant to imply conversation over. The nod fell on stony ground.

'Have you charged anyone?' The reporter was young and Warlow had a vague memory of him doing a set piece outside headquarters a month or two ago. Something vital to the public interest, like the police being sensitive to people's pronouns of choice when they were being charged. In Warlow's mind, most of the buggers qualified as an 'it' anyway.

'I can't comment on that.'

'At this stage, do you fear for Osian's safety, Mr Warlow?'

Warlow suppressed a scream. He often wondered if any of these people really knew what they were doing.

What effect such a throwaway statement might have on Osian's parents watching this from their living room either live or on some news bulletin. The DCI's every thought brimmed with fear for Osian's safety. But you didn't say that. Because fearing for the safety of someone put the investigation on a different footing. It wasn't time to lay the ground for that kind of outcome. Not yet. You lived in hope. That thin strand of faith that things might yet still turn out okay. This idiot should have known not to put words into his mouth.

'Osian's safety is at the forefront of our investigation. The response from the public so far has been encouraging and we've been inundated with offers of help. It's good that people are motivated. But it would be doing the police service and the community an injustice by speculating anything without evidence.'

Christ, not bad, Evan, he thought. You dragged that little nugget out from the vault somewhere and avoided any words beginning with f.

'James Ryan is in custody. Is he your prime suspect?'

The rat-muff wielder half stepped in front of Warlow in an attempt to delay his progress. He was a persistent little oik. Warlow did not slow down. 'Several people have come forward to help. No charges have been made. Mr Ryan is not a suspect.'

Cameras flashed. More press were arriving, like piranhas around a carcass.

'Do you think Osian is—'

Warlow trod on that one without waiting for the end of the sentence. 'Now if you'll excuse me, I have work to do.'

Rat-muff man, emboldened, tried one more obstructive manoeuvre. Unfortunately, Warlow turned towards his car at that point and, to avoid a collision, rat-muff stepped back, misjudged the gap between kerb and road and fell backwards onto his arse.

Warlow hesitated and looked down. Luckily, he'd been four feet away when the man fell.

'Careful,' the DCI said. 'You could do yourself an injury there.'

He didn't offer to help him up and one corner of his brain fervently hoped that the camera person had that one on film. No one laughed, but it would be a YouTube classic.

Shouts followed him as he opened the car door. Some of the sods even stood in front of the bonnet to get a photo. Warlow's foot hovered on the clutch. One slip and he could almost hear the bang and squelch as one of the vermin fell under his wheel.

Instead, he pulled slowly out and accelerated smoothly away until they were just a bunch of leeches in his rear-view mirror.

As encounters went it was not a bad one. He hadn't screamed or hit anyone. And the slapstick had been provided by one of their own. Sion Buchannan would be proud. He drove away with the burning question of just how far you could stick a rat on a stick up someone's rectum at the very forefront of his mind.

———

No one had seen hide nor hair of Grimshaw when Rhys called back to the Reading Room. A group of Uniforms, tired from the search, sat around drinking tea and eating sandwiches but there was no sign of the social worker, nor Sergeant Ken Morris, the PolSA.

'Just missed him by five minutes,' one of the Uniforms said. 'Got called away. Someone thought they'd seen something in a field.'

'One of many,' muttered the bloke next to him. 'Reports, I mean. Not fields. Seen enough of those today.'

Rhys thanked them and headed up the road towards the Howells' property. He'd turned in and was approaching the cordon, where a group of uniformed officers were chatting, when one of them looked up and hailed him.

'Ah, the very man. Your boss about?'

Rhys recognised the thick glasses. Sergeant Ken Morris's other trademark feature, his bald head, now nestled under a regulation baseball cap. 'He's on the way back to HQ, Sarge,' Rhys explained.

'Oh, well, you'll do. Follow me.'

Rhys didn't argue, and the PolSA filled him in as they walked past the Howells' place to the gate leading to the field opposite that he and Warlow had walked across on their first visit to the scene that afternoon.

Rhys threw a glance towards the house as he passed it. Gina was in there, and likely with a nice warm cup of tea. But they'd both still be there in fifteen minutes. So long as the PolSA wasn't intending on taking him on a cross-country trek.

'One of our lads stopped a boy racer doing a ton on the A40 between here and Whitemill. Two youths in the car, one of them couldn't stop talking once they had them out of the vehicle,' Morris told Rhys.

The DC followed Morris, and they both made their way up along the hedge. 'What did they say?'

'They said that they'd been trying to get some photos of the Howells' property for their Insta feeds.'

Rhys stopped. 'Was the car a vomit yellow Astra?'

Morris snorted. 'My boys said canary. I prefer your vomit. You remember them?'

'I do, uh…Stebbings, was it?'

Morris recommenced his ascent until he stood on slightly higher ground, then stopped and looked down at Rhys. 'I'm impressed. Yes, Stebbings is the driver. The one who can't shut up is called Ben Mainwaring. They're up here.'

Morris led the way to the copse but never got to the fence. A few yards to their right, torchlight and voices showed a spot where a couple of Uniforms stood with the two boys. Someone had set a lantern down on an upturned stump. The youths, hands in the pouches of their hoodies, looked small with two big Uniforms, bulked out by all their equipment, standing next to them. All four of them stood staring at a pile of branches.

'We waiting for a voice to emerge or for it to catch fire first?' Ken Morris asked.

'Wha—?' One of the boys turned, too lazy to even add a 't' to the end of his mouth-breather response. Rhys couldn't read expressions nor see faces clearly in the failing light, but he recognised Mainwaring's whining voice instantly.

'You know, as in the burning bush,' Morris added.

Stony silence.

'Right, note to self, no more biblical references. In your own time, then,' the PolSA muttered.

'I swear on my mother's life it was there. Definitely a UAV, man. Expensive like. In a bag and all,' Mainwaring gushed.

'UAV?' Morris asked.

'He means a drone,' Stebbings explained.

'What were you doing back here?' Rhys asked.

'Not doing anything, man,' Mainwaring protested.

'So what, you woke up from a dream in which you'd been magically transported and here you were standing in this field, is that it?' Morris asked.

Silence.

'Start talking, boys. Detective Constable Harries here has you already interfering in his investigation. Now's your chance to exonerate yourselves or end up in court. You have ten seconds.'

Both boys started talking at once. From what Rhys could piece together, Mainwaring had planned on getting his photograph and convinced Stebbings to return. They'd seen the drone when they'd crossed the fence and described it in its plastic sack. They'd run for it when they'd been disturbed.

'What kind of drone?'

'I dunno,' Mainwaring said. 'Looked expensive though.'

'And the bag it was in?'

'Green. Too big for the drone,' Stebbings explained.

'Why the hell did you not report this?' Rhys spat.

'We thought it must have been one of yours that shouted at us,' Stebbings answered.

Rhys shook his head.

'Someone saw us, so we buggered off.'

'Jesus,' Morris muttered under his breath.

Mainwaring looked at Stebbings and then back at Morris. 'You mean…that might have been the bloke?'

'I'd say it was definitely the bloke,' Rhys said.

'Shit,' Stebbings swore under his breath.

'Well, we didn't know, did we?' Mainwaring objected; his voice even more wheedling than usual.

'Right,' Morris said, not wanting to hear anymore because all it made him want to do was to smack these two twits' heads together until they clanged. 'Phone numbers, addresses and bugger off. We'll need statements in the morning, so don't try to be clever.'

The boys left with the Uniforms and Rhys stood with Morris next to the collected branches. 'What's your take, Sarge?' Rhys asked.

'Having met those two, I don't hold out much hope for humanity. The sooner an asteroid hits and wipes us all out, the better,' Morris muttered. 'But as for this case, I don't see any reason for either of them making this up.'

'It doesn't make sense,' Rhys said. 'This area would have been easily observed.'

'Not that easily. It's higher ground. Plus, it had already been searched.'

'But there are Uniforms not fifty yards down the slope,' Rhys objected. 'The Howells' property is just a stone's throw away.'

'Yep. Hide in plain sight,' Morris said.

'Bloody hell. That would take some balls.'

Morris sighed. 'The one thing that's certain about this bloke is that he is organised and savvy. I wouldn't put anything past him.'

'You don't think it's a double bluff from those two?'

'Who, Batman and Robin in the vomitmobile? No chance. We'll secure the site tonight and get some forensics out here. But they're pretty busy down at the house right now.'

'I'd better get my lot up to speed.'

'You do that. Oh, and watch your footing on the way back. The farmer had some cows in here yesterday. Their pancakes are easy to spot in daylight. A squelchy surprise in the dark.'

When he got to the front gate of the Howells' property, Rhys used the torch on his phone to check his shoes. Not too bad, but he'd take them off before going inside.

Gina met him at the door, all smiles.

'News?'

'Some. Nothing that helpful. But once again, the boss wants me to keep Nerys and Lloyd in the loop.'

Gina scowled. 'People are texting and messaging them. Something about the estate.'

'That's where I've just come from. We may know who the Green Man is.'

'Really?'

'Who is it, Gina?' A shout from the living room.

'It's Rhys…uh Detective Constable Harries.'

'What's going on?'

'I'd better go through,' Rhys said.

'Tea?' Gina asked, grabbing on to his arm.

Rhys nodded, slipped off his shoes and for the second time in an hour walked into the Howells' living room to be confronted by two anxious and expectant faces.

And for the second time, what he had to tell them did nothing to assuage their terror.

CHAPTER THIRTY-FOUR

Thirteen hours, thirty minutes missing…

THE NIGHT WAS SLIPPING AWAY. In fact, it was already tomorrow. In the morning, the press could officially label Osian Howells as missing since yesterday. One more ratchet with which to heighten the emotional tension and suck more readers or listeners or watchers in. Warlow couldn't blame them, not really. It was their job after all.

But he didn't have to like it.

What he'd said to the press was true: they were making progress. And yes, he was knackered, but that didn't matter. What mattered was finding Osian.

When he pushed open the door of the Incident Room, Gil stood at the Job Centre pinning an index card to the end of a long snake of similar index cards stretching across at least three feet.

'If that's its tail, I cannot wait to see the size of that donkey's arse,' Warlow said.

Gil pivoted; glasses balanced on the end of his nose. 'Not as pretty as Catrin's efforts, I admit, but I couldn't find any post-it notes.'

'No, it's…impressive.' Warlow stood behind and read the left-hand card. Gil had written: 10.30 AM OSIAN RETURNS FROM SUPERMARKET. 10.45, FIRE LIT. 11 AM ABDUCTION. He scanned right across to the latest card. It read. 11.15 PM, EW FINDS EVIDENCE OF VODEN IN ATTIC. In between, all the other cards had statements and times written in capitals.

'Where's Rhys?' Gil asked.

'With the Howells, explaining all about that last card.' Warlow nodded at the timeline.

'Did he text you?'

'Maybe, I'm working through them.' Warlow glanced at his phone.

'Right, that means you won't have seen this.' Gil held up a new card for Warlow to read. 10.20 PM, REPORTED SIGHTING OF DRONE IN FIELD OPPOSITE MAES AWELON.

'What?' Warlow scrolled to his messages and read what Rhys had texted.

'A couple of oiks, apparently.'

Warlow nodded. 'The two kids we warned off this morning in the field opposite the house.' He shook his head.

'Exactly,' Gil said. 'Brazen, right?'

Warlow huffed out air and stared at the timeline but didn't register it because his brain was suddenly doing cartwheels. A Green Man in a bloody attic, a drone, and still nothing concrete to go on.

'Still,' Gil stuck the last index card up, 'at least we know the Vodens are involved somehow.'

Warlow's hand rubbed across the hair on the back of his head. 'Catrin's hunch about him was spot on. Shame she can't be here to follow up on that.'

As statements went, Warlow's timing could not have been better. The door to the Incident Room opened, and both men looked up as Jess walked in, shedding her coat in a means business sort of way, followed by Catrin in a pair of dark glasses. She might have been able to carry off the shades-always-on rock star look were it not for the white eye pad jutting out from under the lens on the right-hand side of her face.

'What the hell are you doing here?' Warlow demanded, but more in surprise than as a reprimand.

'For the record, I tried. I even ordered, but she said she'd get a taxi and come straight back in.' Jess shook her head.

'Sir, I'm aware I'm not fully functional, but DI Allanby showed me your text. I did all the donkey work on Thomas Voden. Be silly to make someone start from scratch.'

'But you're only seeing through your left eye?' Gil said.

'It's fine,' Catrin said. 'I'm only going to be looking at a computer screen, not driving an HGV.'

'Are you sure?' Warlow asked, trying to disguise his relief at seeing her.

'Whatever they did to me at the hospital worked. I'm not in any pain. I want to be here.'

'You're absolutely certain about that?' Warlow repeated.

'Sir, I—'

'Because you are going to be providing all sorts of eye-related ammunition for dad-joke Bob over there.' Warlow jerked his head towards Gil, who blinked, and offered up a look of pure innocence.

'I find that deeply insulting,' the DS said. 'I wouldn't dream of doing such a thing. I was always taught never to mock the afflicted.' He sent Catrin a side-eyed glance.

'I'll put up with it, sir,' Catrin said, ignoring her fellow sergeant.

'I mean, if I was the sort of person wanting to zero in on the pirate theme eye-patch,' Gil persisted, 'I'd be thinking of sending out for a wooden leg and parrot with deep frozen pizza from Treasure Iceland. Luckily, I'm not. That kind of person I mean.'

Catrin pulled out the chair under her desk, took off her dark glasses and shook her head.

'Why are you using the desktop?' Gil asked. 'I mean you've already got an eye pad.'

Catrin groaned.

'At least let me get you a cup of tea.'

Catrin looked at him, smiled appreciatively and said, 'Thank you, Gil.'

'I'll even break out the HUMAN TISSUE FOR TRANSPLANT BOX. May even be a few chocs in there left over from my granddaughter's last birthday bash. Fancy one of those?'

'What have you got?' Catrin asked, but warily, as if she was expecting the worst.

'Might be a Mutiny on the Bounty in there. Or even a few pieces of After Eight.'

Catrin dipped her head into her hands. 'I should have known.'

Gil, grinning, was already walking through the door whistling Drunken Sailor.

Five minutes later, all armed with mugs of fresh tea in one hand and a biscuit in the other, the team, minus Rhys, stood, or leaned against their desks, staring at the Job Centre and the Gallery that had been added to significantly in the time it took for the tea to brew. Now that Jess and Catrin were back, Warlow felt something different in the atmosphere. They had information, quite a lot of information. What they needed to do was sort through it and piece it all together. He couldn't help the feeling that they were approaching the water jump in the steeplechase. Once over that, they might get a crack at the finish line.

Or perhaps it was the tea and biscuits that had ener-
gised him.

Sometimes it was impossible to separate the two.

'Okay,' Warlow said. 'Let's go through how we see this.
Jess?'

'Absolutely nothing back from Povey on the drone-
dropped glove except that it was definitely Osian's. Pig's
blood, not human. And I agree, that's simply the abductor
having his kicks. He wanted us, or perhaps the parents, to
think that it was blood. Osian's blood, possibly. To get a
reaction.'

'One that he could see, you think?' Gil asked.

'What do you mean?' Jess frowned.

'I mean, was it in any way possible that he was
watching when the glove was found. If what these two boy
racers say is true and he stored the drone in the field opposite, could the abductor have set up observation points?'

Jess seemed nonplussed. 'Possibly. You think he's got
cameras set up?'

'It's a point,' Warlow conceded. 'This bloke is organised and sophisticated enough to own and fly a bloody
drone so I wouldn't put anything past him.'

'I'll liaise with the PolSA, let him know our thinking.'
Jess made a note.

'Catrin, our Green Man.'

She nodded. 'So, I've brought up the case again on the
PNC. There's not much to add for now.'

'Okay, so we assume that Thomas Voden has tracked
his sister and mother down to the Caeglas estate, yes?'
Warlow asked.

'Really?' Gil sounded sceptical.

'Or,' Catrin said, 'the other possibility is that his sister
or his mother have kept in touch. Did one of them tell him
where they were and he visited, scoped the place out and
twigged that there's an empty flat next door? Mrs Sibley is

partially blind, and she thinks he's going to be her new upstairs neighbour. But all the while he's been trying to burrow through into his mother's house.'

'And where does Osian fit in?' Jess asked.

'Collateral damage?' Gil said and earned an immediate glare that was half inquisitive and half loaded with distaste from the others.

The DS explained his thinking. 'Leopard, spots, changes, never. Rearrange the well-known phrase. The bloke is in an institution. He absconds and comes down and finds himself next to a bloody school. He has a thing for kids, so he follows them on their nature trail and almost grabs Nia Owen. When that fails, he tries again, this time with a bit of planning.'

'But all the while, he's trying to get to his mother and sister. They're the ones who let him be taken away,' Jess added. 'So, what, we think he broke through tonight?'

Warlow shrugged.

'Broke through and used diluted vinegar to subdue his mother and sister and cart them off to wherever the hell he already has Osian,' Gil muttered.

'Which brings us back around to the Vodens and what we don't know about them.' Warlow stood up. 'I can't help thinking about the father. The family relationship may be broken, but he needs to be made aware of what's happening here. All this secrecy isn't helping anyone.'

'I'll try to get back in touch with the sergeant I spoke to earlier, sir. The one who gave me the initial intel.' Catrin turned to her desktop and started tapping the keys. 'It's late, but…'

Warlow nodded. 'Good.' This was progress of a sort. 'But it still leaves us not knowing where the Vodens are.'

'The Green Man enjoys being outside,' Gil suggested. 'We know that.'

Warlow nodded. 'We have the PolSA on that. He can't be very far if he is out in the wilds. They'll find him.'

'But not tonight,' Jess said.

'No, not tonight,' Gil agreed.

Warlow got up and walked towards the Gallery and the photographs of number ten Beili Road. There were no photographs of the Vodens. He stared for a few seconds and then swung back around. 'Why is it we're still playing this stupid bloody game with social care? The Vodens cover is already blown. And the one man with the information we need is nowhere to be found.'

'Grimshaw?'

'Yes. Grimshaw.'

'I forgot to tell you, Rhys said he wasn't anywhere near the Reading Room,' Gil said.

'We need him in here helping,' Warlow said. 'I don't care if it upset him seeing Catrin writhing on the floor because she had acid thrown in her face.'

'Writhing? Really?' Gil said.

Catrin threw him a filthy look before turning to Warlow. 'He's still not answering his phone, sir.'

'Right, that's it. I'm going to find the bastard. It's an unusual name. Can't be that difficult to find an address.'

Catrin nodded. 'Social care always has someone on call, sir. For children needing care and that. They might be able to help.'

'Okay. Ring the buggers. We need Grimshaw's address. I'll be in the car heading towards the A40 because I can't sit here anymore. I'm going to get him in here so he can't bury his namby-pamby hippy head in the bloody sand. It's late but, if the Vodens have any friends or relations down here, we need to know.'

'I've got a contact. Worked with me on Operation Alice. She might know Grimshaw.' Gil picked up the handpiece of his desk phone and began scrolling through his mobile with his left hand.

'I didn't know you could multi-task, Gil,' Catrin said.

Warlow was already walking through the door. The last thing he heard was Gil's voice. 'Know what, neither did ayyyye.'

CHAPTER THIRTY-FIVE

WARLOW SAT in his car with his phone to his ear, listening to Gil explain how he'd struck gold immediately. His contact from Op Alice, now a team leader in social care, was an Amazon Prime nightbird and had not yet turned off her phone. She knew who Grimshaw was and had his address to hand, given that he'd attended a workshop six weeks ago and she'd had to oversee the letters of invitation. She and Gil exchanged a few pleasantries and, two minutes after hanging up, Gil had the address in his messaging app.

He'd promised to forward it but had to ring off in order to send the message as his multi-tasking skills did not stretch to that little nugget of techno wizardry. Warlow waited for the chirp, read Gil's message and rang Gil back.

'I'm on my way.'

'Good for you.' Gil's voice came through the Jeep's dashboard speaker. 'We could, of course, send a response vehicle to pick him up.'

'No. I can't sit around waiting for things to happen. And I still have a bit more clout than two fresh-faced PCs straight off the hay wagon.'

'And a way with words, if I may be so bold.'

Warlow heard Jess snorting in the background.

'Okay, it's up to you, sir.' Gil went for formality. The two men had already abandoned all forms of it when not in the company of other officers. But sometimes, Gil used it when he disagreed. 'Give us the nod if you need backup.'

'Backup?' Warlow repeated the word as if he'd misheard it. 'I'm not arresting him. All I want to do is prise what information he has about the Vodens out of his touchy-feely hands.'

'It is late though,' Gil pointed out.

'Well, neither one of us is asleep nor will Osian's parents be.'

'Fair point. You familiar with Golden Grove?'

Warlow glanced at the texted address. 'I know where the church is, and I've walked Cadi in the country park there.'

'Right. Grimshaw's place is a bungalow near the top of the hill. He lived there with his mother. She died a couple of years ago and he inherited it.'

'I needn't ask if he has a wife or a girlfriend. One look at him will tell you that.'

'Now, now. *Ma bran i bob bran*, as my mother used to say.'

'What does that mean?' Jess's voice in the background.

'A crow for every crow. No matter who you are or what you look like, there's someone out there for you,' Gil explained.

Warlow snorted. 'Poetry? At this time of night?'

Gil ignored the jibe. 'He lives alone. Park the car at the church and walk back down the hill. The house is called Nyth yr Aur.'

Rain started to spit at the windscreen and Warlow flicked on the wipers as he coasted down towards the

Capel Dewi turn-off. 'I'm taking the back road. Should be there in ten minutes.'

'What are you in, a helicopter?'

'The old Jeep can shift when it needs to.'

'Of course. Stay safe, Starsky out.'

———

WHEREAS GIL HAD COME up trumps with Grimshaw's address, Jess was having no such luck in finding Geoff Voden, Thomas and Jaydon's father, and Patricia Munro's estranged husband. Her attempts at finding the DS that Catrin had spoken to fizzled out pretty quickly. He was not on duty and would, like any sensible copper not on duty, have turned his phone off. But her persistence eventually paid off when she was put through to a Duty DI in Hampshire by the name of Lorraine Pyatt.

Jess explained the circumstances, that she was part of the investigation team looking for Osian Howells.

'Commiseration,' Pyatt said. 'I saw the reports on TV. How is it looking?'

'Like a deep, dark hole. We're desperate to shed some light on this,' Jess said. 'We're thinking stranger abduction now, though we have a strong lead with the stranger.'

'Really?'

'That's where you come in. I'm trying to get hold of Geoff Voden.'

The line went quiet. For a moment, Jess wondered if it had been lost, but then Pyatt, who'd clearly been holding her breath, exhaled.

'DI Pyatt? Are you still there?'

'I am,' Pyatt answered, but something in her voice had changed. It had an edge now. Sharp enough to cut yourself on if you weren't careful, thought Jess.

She pressed on. 'Okay, so it's complicated, but we

suspect Voden's family had to be moved down here. You know Geoff Voden?'

'I do.' Once again, Pyatt's reply was brief and stilted.

'Then you'll be familiar with the son, Thomas's story. He absconded from the secure unit he was being held at and may have travelled down to our patch in search of his mother and sister. They're in social housing, using a different name to keep their identity hidden. Thomas is disturbed. We know he has a thing about camouflage jackets. It's possible that Thomas is responsible for Osian Howells' abduction and that he has now also abducted his mother and sister.' Jess paused, 'Still with me?'

'I am.'

'Right. So, the SIO thinks it's only fair that Geoffrey Voden learns all this from us before the shit hits the press fan.'

'You think so?'

Not exactly the empathetic response Jess was expecting. 'You don't agree?'

'Have you spoken to anyone else down there about Sergeant Voden?'

Jess sat back. Answering a question with another question usually implied she was missing something. 'Personally, no. But one of the team spoke to a DS who told us that Thomas Voden's arrest had a destructive effect on the family.'

'It did. And there's truth in the fact that it almost cost Geoff Voden his career. Still might since he's suspended pending an enquiry.'

'An enquiry into what?'

'Allegations of…impropriety.'

This time, the line went quiet because Jess was lost for words. Impropriety covered a multitude of sins. Which one fitted this scenario?

Pyatt broke the silence. 'I'd put money on the fact that

whoever you spoke to was a mate of Voden's. And that he was a bloke. We've found that to be a toxic combination.'

'Lorraine, we're floundering here. I appreciate the fact that you may not want to speak to me about a colleague, but Osian's been missing for over twelve hours now.'

The line ticked and hummed. Pyatt said, 'Let me try Voden's number. See if he'll talk to you.'

The line went dead again. Jess sat and waited, watching the clock on the wall, and listening to Catrin's keyboard click and Gil tutting and mouthing oaths at whatever he was seeing on the screen. Two long minutes later, her phone rang.

'He's not answering,' Pyatt said.

'It's late. Thanks for trying,' Jess replied, expecting her to kill the call a second time. But the line stayed open.

'I wanted to give him the opportunity to talk. That's gone. My conscience is clear.'

'I don't follow,' Jess said.

'No, I'm sure you don't. But give me five minutes and I suspect you will.'

———

WARLOW PARKED the Jeep halfway up a hill in a wide area in front of St Michael's Church, opposite a little hall made of the same grey stone. Another entrance a couple of hundred yards up the road led to the old Cawdor family seat, now Gellu Aur Country Park. Opposite where he sat, the southern limit of the park grounds loomed dark and unlit behind a stone wall.

The rain had turned into a drizzle, and he managed to get damp before he could slide on a coat as he exited the car and made his way back down the hill, passing a few bungalows and peering at their names. He reached a gap between the houses. Further down, a row of cladded semis stood sentinel. Warlow turned and looked towards the woods and the bungalow at the end.

'It would be,' he muttered.

And sure enough, the gravelly track he walked along, already accumulating puddles, ended in the dark low building called Nyth yr Aur. He passed some cars and a people carrier parked on the track and half on the grass. The nearest streetlight stood fifty yards back on the road behind him, and only the thinnest vestiges of light showed him the entrance to the path leading to a front door. Warlow took out his torch. No triggered light came on when he walked up to the door.

He knocked. Three loud raps to make sure Grimshaw heard him. But though he repeated it twice, no light came on and no footsteps approached.

'Shit,' Warlow muttered. 'Where the hell are you?'

He retraced his steps back to the street and, on the paved area downhill, caught sight of a dog sniffing a lamp-post. Behind him, a man leaned on a gate, eyeing Warlow's purposeful approach warily.

'Here, Jack. Come here.'

The terrier paused, leg up, and watched Warlow equally warily. The DCI stopped ten yards away and held up his hand, warrant card showing. 'Evening. I'm DCI Warlow, Dyfed Powys Police. I'm looking for a chap called Grimshaw.'

The man, still wary, pointed back to where Warlow had come from. 'That's where he lives. Nyth yr Aur. But I haven't seen Adrian for a couple of days. Busy at work, they say.'

'You haven't seen him this evening?'

'Thought I saw a car or a van up there about an hour ago, but no, nothing since.'

Jack trotted up and sniffed at Warlow's trousers. 'Hello, Jack,' he said.

The dog wagged its tail.

'I take Jack out last thing,' the man explained. 'Up and down the hill the once. Settles him for the night.'

Warlow nodded.

'In trouble, is he?' Jack's owner asked.

The answer was yes, for not bloody doing his job, but Warlow toned down his response. 'No, he should have been somewhere else, that's all. I wondered if he'd made it home.'

'He's a good sort, Adrian. Looked after his mother for years. Works for the council.'

'He does. Ah well, I daresay he'll turn up. Take care.' He turned, and retraced his steps up the hill, head bent against the drizzle that was now being driven into his eyes by the southerly breeze.

It sounded as if Grimshaw had come home but must have left again. Too late for the pub, so a date? He reached his car, took off his wet coat and slid into the driving seat, unable to suppress the sigh that emerged. He could go back to the Reading Room, see if anyone there had come up with something. The car's lights lit up the church hall opposite. As he swung forward in order to do a three-point turn, his lights picked out a vehicle parked in the dog leg the parking area made. A dark Renault Captur had been tucked away, not visible from the road. Away from prying eyes and thieves, Warlow thought.

Good plan.

Then he reversed, swung the car around and drove the Jeep back out to point his nose downhill, and across the valley to Cwrt Y Waun.

CHAPTER THIRTY-SIX

ADRIAN GRIMSHAW SAW the flash of torchlight outside the window. He heard the dull thud of footsteps on the concrete path, then the firm knock on the front door. He wanted desperately to answer it. So desperate that tears of frustrated effort coursed down his cheeks.

But he couldn't because the tape around his mouth held the gag in place so firmly that he was in danger of choking unless he concentrated on heaving air in through his nose. Any noise he made would be a subdued groan damped down by the ripped piece of tea towel stuffed inside his mouth that was sucking all the saliva from his tongue.

He couldn't move either. The duct tape around his legs and arms and shoulders pinned him to the chair, which, in turn, had been glued to a La-Z-Boy with even more tape. The La-Z-Boy was heavy. It meant he'd been rendered immobile, though he'd managed to see the torchlight by straining his neck, and even then, it had been but a flicker in his peripheral vision.

There were other people in the house. A whimpering occasionally from the middle room, the one his mother had liked to call the TV room. And earlier, there'd been other noises, high-pitched, women's voices, but garbled and strained, like he'd been before the tape had been wrapped even tighter. He assumed they were gagged, too.

Blood had congealed in his left eye, but gradually, his tears washed enough of it away for him to see. His head hurt from being struck with something hard and metallic. He'd tried to move when he'd been constrained the first time. Then with only plastic ties around his wrists and ankles looped around the chair. But he'd fallen, and the noise alerted *him*. Brought *him* into the room. He'd been so angry. No words, just blows. And then, the half-conscious Grimshaw'd been trussed to the chair with the duct tape. Yards of it, so that now he was virtually immobile.

He'd tried asking what the man wanted at the beginning. When he'd barged in. A big man. Used to violence, unlike Adrian. But he'd said nothing. Nothing but 'Shut up and do as you're told.'

There was little to rob in the house. And so, Adrian assumed the worst. That he'd be attacked or tortured. Sexually assaulted, probably. He'd seen enough films about home invasions to know they never ended well.

But nothing had happened. Not yet.

Except for the comings and goings. And the noises of first a child and then the women.

But the man was in the house. He could hear him. At least he had until the torchlight arrived. Then all went quiet. But before that, though the man's voice had not been raised, it sounded harsh, seething with anger. Followed by the pitiful cries of the women.

Still, the torch and the steps brought with them a brief flicker of hope.

Someone outside. Perhaps the police.

But they'd gone.

Abandoned him. And Adrian realised then that he was

probably going to die in this house that he'd shared with
his mother for so long.

———

GIL WAS STICKING another index card on his timeline, this
one simply saying, SIO VISITS GRIMSHAW'S
ADDRESS, with the time at 12.30 AM. Behind him
Catrin groaned in frustration at her screen.

'Mouse died on you?' Gil asked.

'No. It's sodding Facebook. I've had two dozen Adrian
Grimshaws up here and no luck so far.'

She'd been searching to find the right Grimshaw
because he might have a photo wall of friends or significant others they might contact. Strands of a web that
might lead somewhere.

'No website?' Gil asked.

'Why would he have a website?'

Gil shrugged. 'I don't know. Doesn't everybody these
days. Try www.socialcaregelliaur.com?'

'Why on earth would he have a site called that?'

Gil paused in his Timeline endeavours and turned
towards Catrin. 'My granddaughter says I should have a
website – www.Ilovegrandad.com.'

Catrin's expression melted into one of horror. 'Please
tell me you've never typed that into a search engine?'

'Not yet. Why, has someone else got that website?'

Catrin sagged visibly. 'Search engines have a tendency
to extend the search terms and…please don't make me
explain.'

Gil looked very disappointed but then frowned. 'You
mean…?'

'Yes, I do.' Her reply was animated, her one good eye
large with warning.

'What the hell is the world coming to? That's what I

want to know.' But Gil's face, composed as it was into a trademark mask of distraught innocence, gave the game away.

'Very funny,' Catrin said, shaking her head.

Gil grinned and turned from his index cards. Across the room, Jess seemed to be in an earnest telephone conversation with someone. Gil joined Catrin to study her screen. 'Let's have a look. Perhaps he's put himself up there as someone else. An aviator of some kind.'

Catrin shook her head. 'I know you mean avatar. At least I hope you mean avatar. But the really annoying thing is, I'm not one hundred per cent sure because you might not. And you know I would think that. And that makes the whole thing a thousand times worse.'

Gil, still grinning, kept his eyes on the screen. 'What about this one? He has his address as Golden Grove, Carmarthen.'

'He does.'

'He's even got a photograph of the country park as his banner.'

Catrin looked at her fellow sergeant. 'See, Facebook banner. All this pretending to be computer illiterate is a show.'

'Works with Rhys,' Gil said.

'He feels sorry for you.'

Gil kept staring at the screen. 'So, Grimshaw and Golden Grove, it must be him. Let's peep at his profile.'

'It's not him.' Catrin clicked and an image of a man in his early thirties appeared. Short dark hair, a face so fresh it looked incapable of growing a beard or a moustache, wearing a knitted bobble hat and a comedy red blob. The caption read, 'red nose day at work'.

'Christ, that screams social worker to me,' Gil commented.

'Maybe it does. But this isn't Grimshaw. I've seen him,

don't forget. Long hair, beard, moustache. More Shaggy than hipster. But nothing at all like this bloke.'

Across the room, Jess had put the phone down and was staring at her two fellow officers. 'What did you say?'

'Sorry ma'am. I didn't mean to shout.'

'You were a bit loud,' Gil pointed out.

'That's your fault. It's sheer frustration. Apologies, ma'am.'

Jess sat up. 'Never mind that, what did you say about Grimshaw.'

Catrin frowned. 'It's not him. The profile is perfect. So maybe it's his cousin or something. The Grimshaw I met was…' She stopped talking and a look of dawning horror crept over her face. 'DVLA,' she said.

Jess got up and joined them as Catrin punched Adrian Grimshaw's name and address into the DVLA database. It took seconds to call up his record. A record that included his photo ID.

'Oh, shit,' whispered Catrin. The image that appeared matched exactly the photographs of Adrian Grimshaw from Golden Grove on Facebook. 'This isn't the Adrian Grimshaw that DCI Warlow and I met at the Reading Room, ma'am. Nor the one that stayed with me while the ambulance came.'

Gil, this time genuinely confused, looked from Jess's face to Catrin's and back again.

'So, who is the Grimshaw you've been speaking to?'

'I think I have the answer to that one,' Jess said. 'Someone get DCI Warlow on the phone, now.'

CHAPTER THIRTY-SEVEN

Fourteen hours missing…

WARLOW WAS APPROACHING the bridge over the River Towy when his phone rang. The night had turned dark and wet, and this part of the valley floor often flooded. Indeed, a couple of people had been swept away within yards of the bridge when the river was in full flow. But they needed days of rain to get to that stage. One advantage of having so many hills was that there were lots of slopes for water to run down. Still, it always reached bottom somewhere.

It wasn't uncommon to find gawkers parked right on the crest of the bridge, completely oblivious to the fact that oncoming traffic could not tell what was on the other side and coming their way.

Tonight, there was no traffic. And much to his disgust, as of this moment, he was in no hurry either. They'd hit a wall. Finding Grimshaw had given him some focus. But now even that was fading into the mush the rest of the case had become. He stopped the car and picked up the handset.

'Gil. Any news?'

'We have you on speakerphone, sir,' Catrin's voice, sparky and animated.

He picked up on it immediately. 'What have you found out?'

'Where are you, Evan?' Jess this time.

'About to cross the river and head back towards Cwrt Y Waun. No joy at Grimshaw's. No one home.'

'It isn't him, sir,' Catrin again. 'The Grimshaw we met isn't him.'

An icy hand seemed to clutch at his insides and wrench his gut. 'What?'

'The images on his Facebook page, they're not of a bloke with thick glasses and a ponytail. We've checked it against his driver's licence.'

Warlow didn't move. Grimshaw? A hundred thoughts cascaded through his brain, not one of them lasting long enough to take hold.

'There's worse,' Jess said. 'The Munros didn't change their name and relocate to get away from the son. They did all that to get away from the husband. Geoffrey Voden.'

Shit. 'Who the hell is—'

'He's a serving officer on extended leave with the Hampshire Force,' Jess explained quickly. 'Worse, he's a PolSA and a surveillance expert.'

The truth fell like a hammer on Warlow's heart. Searingly, disgustingly, it all clattered into place and made horrifying sense.

The man they were looking for had never been in hiding. Had never been running. Instead, he'd been a cuckoo in the nest. Right in the middle of it, watching them run around like headless chickens.

Surveillance. Something Catrin had said about Grimshaw's phone. He'd misplaced it. Left in the Reading Room to be found by Ken Morris, Dyfed Powys's PolSA and returned to him. But it could have been in that room when Warlow had briefed the team. Recording every word he'd said.

Shit.

The same thought would have occurred to Catrin. He didn't need to spell it out. 'Sir, we're getting hold of Voden's phone number and accessing his calls. We may pinpoint where he's been.'

'No need,' Warlow said.

The line fell silent.

'Evan? What do you know?' Jess asked.

'What kind of car does Grimshaw drive?'

Clicks on the line. He knew his sergeant. She'd have done the background work. Catrin came back. 'A black Renault Captur.'

Warlow gunned the Jeep's engine and raced over the bridge to a junction a hundred yards further on where he turned around. 'Get hold of Rhys. Tell him to bring some Uniforms to Golden Grove. To the church. No blue lights. And not in bloody convoy. They park there and wait for my signal.'

'Where will you be?' Jess demanded.

'Finding Osian.'

———

TWO MINUTES LATER, Warlow passed Jack the terrier and his owner trudging back up the hill towards their house. A thought made him brake suddenly. He waited until the man caught up and rolled down the window. Jack's owner leaned in to listen.

'He hasn't come back since you've been away, if that's what you're going to ask me.'

'I know. I have a different question for you. Do you strim?'

'What?'

'Lawns. Do you strim your lawn?'

'Occasionally.'

'Do you wear protective goggles when you do?'

The man, whose wheezing effort to walk up the hill sounded like a leaking bellow, leaned an elbow on the Jeep's one window. 'Is this some random check? Did someone complain? And anyway, it's not the law, is it?'

'No. Simple question, that's all.'

'As it happens, I do. My neighbour laughs at me all kitted up, but then he has a tattoo on his arm that says, "thudder only happens when it's raining". Spelled t, h, u, d, d, e, r. Got it in Bangkok, along with a couple of difficult to shift STDs.'

'But you wear safety goggles?'

'I do.'

'Good. Can I borrow them?'

The man went a little quiet before adding. 'It's a bit dark for strimming.'

'Fair point. I won't be strimming. I'll be doing something else.' Warlow reached a hand across and offered it. 'Evan Warlow.'

'Stan Thomas.'

Once Stan had delivered, Warlow drove up the hill and this time parked the Jeep next to the Renault, out of sight of anyone driving past. He crossed the road and took a track running parallel to the estate wall and crossed a field that brought him behind Grimshaw's still dark house. To his right, darkness, fields and trees. Next door, separated by a post and rail fence, a newer bungalow's lights glowed through the rain. The fence completed the three sides of Grimshaw's large back garden, broken only by a locked five-bar gate that led to a stoned path leading to the back door.

Behind all of this sat a grey panel van on some gravel

hardstanding. When Warlow touched the bonnet with the palm of his hand, it felt warm. Warlow climbed the fence, not wanting to chance the gate making a noise even if he could open it. Besides, he wanted to stay in the shadows, away from the faint illumination thrown off from the house next door. He hurried forward, crouching low, hoping there wouldn't be a security light above the back door set in a small, flat-roof, lean-to extension.

He got to the rear wall of the house and looked across. An infra-red movement detector stuck out from the soffit above the back door, but someone had removed the bulb and its housing from the light itself. Someone who didn't want to be disturbed, perhaps? Or who might not have wanted to give their own presence away?

The rendered wall was damp to Warlow's touch.

As for the bungalow, all was dark, all was quiet.

Yet every fibre of his being told him to be wary.

What he should do, of course, was sit tight and wait for Rhys and the Uniforms. But the slightest chance of Osian being here in this house drove all other thoughts away. He crouched under a closed window. Above him, rain spattered against the glass like fingers on a drum skin. He stood and cupped his hands against the glass to peer inside.

There was nothing except the vague outline of some words. He stood back and looked at the dark window afresh in the dim glow from next door. There were words plastered inside the window. Words from stuck up newspapers. Someone did not want anyone to see what was going on in there.

He put his ear to the glass.

Nothing except the sound of his own thumping heart.

He should wait for Rhys and the— Then he heard it.

Only the once. And only faintly. A sharp crack followed by a muffled wail.

Barely audible but audible enough. The building was

not empty. The time for crouching was over. He stood up. There'd be no security light, that was for sure. He walked to the back door and took in the broken pane of glass boarded up from the inside with thick cardboard. The sort of breakage he'd seen a hundred times in B & E cases.

He turned away, faced the wall, sank to his haunches, and took out his phone. He texted Rhys:

COME NOW. Stan, the man with the dog will point the way. Cover front and back. Come in on my signal.

THEN WARLOW STOOD up and prepared to kick the door in. But before he did that, he tried the handle. The broken lock gave with no resistance and he stepped over the threshold into the black interior.

CHAPTER THIRTY-EIGHT

R<small>HYS</small> <small>LED</small> the way with four Uniforms in tow. They followed instructions and parked in the church. They'd left their vehicles and were now walking down the hill, not making any sound. Rhys had the address but had no idea where it was. And who the hell was Stan The Man?

He needn't have worried.

Halfway down the hill, a light flashed.

One of the Uniforms whispered, 'Rhys, there's a—'

'Seen it,' he said. 'You lot stay here.' He trotted down towards the first in a row of wooden, cladded, semi-detached houses. The light came from a torch being held by a man standing inside his gate.

'Are you Stan?' Rhys asked when he approached.

'I am. Warrant card?'

'What?'

'He said to ask for your warrant card.'

Rhys fumbled in his pocket and then Stan shone the torch on the wallet. 'Twenty yards back the way you came, first left. Follow the lane to the end. It's the last dormer bungalow.'

Rhys turned, but before he'd gone five yards, Stan called him back.

'Hey, just one thing. He your boss, is he?'

'DCI Warlow, yes.'

'He's okay, is he?'

'What do you mean?'

'Well, it's not my place to say anything because I know bugger all about police tactics and that, but he asked to borrow some safety goggles.'

'Did he?' Rhys said.

Stan shone the torch into the DC's face until Rhys pushed his hand down and away.

'That's not normal, is it?' Stan asked.

'Look around,' Rhys said. 'It's past midnight, it's drizzling and we're all out here looking for a kidnapped six-year-old boy. What's normal?'

Stan nodded and flicked the torch off, leaving both men bathed in the glow from the streetlight above.

'Last house, dormer bungalow, right?' Rhys asked.

'That's it.'

'Thanks.' With that, Rhys loped back up the hill and signalled for the Uniforms to join him.

———

WARLOW STOOD STOCK STILL, listening. Another whimper and a voice. This time, definitely male and deep. He couldn't make out the words, but from the tone, they sounded at the least accusatory, at the worst angry. He smelled blood in the air. Blood and something else. Something worse.

He'd once had to follow a suspect through an unlit park and spent an age finding a red filter for his phone's screen. Since that time, he'd had the filter on a triple-click shortcut. He did that now and the phone's screen lit up red.

The lurid light showed him the layout. He stood in a hall with a stairway running up to his left. The landing above, where the noises came from, showed two shut doors. On the ground floor, a kitchen to the left, two closed doors to the right. Warlow went to the kitchen first. He had no weapon. From the knife block near the sink, he picked up a long, thin, sharpening steel. Not exactly a baton, but it would do. From the slot next to it, he picked up a small knife and slid it into his coat pocket.

Back in the squat hallway, Warlow covered up his phone and opened the door furthest from the stairs.

Darkness.

No, not quite. The thinnest glimmer of distant street-light through the newspaper-covered window.

A dark outline, vaguely body shaped, silhouetted against it.

Warlow brought the phone up.

The shape whimpered and shivered.

The DCI stepped in; steel rod raised. The shape didn't move but its head, encased in silver duct tape, trembled. Warlow checked the floor. Scattered debris, more signs of violence, dark splashes of what looked like drying blood. Then he stepped around to face the captive. Someone had used yards of tape to secure whoever this was, first to a chair and then the chair to a large armchair. It looks almost as if a gigantic spider had cocooned a victim, ready to return and devour it.

There were two slits in the tape. One showed a silver of eye and a dancing pupil behind it, peeping through. A gap no wider than a couple of millimetres. A second gap around the bloodied nose. The sound of gasped breathing came through the tape. On seeing Warlow, the trembling got worse and the head, unable to move more than an inch, strained away.

Warlow said nothing. He held a finger to his lips, and quickly took out his warrant card and shone the red light of the torch on it so that the eye could see.

The trembling slowed.

He fished for the knife and started sawing through the tape around the head until he freed up the end of one section and tore it away from eyes and nose and mouth. Underneath the tape was a mess. Dried cuts, a broken nose, one eye completely swollen shut from a haematoma.

The man's breathing sped up and tears ran down his face.

In the lowest of whispers, Warlow asked, 'Grimshaw?'

The care worker nodded. Quickly Warlow cut the tape from around legs and arms. No point trying to strip it all away. What they needed was to make the man mobile.

Warlow helped him to his feet only to see him half stumble.

He grabbed Grimshaw and pointed towards the ceiling.

Grimshaw, blood streaked and wild looking, his breath still heaving, nodded.

'Get out through the back,' Warlow whispered.

Grimshaw shook his head.

'Don't bloody argue. Just leave,' Warlow hissed. 'I'm going to get the boy.'

Grimshaw held up a hand, nodding and shaking at the same time. He either couldn't or wouldn't speak. Warlow wondered if anything had been done to his tongue. Or maybe his jaw was broken. It looked swollen enough. But the man pointed up and then held his hand palm down against his hip and shook his head vehemently.

Warlow scowled and looked at the hand and then at Grimshaw.

'The boy isn't upstairs, is that it?'

Grimshaw nodded.

'Shit, then where—'

Grimshaw pointed to the far wall. To the room next door.

Warlow made Grimshaw stand inside the door of the room that had been his prison. He looked like something from a maniac's attempt at a drawing of a Marvel superhero. Bits of silver tape still clung to him, all over his chest and abdomen, a few on his neck and hair.

Duct Tape Man.

Warlow stepped out. Another moan from above.

The second door opened onto a room lit by the light from a TV. Some owlets were feeding. Country File reruns by the look of it. But there was no sign of Osian. Food debris lay on the sofa and on the floor. Crisps, some sandwich crusts. Warlow stepped quietly inside. The room stank of food and urine. Not strong, but definite. Foetid notes to accompany the metallic blood from the corridor. He walked in. The sofa stood unoccupied. The chair too. And then, as he moved towards the middle of the room, he saw the feet.

Two small feet. Unmoving. Lying on the floor next to the chair, the rest of Osian's body out of sight between the furniture.

Warlow suppressed a moan.

'No, no, no,' he whispered. 'Not this. For Christ's sake, not this.'

He knelt down, touched the leg, feeling for the cold clamminess that would confirm the worst.

The leg felt warm.

Warlow thrust the armchair away. Osian lay there, stretched out, the sudden movement waking him from sleep. Waking him had triggered a wail of fright at seeing this red-lit man leaning over him.

'Osian, no, it's okay, it's okay.'

But the wail persisted. And so Warlow did something that he'd always regret. He plucked the child off the floor and clamped his hand over his mouth. Then he was in the hall and hurrying towards the back door, with Grimshaw hobbling behind him. Warlow ran into the garden just as a Uniform came around the corner.

'Sorry Osian, I'm sorry,' he said to the terrified child. He handed him over and whispered an order to the officer, 'Get an ambulance here, yesterday.'

But he didn't wait for a reply. He only hesitated for one second when Rhys appeared around the corner and almost collided with him as he made his way back to the bungalow's rear entrance.

'Alright, sir?'

'No. Definitely not.'

'You're wearing safety goggles, sir.'

'I am. Now, follow me, but stay behind with your head down, understand?'

'Head down. Right, sir.' Rhys's eyes kept flicking from Warlow's face to the rod of sharpening steel he held in his right hand. 'Is there a reason…?'

'Don't ask, just do, understand?'

Rhys nodded.

Once he reached the door, Warlow stopped and yelled up the stairs. 'Voden, we know you're up there. You can't hide now. It's all over.'

No reply. Warlow crept in and started up the stairs. He heard a creak behind him and turned to see Rhys following. 'Head down,' he ordered.

Rhys nodded and complied, turning his face down towards the stair.

Warlow spoke as he climbed. 'We've got a van load of Uniforms on the way. This will not end well unless you give yourself up now.' He was halfway up but paused to sniff the air. A new aroma. It took a second, but then it registered.

Petrol.

'Jesus,' Warlow muttered before shouting. 'Geoff, come on, man. This is finished. Come out now.'

Another three steps to the landing. He got there, tried the light switch. No light came on and the landing stayed dark. He guessed there'd be two rooms, one on either side, together with a bathroom at the end. One bedroom for Grimshaw, one for his mother. But God alone knew what was in them now.

'Geoff, talk to me. This has been hard for you—'

A shape came out of the bathroom. Big, holding something in its hands. Warlow felt the fluid hit his face, and he clamped his eyes shut. He tasted vinegar. Behind him, Rhys cursed.

'It's vinegar, Rhys. Keep your head down,' Warlow ordered.

He opened his eyes. His face was drenched, so were his clothes, but his eyes, under the goggles, were clear. He took the last two steps in one bound. But Voden had already gone through one door, slamming it behind him. Warlow ran forward, turned to the right and opened the other door. He flicked on his phone again. Two bound and gagged people lay on the bed, one male, one female. Both struggling against their bonds on seeing him.

Struggling and alive.

Therefore, not his priority.

He turned back. The door to the second room stood closed. Warlow reached for the handle and pushed.

Not locked.

It didn't need to be. Inside, a bedside lamp provided the illumination. Later, Warlow would wish it had been dark. That way, he would not have had to remember the scene.

But there would be no escaping the image of violence and hatred that he saw. A woman in her forties lay face down on the bed, her head turned to the door, her face swollen and bloody, one arm looking as if it wasn't hinged properly at the elbow.

Geoff Voden stood dressed in his black police uniform, cap pulled down, a different logo to the usual Fleur de Lys of Dyfed Powys on the front. No beard or moustache now, only a grizzled dark stubble under a pair of glittering sunken eyes. The room stank of petrol. Warlow took in the smear of it all over the woman and the mattress. Half a dozen candles stood lit on the bedside table and a dresser. Dim illumination for the job in hand.

Voden had a knife in one hand, held a burning candle in the other, and had his knee on his wife's neck as he regarded Warlow with a look of uncaring defiance. Her naked back had a dull sheen like thin milk where Voden had been dripping hot candle wax onto her skin. On the floor between the door and Voden were a toy water pistol with a bulbous green cylindrical reservoir and an upturned petrol can, bedclothes and duvet rumpled in a pile.

'Or what, Evan, eh?' The words came out through gritted teeth.

Warlow stared.

'Oh yeah, I know who you are. I've listened to everything you said to the team. They think you're fucking God.'

'Your kids are next door, man. Spare a thought for—'

'Piss off. That little moron Thomas ain't mine. Something wrong up here,' Voden tapped his head. 'Not mine. No fucking way. Jaydon, she's smart. She's mine. But she sided with her mum and that fucking cretin of a brother of hers. He cost me my job and my family, the fucker. I warned them. A thousand fucking times, I warned them. Don't cut me out. If you do, there will be consequences.'

He grinned; teeth bared between trembling lips. 'These are the consequences.'

'Why Osian? For God's sake—'

'Ocean. Stupid bloody name. Stupid fucking language. He's just collateral damage. I knew that turd Thomas would try to find his mother and sister. Jaydon would have stayed connected with him. Too soft by half. She'd tell him where they were. As soon as I saw the Green Man come up on Facebook, I knew they'd be here. Grimshaw said he didn't know, even after I beat the shit out of him. He only knew some families had been relocated. I still needed you lot to do the donkey work and find out where they were hiding. Play the dumb social worker and let you lead me to them. Thanks for that.' His grin was sickening.

'That can't justify kidnapping a child.'

'Worked though, didn't it?' Voden spat. 'Had you all running around.'

'Grimshaw's in a bad way. You might have killed him,' Warlow said.

'Boo fucking hoo.' Voden smiled, but his lips stayed razor thin. 'Nice touch with the goggles. I used vinegar spray when I was undercover. Amazing what a shot of that in the peepers will do. Drives people nuts.'

'It's finished, man. You can see that.'

'No, it's not finished. Not yet. I'm screwed. We all know that. But I'm not finished.'

Warlow shook his head. 'You're better than this, Geoff.'

'Oh yeah? You know fuck all. No idea what this bitch has put me through.' He gritted his teeth and knelt harder. On the bed, Patricia's breathing became a stertorous wheeze.

Voden was right, of course. He had the upper hand. Had the weapons and the victim.

'So, what now? Within minutes this place will swarm with coppers,' Warlow said.

'Think I give a shit? And forget the hostage bullshit. I'm not interested in chatting or making a connection. I've read all the fucking manuals. No more chat.' Voden's eyes had a dullness to them. A death row stare. Still looking at Warlow, he calmly slid the knife an inch into the back of his wife's shoulder.

She screamed through the gag.

'Now fuck off, close the door and let me finish my work,' Voden said.

CHAPTER THIRTY-NINE

WARLOW HELD UP BOTH HANDS, including the one holding his phone, and stepped back. 'Okay, Geoff. Okay. I'm backing off.'

Voden was going to kill his wife. Of that, there was no doubt. But before he did, he clearly wanted her to suffer. What would be the final act? Setting fire to her alive on the bed?

Voden twisted the knife. It made a noise of metal against bone. Patricia screamed again. Warlow took a shuffling step back, his feet catching in the discarded jumble of bedclothes, the phone in his hand the only solid object he had. But what use was an oblong of metal and plastic faced with an armed man?

No use at all, unless…

Warlow dropped the phone. It clattered to the floor, and he fell to his haunches, making a show of finding it, groping over the bedclothes.

'Leave it. Get out, you bastard,' Voden growled.

Warlow half-turned away from the man, grabbed as much of the bedding as he could in one movement and, still crouching, charged at Voden, at the same time yelling. 'Rhys, get her out!'

Holding the blankets and trailing duvet like a shield in front of him, Warlow barged into the bigger man, catching him off balance. A knife thrust narrowly missed his shoulder but got caught up in the material. Behind him, Rhys appeared. To his credit, he did not hesitate and did exactly as asked. His enormous hands grabbed Patricia and tore her off the bed, dragging her out in one movement.

Warlow's scramble had pushed Voden against the wall, but the violent movements shifted the bed and it rattled against the bedside table. The contents fell with a clatter: lamp, clock radio, and the candles that Voden had lit.

'You fuck,' Voden screamed. 'You fuck.' This time his knife thrust hit home. Warlow felt a stab of pain in his upper arm and staggered back, letting go of the bed linen. The sudden easing of pressure let Voden step forwards. But his legs caught in the fallen bedclothes, and he fell sideways onto the bed just as a candle flame ignited the petrol-soaked mattress. Flames erupted with a soft whumping noise.

A sudden stench of burning hair filled the room.

Voden screamed.

Warlow staggered back, feeling for the wall and the door frame. Blue and yellow flames danced over and around Voden as he pushed himself back up and away from the burning bed. But the flame came with him, over his arms and his hair. Later, the DCI remembered only how quickly the accelerant fed the fire. How rapidly the room succumbed to the beast. Voden had obviously been generous with the petrol. It must have splashed on his clothes and skin. The hungry fire leapt on both.

Voden screamed, batting at the flames on his clothes and hair. He couldn't see for the smoke. That was obvious.

As Warlow found the doorway and fell through, coughing and spluttering, acrid smoke and fumes from the bed turned the room into a smoke-filled gas chamber. Voden stumbled blindly forward, reaching for the door, but his groping hand pushed instead of pulled and the door closed in front of him. Down on his knees on the landing floor, Warlow peered up through the smoke in time to catch Voden stumble again, and his shoulder strike the half-closed door, slamming it fully shut.

Hands pulled Warlow away, helped him down the stairs. 'The other room. Two in there,' he said, waving his good arm.

'We're on it, sir,' Rhys said, his big arm around Warlow's shoulder.

'Then get Voden out.'

'Yes, sir.' Rhys disappeared back up the stairs. Through watery eyes, Warlow watched the young DC pummelling the door with his shoulder, but it wouldn't move. Smoke billowed out from the gap between door and floor, grey and toxic.

'I can't budge it, sir,' Rhys spluttered, between coughs. 'He must have fallen against it.'

The Uniforms brought the younger Vodens out. Both could barely walk, but they got past Warlow, down the stairs and out into the garden.

'I can get a crowbar, sir.' Rhys coughed out the words.

'No,' Warlow said. 'The smoke…it's too dangerous.'

'But he's in there, sir.'

'I know. But he's used petrol, and that mattress is old. Christ knows what fumes are coming from it.'

'But sir…'

A loud bang in the room shook the rafters as something exploded. Both men flinched. They had no way of knowing what other goodies Voden had brought with him.

'Come down. We need to get out.'

'Sir?'

'That's an order, DC Harries.'

Rhys came down and helped Warlow out. It took eight minutes for the fire engine to arrive. By the time it did, the whole of the bungalow's dormer rooms were alight, and Geoff Voden did not survive to answer for his crimes.

———

WARLOW HAD INHALED little smoke and recovered quickly from that but the injury to his arm was a bleeder. He kept pressure on it. Paramedics and fire-crew took over the scene. Povey would descend on the place later, but what evidence remained would be a charred mess. Fire destroyed everything. Osian and Grimshaw went off to hospital, but Warlow waited until they were away before telling Rhys that he would follow in his own car.

'I can drive you, sir,' the DC insisted.

'You could, but you're needed here to be my eyes and ears, got it?'

'But you're injured, sir,' Rhys objected.

'I'd better get a bloody move on then.'

He left Rhys looking unhappy with his hands on his hips, but at least the kid didn't escort him to his car.

Tying a bandage around the wound proved to be a challenge, involving teeth and a cloth he normally used to clean steam from the car's windows. But he managed and ten minutes after leaving the still burning bungalow, Warlow drove off to the hospital. Bad enough that he'd have to explain his HIV status to the staff there again. No need to have it broadcast to the whole of HQ. Which is what might have happened had Rhys come with him. Not that the DC would have given up Warlow's dirty washing if he asked him not to. But this was blood and being anywhere near someone while he was bleeding filled

Warlow with horror. Best if this stayed his dirty little secret. No need for the world and his wife to have that knowledge. Or should that be the world and his partner these days?

'Balls,' Warlow said, and drove away. He phoned through to A&E, found the night sister in charge and got fast-tracked past the mournful throng in reception. He was dealt with swiftly by a doctor called Imran in full PPE and didn't see Osian or Grimshaw again that evening. Now that they were safe, they could wait.

It was almost 2.30 in the morning when he opened the Incident Room door to find Gil, feet up on a chair, doing the crossword.

'Ah, the hero returns. You okay, Evan?'

'Right as rain. What the hell are you doing here?'

'Obeying direct orders from on high.'

'Buchannan?'

'Higher still if you take their combined score. That is DI Allanby and Anwen, the present Mrs Jones, both of whom insisted I make sure, absolutely sure mind you, that you did not doss down in the SIO room because you were too knackered to go home.'

Warlow toyed with denying it, but damn them both, they got it spot on. In all honesty, he didn't think he was safe to drive and kipping in the SIO room seemed a lot better prospect than in his car, such was his tiredness level. He felt drained and his only misgiving was not being able to see his dog tomorrow morning if he stayed here. But if he drove home in this state, there'd be a chance he'd go off the road and not see her ever again.

'Are you here to shoo me off home, then?'

'On the very contrary. I'm here to offer you a proper bed at chez Jones.' Gil looked at his watch. 'We can be in Llandeilo in twenty minutes. I'll drive. The lady Anwen will have a cup of tea and a slice of buttered *bara brith* awaiting us. Plus, I guarantee to have you back here at eight.'

'Seven forty-five.'

'Slave driver.'

A sigh as deep as the Mariana Trench escaped Warlow. He took one look around the Incident Room, now deathly quiet after the day's frenetic activity, and shrugged. 'Can I upgrade to a superior room?'

'No such thing. Only one class. Tidy.'

Warlow succumbed to the offer and promptly fell asleep in Gil's car.

To Anwen's credit, she didn't disturb the men when they arrived, but the tea steamed on the table and the cake had been cut. Warlow came to, ate and drank in silence. But like elven bread, the food and drink revived him enough to talk a little.

'You did a good thing tonight, Evan,' Gil said between munches.

'Did I? We lost Voden.'

'Nothing you could have done, so Rhys told me. Besides, I think Voden got lost a long time ago.'

'Hmmm,' Warlow grunted. He paused, enjoying the contrast of the cake's sweetness with the saltiness of the butter before asking, 'Osian back with his parents?'

'Voden didn't lay a finger on him, so yes, he is back home. I ought to warn you, Gina Mellings says the next time she sees you she is going to kiss you.'

Warlow's mouth twitched into a smile. 'Does Rhys know about this? He's a big bugger, you know?'

'He has no say in the matter. Christ, I feel like kissing you myself.'

Warlow looked up under lowered brows. 'Get a bloody grip, man.'

When they'd finished the tea and cake, Gil walked Warlow up to his room. Simply furnished, with tasteful curtains and towels folded on the bed. A bed that looked inviting. 'You are ensuite.' Gil flicked a light on in the little adjacent bathroom. 'Fancy anything for breakfast?'

'Piece of toast will do fine.'

'Brown or white?'

'Ooh, better make an effort after that *bara brith*. Brown, then.'

'Tidy. See you in the morning.' Gil closed the door.

Warlow knew he should take a shower. He stank of smoke and his arm had dried blood caked below the elbow. So, a quick shower and…he made the mistake of sitting on the edge of the bed to take his socks off.

———

THE NEXT THING HE KNEW, someone knocked on the door.

'Rise and shine. It's just before seven. Anwen put a clean shirt outside the door. One of my old ones, so it might be a bit big for you, but you'd drown in one from my current wardrobe.'

'Is that bacon I can smell?' Warlow asked, blinking in the light coming through the window.

'It is indeed. Thick and hand cut.'

'Right, I'll be down in ten minutes,' Warlow said, glad they hadn't listened to his simple order of toast.

CHAPTER FORTY

EVERYONE GOT IN ON TIME. Everyone looked tired, too, Warlow most of all. But no one wanted to miss the catch up. There'd be a ton of work to do before it could all be signed off. But everyone knew how rare it was to have tied up an abduction case so quickly.

Rarer still to have the victim home, safe and sound.

It was ten o'clock by the time they'd all made phone calls or spoken to the people who wanted reports or to offer congratulations. But, armed with tea and with the HUMAN TISSUE FOR TRANSPLANT box well and truly open, Warlow held the briefing, detailed what happened the night before and then called on each one of them to fill in the blanks.

Jess had been on the phone to Lorraine Pyatt for an hour that morning.

'Questions are going to be asked,' she said darkly. 'Geoff Voden had a history of violence. It's the usual story. Partner ends up in hospital five times but drops the charges. Except this time, he fractured her orbit, so she was going through with it.'

'Is that why he was on suspension?' Catrin asked.

Jess nodded.

'Why the hell was he still in the job?' Warlow asked.

Jess shook her head but told the team what she'd learned from a much more candid Pyatt that morning. It looked like Hampshire police had decided, wisely, that closing ranks might not be the best way forward when it came to outing a police officer who'd kidnapped a child and almost beaten his wife and others to death.

The fact that he'd burned to death was also a good reason to no longer keep quiet.

They all knew the answer. Already it had emerged that Voden had a reputation for inappropriate behaviour around female colleagues. He'd been unofficially reprimanded for using sexualised language and had been reported for slapping a female officer's bottom at a police station. No action followed the report.

It made for grim reading.

'Anyone talked to Grimshaw, yet?'

Catrin nodded. The eye pad and glasses were long gone, though one eye still looked a little red. Gil had told her it matched her hair.

'Still in hospital, sir, but they don't think he'll need to stay in. He has a hairline jaw fracture and a broken nose, but nothing else. He'll come in and give a statement as soon as he's released.'

'Has he been able to give us any details?'

Catrin stood and walked to the Gallery. Grimshaw's DVLA photos had been pinned up next to one of Voden. 'We've already obtained Voden's phone records, sir. He placed a call to Grimshaw an hour after the abduction.' She pointed to a highlighted line on the printout. 'Grimshaw remembers it. He said that Voden told him he was part of the investigating team and that they'd be wanting to interview people in the vicinity. Asked him if there were any relocated families in the area. Grimshaw told him he was aware that the estate had been used for relocations in the past but that he was not given details of cases for the same security reasons. In those instances where a protection element was involved, they used individual case workers. Voden then asked for a meeting.'

'Why did he pick Grimshaw?'

'Male. Lived alone. He features on the local authority's website. It would have taken him minutes to find out Grimshaw worked in social care, so he'd have ID.'

'But he looks nothing like Grimshaw,' Rhys pointed out.

'Did you double check his ID?' Warlow asked.

Rhys frowned and shook his head.

'No, none of us did.' Warlow let out a mirthless huff. 'Voden didn't know where his wife and daughter were because they'd gone into hiding. He had no idea where to look. But then social media lights up with a Green Man report. He learns that Thomas Voden has gone missing and puts two and two together. The Green Man has come to Wales to see his mother and sister. So, he comes down, kidnaps Osian in order to get us to do all his investigative work for him. He meets up with Grimshaw, pretends to be one of us – not difficult because he was – and steals and doctors the ID to become a hippy version of Grimshaw the social worker with the ponytail and the beard. It worked because it's what we expected to see. That way he could be a part of the investigation. Hide in plain bloody sight while we join the dots and flush out the Munros. Do all his dirty work for him.'

He told them of his theory about the fake Grimshaw's lost phone, left in the Reading Room to listen in on Warlow's briefing. It had been Voden who'd been in the house when Catrin had got sprayed with vinegar. Which one of the family he'd been carrying out at that point it didn't matter. And to cap it all, he'd had the nerve to come back to the house and babysit Catrin until the paramedics came before driving calmly away in his hired panel van. That way he'd bought himself an hour in which to have his sick revenge.

'*Arglwydd Mawr,*' Gil said. 'And he almost got away with it.'

'Almost,' Warlow muttered.

'Do you think he would have set fire to the house with Osian and Grimshaw inside it, sir?' Rhys asked.

Warlow had thought about it. He'd thought about nothing else since waking up that morning. 'Who knows. All he wanted was to have his revenge on Patricia Munro. Everything else was collateral damage. How is she, by the way?'

'In ICU,' Catrin answered. 'Ruptured spleen and torn liver as well as fractures to ribs and her arm. She's due in surgery later today.'

Warlow glanced at his watch. There were a ton of loose ends to tie up. He had meetings and paperwork. But there was no denying it. Voden had paid the price, but a win was a win.

'Let's get to it. But at five thirty, we stop, no matter what. Pub at six. My round.'

'Now you're talking my kind of language,' Gil said.

———

THE REST of the morning progressed as what needed to be done got done. Statements were taken and discussions with Buchannan took place about what they could release to the press. At lunchtime, Warlow found himself alone in the SIO room, staring at another update in his inbox and running his finger around his neck inside the collar of the shirt Anwen had put out for him. It had begun to itch like mad.

'Yeah, she's a bit old fashioned like that. Starches the buggers like billy-oh,' had been Gil's explanation. Little consolation.

A knock on the door came as a welcome distraction. Jess stood there, a concerned look on her face.

'What?' he asked.

'You look like crap is what.' She glanced at his neck. 'What is that shirt you're wearing? Last time I saw collars like that John Travolta was Staying Alive. Why don't you go home and change?'

Warlow shook his head. 'Too much to do.'

Jess tilted her head and lowered her chin. 'No there isn't. This case and the world in general will not stop turning because Evan Warlow takes a few hours off. Go home, change, walk the dog and come back in later. You're not getting out of the pub. No one will forgive you that.'

He thought of objecting, but knew she was right. Accepting responsibility for the whole shebang was part of being the SIO. Murders were the worst. You became the victim's advocates. Their angels seeking retribution. But no one was going to cry too much for Geoff Voden. And damn it, Osian Howells and Grimshaw were alive. And the person telling him to bugger off was an SIO in training. Jess could do all this with her eyes shut.

'Maybe you're right.'

'I know I am. Turn your phone off for a couple of hours and reboot. Or even leave it with me.'

'Can't do that. You'd learn all my dark secrets.'

'I know most of them already, Evan. I can read you like a book.'

'Thriller, I hope?'

'Mystery, definitely.'

Warlow stared at the screen and the email he'd read four times and not absorbed one word of. 'Okay, I'll do that. If the Buccaneer—'

'Leave the superintendent to me and the team.'

Warlow pushed back in his chair and heard the wheels squeak. 'I need one favour. I know you're new to the patch, but I want to send someone some flowers. Can you find out about florists—'

'Jesus, did you not get the memo about leaving the twentieth century?' Jess shook her head. 'You can do all that stuff online. Who are they for?'

'Anwen, Gil's wife.'

'I'll sort it and send you the bill.'

He toyed with discussing a budget but wisely buried the idea before he got turned to stone by Jess's look if he even mentioned it.

And so, at twenty minutes before one, Evan Warlow left the building. He picked Cadi up from the Dawes, threw his shirt in the boot, put on a T-shirt and fleece he kept in the back of the car, and man and dog walked one of their favourite spots along the Nevern estuary. He got back to his cottage, Ffau'r Blaidd a little after three, showered again and changed into a fresh shirt and a jacket that didn't stink of smoke; that didn't remind him of Voden on fire in that dormer bedroom and the betrayed and battered face of Patricia Munro on the bed.

Then he fed Cadi, ate something himself, and sat and talked to the dog with his hands in the soft fur of her neck as she sat with her head in his lap for twenty minutes. What he said didn't matter to neither man nor beast. All she wanted to hear was his voice. All he wanted was to touch her.

He felt a damn sight better for having done it.

Cadi therapy. You couldn't beat it.

Once the painkillers he'd taken had kicked in and his arm finally stopped aching, he locked up and got back into the Jeep to do the one thing he knew he had left to do that day before the pub. A duty that there was no shirking.

CHAPTER FORTY-ONE

THERE WAS no real reason for a FLO to be at the Howells' property anymore. After all, everything should have been back to normal. But Warlow had insisted the family continued to have support if only to fend off the press who stubbornly persisted to infest the road outside the property. On the off chance that she'd be the one on duty, he rang Mellings.

'Gina?' he asked, when she picked up.

'Mr Warlow, it's you.'

'Yes. You at the Howells'?'

'Still here, sir.'

'Good. I'd like to see Osian and his parents. Is he there?'

'Yes, sir, of course he's here. And that's all thanks to you.'

'Never mind that. Look, I don't want to walk through the hyenas. If one of them asks me a question I might clock the bastard. I seem to remember the Howells parked their car at the side. Is there a gate?'

'There is sir. I'll make sure it's unlocked.'

He parked at the school again. All the kids had gone home by the time he arrived, and the road was deserted. The press attention had switched to Golden Grove and the burnt-out bungalow. The rest of them were encamped outside the Howells' property. Quickly he took the lane to the treatment works and wound his way towards the rear of the Howells' place. Probably the way Voden had accessed the field behind and set his fire. No one was watching him. No cars could come this way and the press were only interested in official comings and goings. People of importance they could badger.

Well today, they could badger off.

Warlow stepped in through the side gate at Maes Awelon and walked up to the back door. He didn't have to knock as Gina Mellings opened it accompanied by Fflur Howells who stood behind the FLO, smiling.

'They're expecting you, sir,' the FLO said. A minute later he was sitting on the same seat he'd sat in before, in the presence of all the Howells and Gina Mellings. They listened to what he had to say in rapt attention, at how someone else's personal problems had caused an earth-quake in their lives. He drank tea, made to his specification with no need to repeat his preferences to Gina, and answered as many of the family's questions as he could.

Throughout it all, the boy, Osian, sat in his father's arms eyeing Warlow with a look of abject suspicion.

But they got through it. When they'd almost finished, Warlow brought up one last thorny subject. 'I also wanted a word about your brother, James.'

'What about him?' Nerys said, her voice terse. 'He's going to jail, isn't he?'

'That's up to the courts, but I suspect he will do time, yes. Even with mitigation. And there is no excuse for what he did. He'll pay.'

Lloyd shook his head. 'Sometimes there is no reasoning with him.'

Warlow nodded. 'But when it's over and he's paid his dues, don't shut him out. The kids love him, and I know he loves your kids.'

Gina frowned, confused by this show of sympathy from her hard-nosed boss.

'Really?' Lloyd said. 'I'm all for banning him from the house.'

But Nerys could see where this was coming from. She turned to her husband and put a hand on his arm. 'Come on, Lloyd, you know James would do anything for the kids. It's such a shame that he and Heidi never had any of their own. I think he'd have cooled down if he'd had children.'

'That's his bloody choice, isn't it?' Lloyd said.

More a statement than a question. But it hung in the air like a bad smell.

'Sometimes choices aren't always what they seem to be. Choice implies options, good or bad. But when you have little or no option, then there isn't truly a choice.' Warlow swirled what was left of his tea and finished it off while his audience absorbed this little conundrum.

Lloyd looked confused and Nerys blinked. 'I haven't talked to Heidi about her and James. Truth is, we haven't talked much since they split up.'

'Perhaps you ought to talk to her. She seems like a nice woman. And she knows James Ryan better than most.' Warlow left a lot unsaid, but perhaps the little he'd given away might allow Nerys and Lloyd to forgive James Ryan some of his hotheadedness. They didn't know Ryan couldn't have children and Warlow wasn't about to tell them that. But a nudge in the right direction wouldn't do any harm. For the sake of Osian and Fflur if nothing else.

Finally, after hugs from Nerys Howells and a prolonged

heartfelt handshake from Lloyd, Warlow came to the real reason for his visit.

When his father had stood up to shake Warlow's hand, Osian hurried away to hide behind his mother. Warlow got down on one knee to be at eye level with the boy. What he said next was in the boy's first language, Welsh.

'I'm sorry I frightened you, Osian. I didn't mean to. Waking up and seeing me with my goggles on in that red light was very scary. And I'm sorry I put my hand over your mouth. We needed to stay quiet until we got out. I don't expect you to understand, but I'm apologising anyway. Mae'n ddrwg da fi.'

Osian stayed where he was.

Warlow nodded, gave a thin smile, and stood up. He couldn't expect a six-year-old to understand. He said his final goodbyes and Gina showed him out. At the backdoor, she looked like she wanted to say something.

'You alright, Gina?'

'No, sir. I…I'll probably get into trouble, but I said I would, so, sod it.' She leaned forward and pecked him on the cheek. 'That's from me and Fflur for bringing her brother back.'

Warlow grinned. 'I won't report you, detective constable. And what Rhys doesn't know can't hurt him.'

'Oh, I will tell him, don't you worry.' She grinned.

'You did a good job here, Gina. A fantastic job.'

'So did you, sir.'

Warlow turned away and had taken half a dozen steps towards the side gate when Gina called his name. 'Sir? DCI Warlow? Hang on.'

Warlow pivoted. The family Howells were walking through the back door to stand and see him off. From their midst, Osian appeared and walked forward, with one glance back to receive a nod of encouragement from his mother and a beaming smile from his father. When he got to Warlow, he held out his right hand.

'*Diolch*,' the boy said.

Warlow took the small hand and shook it.

'*Pleser*,' he said. Probably not quite the right word, but it did the job. And helping this family had been a real pleasure.

Gina Mellings' hand flew to her mouth as she furiously blinked away tears. When Warlow caught her eye, she held up a thumb because sometimes gestures are much better than any words.

He walked back along the lane, relishing these few moments of solitude in knowing that they'd teetered on the edge of the abyss and somehow managed to prevent a tragedy. Pleased more than anything, that Osian had been prepared to forgive him. He got to the car, gunned the engine, and pointed it back toward Carmarthen and the pub.

Warlow had some insight into his role in life, even if he rarely admitted it. Few people got to experience moments like this. Moments where the reasons why he remained glued to this roller-coaster job were brought home to him in the simplest terms. The world was changing. Status and possessions were the idols that most people, young people especially, seemed to worship. A notion fed by the media in all its hydra-headed forms. But in his experience, most ordinary people retained core values. Honour, kindness, trust. Pillars on which to build a family and life. Preserving those pillars was what got him up in the morning.

Privilege had become society's dirty word. But not in Warlow's book. It didn't have to mean a tendentious advantage courtesy of position or wealth or skin colour. It also meant an opportunity to do something worth bloody while. Helping the Howells had been his privilege. He'd take that and make sure the rest of the team understood it, too. He was looking forward to a pint with them knowing how rare it was to get this sort of result in a case.

He'd make sure they all made the most of it.

Then, he found his son Alun's number and dialled it. It would be good to hear his voice one last time before he flew back. And then he'd ring Tom. They had plans to make about Australia.

FREE BOOK FOR YOU

Visit my website and join up to the Rhys Dylan VIP Reader's Club and get a FREE novella, *The Wolf Hunts Alone,* by visiting:

www.rhysdylan.com

You will also be the first to hear about new releases via the few but fun emails I'll send you. This includes a no spam promise from me and you can unsubscribe at any time.

ACKNOWLEDGMENTS

As with all writing endeavours, the existence of this novel depends upon me, the author, and a small army of 'others' who turn an idea into a reality. My wife, Eleri, who gives me the space to indulge my imagination and picks out my stupid mistakes. Sian Phillips, Tim Barber and of course, proofers and ARC readers. Thank you all for your help. Special mention goes to Ela the dog who drags me away from the writing cave and the computer for walks, rain or shine. Actually, she's a bit of a princess so the rain is a no-no. Good dog!

But my biggest thanks goes to you, lovely reader, for being there and actually reading this. It's great to have you along and I do appreciate you spending your time in joining me on this roller-caster ride with Evan and the rest of the team.

CAN YOU HELP?

With that in mind, and if you enjoyed it, I do have a favour to ask. Could you spare a moment to **leave a review or a rating**? A few words will do, but it's really the only way to help others like you discover the books. Probably the best way to help authors you like. Just visit my page on Amazon and leave a few words.

AUTHOR'S NOTE

Gravely Concerned is set in one of the most beautiful areas of Carmarthenshire. Still relatively unknown as a tourist destination, in a valley with so many ruined castles, if you turn too quickly you'd trip over one. But, as we know by now, what goes on under the surface of these idyllic settings can be unpleasant in the extreme.

From this little corner of Wales, you can visit the National Botanic Gardens, get to the deserted beaches within half an hour, or be on top of a mountain thirty minutes the other way. But you've always got to be wary of the weather. It'll follow you wherever you go. Best to be prepared.

Of course, Cwrt Y Waun does not exist as such. It's an amalgam of places. A construct to fit the story. But the river is real, so is the valley and the castles and the town of Llandeilo. And, unfortunately, the concept of evil is real, too. In this case, an insidious lust for vengeance that disrupts communities and lives and that is too easy to believe will never affect you.

Until it does. That's when you need Warlow and the

team. But don't let me put you off because the events depicted are rare. West Wales is an amazing part of the world, full of warm and wonderful people, wild coastlines, golden and craggy mountains. But like everywhere, even this little haven is not immune from the woes of the world. Those of you who've read *The Wolf Hunts Alone* will know exactly what I mean. And who knows what and who Warlow is going to come up against next! So once again, thank you for sparing your precious time on this new endeavour. I hope I'll get the chance to show you more of this part of the world and that it'll give you the urge to visit.

Not everyone here is a murderer. Not everyone... Cue tense music!

All the best, and see you all soon, Rhys.

READY FOR MORE?

DCI Evan Warlow and the team are back in...

A Mark Of Imperfection

Know thine enemy...

Evan Warlow is a man with enemies. As a DCI in the Dyfed Powys force, that comes with the territory. But when two of his most vicious critics are abducted and killed and turn up dead in a macabre tableaux in a forestry plantation, questions need to be asked.

The uncomfortable answers lead Evan and the team back to his roots and an old case that has haunted him for years. The deaths in the forest have all the hallmarks of a killer who doesn't fear the consequences. And when one of Evan's fellow officers is targeted it's clear that the murderer isn't finished yet.

There's a coppery aroma of vendetta in the air and unless Evan and the team can get to the root cause of the killer's misplaced anger, it's obvious there'll be more deaths. And guess who's next on the list?

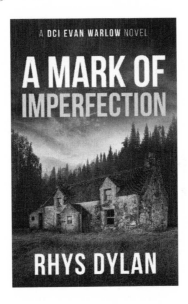

Made in United States
Orlando, FL
25 November 2022

24999228R00193